本书为山东省社会科学规划研究一般项目“网络环境下大学英语课堂教学的探索研究”（编号:14 CWXJ51）的成果。

当代英国移民作家的自传体叙事

Autobiographical Narrative of Contemporary British Writers

李厥云 杨花艳 著

吉林大学出版社
·长春·

图书在版编目（CIP）数据

当代英国移民作家的自传体叙事 / 李厥云，杨花艳著. -- 长春：吉林大学出版社，2021.5
ISBN 978-7-5692-8511-6

Ⅰ. ①当… Ⅱ. ①李… ②杨… Ⅲ. ①石黑一雄—小说研究②萨尔曼·拉什迪—小说研究③奈保尔—小说研究
Ⅳ. ① I561.074

中国版本图书馆 CIP 数据核字 (2021) 第 133638 号

当代英国移民作家的自传体叙事
DANGDAI YINGGUO YIMIN ZUOJIA DE ZIZHUANTI XUSHI.

李厥云　杨花艳 著

策划编辑：张宏亮
责任编辑：代景丽
责任校对：殷丽爽
装帧设计：昌信图文
出版发行：吉林大学出版社
社　　址：长春市人民大街 4059 号
邮政编码：130021
发行电话：0431-89580028/29/21
网　　址：http://www.jlup.com.cn
电子邮箱：jdcbs@jlu.edu.cn
印　　刷：长春市中海彩印厂
开　　本：787mm × 1092mm　1/16
印　　张：15.5
字　　数：250 千字
版　　次：2022 年 1 月第 1 版
印　　次：2022 年 1 月第 1 次
书　　号：ISBN 978-7-5692-8511-6
定　　价：79.80 元

前　　言

自二十世纪七十年代伊始，后现代自传体小说已成为最为流行但备受争议的文体之一，因其能真实反映社会和个体生活现状的特性而迅速占据了自画像、回忆录、日记、反思小说和仿自传等文学场域。鉴于其强调作者个性或者背景的某些特定特征，甚至能一窥作者的自我身份，越来越多的作家和评论家见证了自传体作品的日益涌现以及其伴随的身份政治性和历史反思情结。本书主要关注当代移民作家及其作品，主要或者部分地展现了自我的自传体经历和多元文化遗产。由于移民作家，如奈保尔、拉什迪和石黑一雄，相继获得西方世界的认同并荣获国际文学大奖，这一文化群体也随之受到了更多的关注。

自传体小说不仅适合于浪漫主义作家，比如卢梭和华兹华斯曾利用其艺术作品抒发自我的内在情感，而且也适合于本书所述的当代移民作家。尽管后者继承了自传体的艺术形式，但却部分拒绝了叙事情节的自我指涉性。虽然移民作家作品拥有较高的流行性和关注度，但其自传体小说仍未得到评论家和读者足够的重视和研究，已有的著作和论文也主要集中于后现代和后殖民视角予以解读，对移民作家人生故事的自我指涉及心理分析视角的研究甚是缺乏。本文通过移民作家相似的教育与成长经历但迥异的家庭背景为读者提供了解读作者不约而同地选择旅行者或者国际移民作为自传体叙述者的初衷，唯有如此，叙述者才能真实地描述后现代语境下作者本人的自我意识和社群的集体无意识，才能融合过去和现在的身份认同并成功塑造作为艺术明星和公共知识分子的自画像。本书由五部分构成，前言部分叙述了研究现状和文化背景，其后三章分别研究了石黑一雄与奈保尔等两位作家的小说叙述者，利用历史事件作为传记的社会语境展现了重塑人类生活愿景的可行性意象，由此可见作为读者的文本受众亦将影响或决定叙事结构与作者情感的阐释方式。最后为结语部分，总结了所提出的论点和研究倾向性与意义。鉴于历史语境的重现，此类自传体小说为重绘特定时代历史事件与个体经历彼此依存的共生关系提供了更为个性化与文学性的解读视角。叙述者的生活经历与传记故事之间所存在的想象性空间为移民作家提供了不可或缺的叙事策略或者范式，并以此阐释或辨析他们的过往经历，通过诉说自我的人生故事构建了一副后现代个体自画像和社群浮世绘图景。

Contents

Chapter One Introduction

Since the 1970s and the 1980s the postmodern autobiographical fictions have become one of the most popular and controversial constructs to mirror social and personal life that dominates the marketing of self-portraits, personal narratives, memoirs, journals, self-reflective fictions and mock-autobiographies, to name just a few forms. The autobiographical writings often help to foreground some particular aspects of the author's personalities or backgrounds, and even provide a glimpse of authorial self-fashioning. More and more writers and critics witness a surge of cultural interests in fictional self-portrait writings as a result of the rise of identity politics and commemorations of historical events. Many immigrant authors have written their fictions which largely or partially represent their autobiographical experiences or discoveries about the nature of society, and receive an increasing attention as a result of the fact that the immigrant novelists, such as Naipaul, Rushdie and Ishiguro, were successively awarded the prodigious literary prizes. Despite the popularity and prevalence as a genre, autobiographical fictions of these writers have not yet been profoundly researched and studied in the context of contemporary immigrant writers. Although monographs and essays on these immigrant writers have largely focused on a postcolonial and postmodern reading, which includes theme of globalization, migrancy, and cultural hybridity, critical responses to their autobiographical fictions have not yet focused on the self-referential and psychoanalytical aspects of their life-writings. Here the thesis is intent on examining how and why such immigrant writers connect their past and present selves to establish their fictional self-portraits as literary stars and celebrity intellectuals.

Since the publication of Jean-Jacques Rousseau's *Confessions* (1782), the autobiography has become a distinct genre and sets a model of recounting the narrator's introspective life-stories intertwined with personal or collective memories. In spite of its probably reminding readers of *The Confessions of St. Augustine* (c.397-400), the modern autobiographical narrative has become a witness that can confess his/her life-stories, or some kind of defensive self-portraits about his/her identities and even past experiences. Despite the specific differences between the created characters and the author himself/herself, it is the author that really offers the textual space to feel and then think about certain kind of subjects and events. In his essay, *Autobiography as De-facement*(1979), Paul de Man contends that autobiography should not necessarily be based upon the actual and potentially verifiable events, but that "autobiographical project may itself produce and determine the life and that whatever the writer does is in fact governed by the technical demands of self-portraiture and thus determined in all its aspects, by the resources of the medium"(Paul de Man, 1979: 920). According to Paul de Man's account, the proper name of an author such as Rousseau, Naipaul and Rushdie, is not a stable mode of referentiality, but a figure that produces the illusion of reference to emphasize the assumed truth. That is, the images of the character provide for readers a representation of what the author has portrayed with his/her imagination and a reflection upon the thoughts of the author and his/

her attitudes to the outer reality and life.

If not unconscious mechanisms of self-representation, these autobiographical novels often help to emphasize the particular aspects of their authors' personae or backgrounds, which is essential to form his/her worldly self-portrait. Since the Renaissance, the Western civilization has started its process of secularization which ultimately replaces the close relation of God and mankind with a modern sense of self-definition within the physical world and personal life. Although scandals and doubts of these textual interpretations are undermining the presumption of truth, we still recognize the typicality of a varied formula that overemphasizes the assumed truthfulness of authorial self-fashioning existing in autobiographies and memoirs alike. Together with its crisis of postmodern personal identity, the issue of postmodern self-fashioning has become "a plural, shifting organization, which is patterned around constructive and reparative object relationships and derived from different interpersonal contexts. In this vision, we are all negotiating a complex, contradictory sense of self, and our experience of the world involves multiple perspectives of unity and fragmentation"(Elliott, 1996: 14). The conventional concept of identity featuring in its completeness, linearity and causality of the self-identity has transformed into new models represented by randomness, uncertainty and contingency.

Different from the conventional autobiographies, the texts selected here have in common the employments of first-person narrator as its main character, but void of the identity-contract between the narrator and the author. The changed perception of autobiography not just results in the emergent form of metafiction and intertextuality to mirror the topic of the self and its representation in writing whose status becomes divided and decentralized within the postmodern era. The narrators of immigrant writers placate their moral visions and relationships with others subject to cultural and social forces to unfold their own meanings of human life, upon which exists the artificiality or constructiveness of autobiographical fictions. Instead of foregrounding a coherent, objective and meaningful narrative, Roland Barthes regards autobiographical narrative as a reflection of self-definition deriving from social life, and underlines its performativity as "a rare verbal form (exclusively found in the first person and in the present), in which the speech act has no other content (no other statements) than the act by which it is uttered: something like the'I declare'of kings or the'I sing' of the earliest poets" (Barthes, 1986: 52). This kind of narrative enables human beings to interpret their life experiences as self-understanding stories through a perspective of its first-person narrator who is not identical with the author but painted as self-portrayer to narrate, think and ruminate even if there are not any parallels existing between the author and the narrator themselves.

The autobiographical narration is often polyphonic or an ensemble of voices which constitute the narrating persona inspired by the author's creative and fictional motivations. Furthermore, the destruction of deconstructionist representation destroys the mimetic quality of language and placates its textual meaning for recording and representation in the mire of the gap between the signifier and the signified. Regine Hampel argues that postmodern autobiographical fiction shifts its focus upon the usual coincidence of its new definition of the self, its intertextuality and meta-fictional process of retelling a story as a result of the emergence of twentieth-century post-structural and psychological theories (Hampel, 2001: 88-89). This perception of autobiography has changed dramatically and gradually regarded itself as a literary genre to reflect the author's interpretation and representation of the self. Besides geology and places, all the authors discussed in this book choose to explore their traumatic childhood, and therefore, to solidify their rightful claim of self-identification. Even while they begin to focus on their immigration experiences, they still utilize the juxtaposition between East and West to signify the ambivalence they upheld for their rooted identities or imagined homelands, a feeling that permanently crackles out from the self-fashioning of their auto-fictions. Among these textual voices, the most prominent is the narrated"I", an interior version of self-referential characterization that can privilege a web of external voices stemming from outside society. Furthermore, the writing of postmodern autobiography is regarded not as its representation of his/her factual life, but as a text or sign system existing within the space of different texts. The intertextuality that refers to the already existing characters in human cultures produces the Bakhtinian dialogism, through which heterogeneous discourses of identity are dispersed throughout its fictional autobiography. As an alternative to the conventional self-knowledge, Rushdie presents his characters such as Saleem Sinai and Omar Khayyam with the multiplicity of personal identity under the influence of different, sometimes contradictory, backgrounds through his referential intertextuality for its conjunction of Eastern and Western culture, politics and literature. Another aspect is its metafictional approach to the autobiographical writing process that subverts the conventions and methods of presenting one's life through his/her memory and consciousness.

Due to its inaccessibility to the past, autobiographers question its validity of his/her narration and reliability of memories, and demonstrate their postmodern perception of the reality around us that is based more upon the interpretation and recollection rather than what has really happened. Thus the autobiographical narrative becomes a thorough reinterpretation which does not testify to "the extra-literary past reality of the author (Olney's 'bios') or his/her extra-literary present views of this past (Olney's 'autos')", but starts to concentrate"on the third element in autobiography,'graphe', that is writing and representation"(Hampel, 2001: 63). The notion of preserving an idealized myth of the past has a significant influence upon the present of the diasporic subjects. That is, the nostalgia of the past is positioned against the pragmatics of the present, resulting from the competition for the identity formation by historical and cultural forces.

The epistemological crisis which derives from the developments of modern science contributes to the distrust of realist ic novels of the eighteenth and the nineteenth century and demands a new form to reflect scientific and philosophical concerns. The deconstructionism of self-hood which has its roots in the heart of the Renaissance comes to its heyday as a result of the popularity of postmodernism, and ultimately destroys the conception of conventional representation and of the self-identity. According to Linda Hutcheon,"postmodern writing is metafictional and also parodic intertextuality of or ironically distanced comment on previous texts (literary or historical)"(Hutcheon, 1988: 6). One of its main effects is the deconstruction of the mainstream discourse, which has much in common with postcolonialism. While postcolonialism applies deconstruction to shift its focus from the colonizer to the colonized, postmodernism can account for the centre as a supplement to postcolonial theories.

The fact that autobiographical narrative contains its fictionality and its being double-jointed "autofiction" prefigures the dissolving boundaries of fiction and autobiography. The notion of autofiction first emerged in France in the mid-1970s as part of a revival of hybrid with an autobiographical form and fictive content. Its key feature is probably best "characterized as their promotion of act-value at the expense of truth-value within the set of parameters considered effective in determining autobiography's generic force"(Jolly, 2001: 86). Since its being coined by French writer Serge Doubrovsky in 1977, the term of auto-fiction has undergone an overlapped process of fiction and autobiography to stress its function and form, rather than its conventional content and extra-literary references. The contemporary immigrant writings also blend facts and fiction in a hybrid form of life-writing that purposefully blurs the borderlines of autobiography, autobiographical novel and fictional autobiography through taking on board inter-textual and meta-fictional elements. The increasing awareness of fictionality inherent in autobiographical writings suggests an unstable mixture of fabrication and actual experience that "we need the help of fiction to organize life retrospectively, after the fact, prepared to take as provisions and open to revision any figure of emplotment borrowed from fiction or from history" (Ricoeur, 1992: 162). The self-reflexivity of autobiographical act exceeds beyond the representation of one's past life to include the present self and its narrating discourse which constitutes his/her metafictional process of retelling the life-story. The autobiographical self-hood can only be accessed by readers through the form of narrative evolving from confessional autobiography or memoirs to make up their own self-portraits, and offers a sense of personhood which concentrates on the process of narrating and its constructive meaning.

The definition of autobiographical fiction is not only suited to Romantic writers such as Rousseau and Wordsworth who apply their writing forms to express their inner feelings, but also applicable for the contemporary novelists discussed here for their inheritance of the autobiographical form but rejecting its self-referential authorship. Instead of referring to the author's factual life and his/her past experiences, contemporary authors concentrate more on the relation between the textual narrator and his/her discourse which completely sheds off its referential truthfulness. The narratives of these immigrant writers are considered more fragmentary and marginal than central and linear in relation to Rousseauian criteria and tend to account for a more disjointed personal life to piece together the image of self-identity and its self-representation. This phenomenon probably stems from the self-definition of its narrators and writers as marginal or displaced social roles, of which the self-within-society voice is more obvious in their autobiographical reconfiguration of human life that derives from the transformation of historical accounts. As for the sense of self-reflectivity, Regine Hampel argues that postmodern autobiographical fiction "concentrates on the question of how meaning is created instead of depicting the meaning that is supposedly out there, ready to be represented. Or it even refutes meaning altogether"(Hampel, 2001: 74). For example, Naipaul's preference of telling his own and his family stories, such as in his novels *A House for Mr. Biswas* (1961) and *The Enigma of Arrival* (1987), provides readers with the possibility of delving into his unconscious ness through the self-portraits of his autobiographical fictions. Naipaul's fiction mainly concerns his "imaginary return to the childhood memories"(Anderson, 2001: 118), which initiates him into writing stories as a traveller of displacement participating in his permanent travelling within the former British Empire.

The subjective narrators created in autobiographical fictions and for whom the text is practiced nevertheless trigger the time-space distance of the self-image both as subject and as object. However, the autobiographical text is not only a documentation of the personal past, but also a performative and interpretative narration through which the simultaneous presence between the writer and the narrator can build up the cultural and figurative aspect of the fiction. Yet usually, the historical approach in memoirs of women or ex-slaves and autobiographies implicitly expresses "an ideology of individualism in the very convention of the autobiographical form, an ideology built on the notion of a coherent, self-evident, self-conscious and commanding subject who appropriates literature precisely as a means of 'self-expression' and who in turn constructs textually for the reader the liberal imaginary of a unique,'free' and autonomous ego" (Beverley, 102-103). Through introducing the interfering unconsciousness, Freud subverts the authority of memory and consciousness as a tool to evacuate the past and obtain the cohesiveness of one's selfhood. The foundation of conventional autobiography that can provide its protagonist with a consistent identity through linking his/her past with the present unfortunately surrenders to the collapse of a fixed or self-defined consciousness. The motivation of contemporary autobiographical fiction, through the illusion of reality and credibility, is therefore to make sense of the history of one particular person whose identity is probably marginalized from the mainstream society. For example, the narrator in Naipaul's *A Way in the World (1994)* expresses the confusing ethnic identity of Trinidadians that carries "the memories of thousands of beings" and "all the traits we have inherited. Sometimes we can be strangers to ourselves" (Naipaul, 1995: 9) as a result of the resistance to and disappointment of the collective values and expectations which are imposed from historical documents and people's own experiences. The narrators in autobiographical fictions follow and sometimes parody the earlier types of autobiography such as memoirs, apologia, confession, etc. and consequently exceed beyond individual concerns to focus upon the representation of marginal groups.

As for the immigrant authors mentioned above, the similar English education but different family backgrounds probably account for their common autobiographical narrators as surrogates of homeless or international immigrants to relate not only the story of their self-consciousness, but also one of the stories belonging to their communities. Despite the alleged sincerity, the narrators in these autobiographical fictions choose the reconstructive quality of memories to attach the importance and meaning to the past events and talk away the pain of the trauma they currently suffer. Due to the questioning of one's fixed and stable identity, postmodern authors express their concepts of a fragmented selfhood resulting from the breaking up between his/her present and past self. The autobiographical fictions, in which the first-person narrator introduces and comments on his/her third-person character,"extends the already existing temporal and spatial non-identity between the narrator and the hero [so as] to include grammatical and personal non-identity between narrator and the character" (Hampel, 2001: 105). As for the process of textual reconstruction, certain misrepresentations and even fictive emplotments are inevitably employed to the retrospective self-narrative which leads to the emergence of either self-split narrator or coexisting multiple narrators. Different from conventional autobiographers, postmodern fictions allow different narratives to coexist with and generate one another that can present different textual versions devoid of a reliable and fixed voice. In Naipaul's autobiographical fictions, the extradiegetic narrators provide readers with an autobiographical account which sets the tone for the text, most of which are made up of more general subjects of Trinidad, its history and collective identity that is dispensed with its more than one intradiegetic and sometimes metadiegetic narrators.

Its qualities of subjectivity and self-referentiality within different versions of narrative ultimately underline the notion of personal or collective memories through creatively imitating or modifying the existing imagery of cultural stock, upon which individual or national identity builds the foundation and then apply different sorts of literary forms to transform life experiences into cohesive narrative. Whereas the narrators created by Ishiguro and Rushdie uses historical events as the context of autobiographer's stories to show the imaginative possibilities to make a fable of human life, the imagined addressee they create also impacts and shapes the text of the story. While seeking an intimacy with history, the autobiographical fictions provide a more personal and literary perspective to present the interdependence between individuality and historicity of their times. Marcus Billson regards autobiographical memoirs as "personal act of witnessing the past, of ascertaining the meaning of [people's] participation in the social matrix, and of remembering [people's] experiences as a moral metaphor" (Billson, 1977: 282).

Since the narrators represent certain views and thoughts that can probably echo the author's attitudes to outer reality and life, they are therefore to be analyzed with a psychoanalytical perspective to find out what has hidden behind these auto-fictional self-portraits. The central critical approach in this essay is to focus upon the psychoanalytic theory to analyze the textual characters and to explore why the author chooses such approaches to depict his/her outer reality and personal life. The autobiographical narrative offers the writer its therapeutic effects and can be applied to the Freudian notion of talking cure so as to walk through the traumatic melancholia. Although his narrators desperately pursue the consolation and therapy for traumatic events, Ishiguro's own writing confirms his catharsis of regret or melancholy that probably originates from the Freudian bereavement of emotion associated with his grandparents in Japan. Ishiguro claims that his writing is not, in the simple, direct sense, autobiographical, but one whose autobiographical element is "embodied by any one character. It comes through in the story, the drama [...] if you're in the Shakespeare tradition, it's easier to write from the point of view of character, which involves sexes, different ages and classes" (Groes and Lewis, 2011: 252). His autobiographical fictions can be traced with scattered life scenes from his homeland of memory and imagination, such as the episodes of movie-going by Ono and his grandson Ichiro, and the repairing of the three-generation household ravaged by war. The material that the writer chooses to apply but has not lived out in his personal experiences gives him greater freedom to present a fuller autobiography of self-image, either consciously or unconsciously. Unlike autobiographical convention, Ishiguro's fictions begin with the current anxiety of narrators, and then turn back to measure the moral vision of their present existence against their past one that is passing away as outdated. In writing their own stories, the narrators invite eye-witnesses to participate in their emotional pilgrim, and ultimately reveal "their eventual ease with self-deception to achieve a self-comforting or self-protecting condition" (Wong, 2005: 19). We must recognize that the narrators collude with the indebtedness of memory to build up their coherent narrations of the writings at the expense of the accuracy and sincerity.

Confronted with their present frustrations, the narrators choose to articulate, confess and narrate their autobiographical experiences to come to terms with their depressing legacies. Although his novels anxiously involve the historical and personal realities, Ishiguro is preferably interested in the emotional or psychological upheavals, or just as Freudian defense mechanism entails, how one uses memory for one's own purposes, one's own ends. The therapeutic role of the autobiographical narrative will be elaborated in the following chapters. Here memory embraces writers' imagination and speculation to locate the truth of their personal experiences, because the version of the past they have created is "real [and] tangible, [which is]made of the stuff of a life lived in place and in history [...] We must acquiesce to our experience and our gift to transform experience into meaning and value" (Hampl, 1986: 1007). The psychoanalytic perspective also negates the possibility of absolutely autobiographical veracity, because, according to Freudian terms, the psyche can not let out the truth, but will repress, distort and displace such material to leave the autobiography unreliable, full of gaps and contradictions. Paul Ricoeur argues that life writings acquire the qualities of their "fictive history" or "historical fiction" stemming from the narrative patterns "borrowed from history or fiction" (Ricoeur, 1991: 73). Ricoeur's notion of narrative identity can account for the therapeutic narration of the narrators through reconstructing their self-referential stories to bridge the experienced past and the anxious present for their psychological reconciliation.

The autobiographical narrators engage in their awakening important memories to talk away the haunting emotions they are suffering. Furthermore, the reconstructive quality even enables the narrative to bridge up the gap between unrelated events in order to make sense of their life stories. Donald Polkinghorne elaborates the essential elements of autobiographical narrative as "(a) memory as reconstruction of past events, (b) the smoothing processes of Gestalt-type configuration, and (c) the use of culturally available plots" (Polkinghorne, 2004: 42). The function of the first element which has been explained will be detailedly explored in the following specific works. And the "smoothing" element as a defense mechanism underlines the narrator's selection and rearrangement of past life to achieve the cohesion of its narrative, which is similar to the performance of Freudian talking cure. The emphatic emplotment "to produce a coherent story that leads to denouement and closure" (Polkinghorne, 2004: 43) acts as a framework for divergent events and life experiences to build up a bridge for life and fiction through the autobiographical genres. The fictionalization of the autobiographical writings encourages the greater imaginative engagement with the realistic life through flashing freely across the memories and feelings suited to express the inner life. The life narrative becomes not only a process of rediscovering the preexisting identity, but also an instrument of self-defining his personality through moulding the self-image on its coherence of fictional plots rather than the authenticity of authorial life.

Probably, these immigrant writers choose their autobiographical writings to explain and justify their past for the purpose of creating a self through the process of writing in one's own life stories. The anxiety they have suffered can harken back to a sense of displacement from a world they belong to and of stranding in an estranged reality which subverts the value systems they hold on to. It seems that to some extent these immigrant writers tend to successfully assimilate the sequel of their separation from cultural homeland into their existing self-narratives or integrate this kind of empathy into their previous sufferings and present the identification they now struggle to change. We find that they have intentionally transcended the regressive narrative of their past and transformed into a more cohesive one that directly or indirectly represents the aspects of the protagonists existing in their self-portrait writings.

Like Freudian talking cure, the cathartic quality of self-narration enables writers to account for events in their life through the mediation of symbols, dreams, metaphors and dramatic scenes to accomplish the psychological aims. Donald P. Spence comments that "Freud made us aware of the persuasive power of a coherent narrative [...] that a well constructed story possesses a kind of narrative truth that is real and immediate and carries an important significance for the process of therapeutic change" (Spence, 1982: 21). The unreliable narration based on the reconstruction of memories endows the narrators with its power of therapeutic effect through their selectively "constructed story" to impart a meaning that can heal or relieve the pains of their past experiences. This kind of cure is introduced by Suzette Henke to refer to scriptotherapy, through which "autobiographical writing functions as a mode of self-healing"(Smith and Watson, 2010: 279) to write out the traumatic experience in the mode of therapeutic reenactment. Thanks to its entanglement in current social contexts, autobiographical fiction can not merely be regarded as the retrospective accounts of his lived past, but also his literary performativity to enact the self-fashioning of the narrated discourse.

The awareness of the gap between life-experience and life-story of these immigrant writers constitutes an indispensable factor to foreground the strategies and paradigms employed in their fictions. Through the communication between the past experiences and present story-telling, readers can realize that the way we represent the past shapes our understanding of the present. Life-writings, including history-telling, will always assume a certain point of view which will minimize or miss some aspects while maximize others the author attempts to conceal or repress. The potential values of involuntary memory are followed by an approach of mourning, that is, the retelling of his traumatic story, to adjust to the present conception of social ethics.

Chapter Two Autobiographical Narrative in Ishiguro's Fiction

The autobiographical narrative presents the Narrator's sense of displacement in the cultural upheavals of Japanese reconstruction period, echoing Ishiguro's situation suffering from his bi-cultural legacies, and the alleged international identity he always advocates for the immigrants of postcolonial context. Ishiguro, a Japanese-born writer, selected his Japanese protagonists and settings for the debut of his writing career and created the images of Etsuko in *A Pale View of Hills* (1982) and *Ono in An Artist of the Floating World* (1986) set in post-war Japan. The Booker Prize winning novel *The Remains of the Day* (1989) convert his focus to the British butler Stevens as its narrator to witness British politician Mr. Darlington's fascist conduct. The narrator Banks in *When We Were Orphans* (2000) suffers his displacement from imaginary homeland of Shanghai, and presents his historical memoirs in the 1930s. Ishiguro's motif of displacement, as well as its effects on characters of *Never Let Me Go* (2005), argues that his brief spell of working with the homeless in the 1970s probably accounts for his obsession with struggles between the individual self-hood and the collective ideology that literally house his imagined self-consciousness within a larger historical context.

2.1 Confessions about the Imagined Nagasaki

Despite the Oriental characteristics commented by Barry Lewis and Bruce King, other critics such as Robert Clark and Terrence Rafferty respectively associate his techniques with British and European writers such as Jane Austen and Henry James. Ishiguro also acknowledges his debts to Dostoevsky, Chekhov and Kafka, from whom he learns the exploration skills of psychic dissonances, subterranean currents of emotion and surrealist frustrations of modernist psychology. Ishiguro's background offers him an innovative perspective to scrutinize the similarity and distinction of Japanese and British literary legacies. His earlier works parody the traditional emplotment of Japanese shomin-geki inspired by domestic films such as those of Ozu and Naruse, and portray the generation gaps and estrangements of Japanese families and marriages suffering post-war upheavals of social culture. The Japaneseness of his novels is not based on its historical or accurate authenticity, but on the symbolic homeland of his imagination, memories and speculation, a fictive artifact that can be mapped to satisfy Western curiosity about the images of alien and aesthetic oriental otherness. Gregory Mason even attributes Ishiguro's oriental motifs to the shomin-geki developed by Ozu and Naruse, and underlines that his themes "possess a Japanese resonance but with a Western incisiveness" (Mason, 1989: 50) to explore the psychological and ethical predicament set against the post-war cultural upheaval and reorientation background.

The autobiographical narrative of this debut novel reworks and improvises the genre of confession, and depends on the access of memories to narrate the past so as to reconstruct the narrator's own identities. His first novel, *A Pale View of Hills*, was appreciatively acclaimed and won the Winifred Holtby Memorial Prize. Contingently, the Ishiguro siblings are similar to the two sisters portrayed in his first novel, implying that to some extent he presents an allegory of his own family background. In fact, his mother, who was then a teenager girl, received injuries from the atomic bomb in Nagasaki and passed on her personal memories and anecdotes to her novelist son for his work of testimony and witness of historical events to reach to the public realm. Set in England, the novel recounts Etsuko's confessional meeting with her daughter Niki that triggers her retrospective justification of neglected responsibility leading to the figurative murder of another daughter Keiko. Ishiguro excavates his Japanese memories and infuses the self-referential experiences into the role of a Japanese woman partly because he "felt knowledgeable about the debates that were going on about feminism in my generation [...] serious and interesting cultural magazines where these debates took place from a female perspective" (Groes and Lewis, 2011: 251), which represents a new cultural collage of his Japanese childhood, family education and classically domestic films as his chief raw materials to reinvent his imagined Japan. Etsuko, a middle-aged immigrant Japanese woman who is living alone in her London country house in London, suffers a haunting guilt for Keiko's recent suicide and deliberately confesses the truth of her traumatic past life in Nagasaki. Smith and Watson conceive of confession as one basic genre of autobiography, through which confessants can admit their sins to an addressee who can represent the communal value or integrity, and even decree absolute judgement (Smith and Watson, 2010: 265) .Whereas Etsuko's confession is readily considered as the untruthful account of excuses and justifications of past wrongdoings and continuous attempts to identify with the communal ethics she has violated. Niki, the hybrid of her second marriage with English journalist Sheringham, undertakes the role of moral judgement made possible by her lack of loyalty to and prejudice of any specific culture.

The confessional impulse of excusing oneself from sins inevitably leads to ultimate untruthfulness as a result of its strategies of selective omissions, silences and concealment. The split subjectivity between the present narrator and the past narratee produces a discontinuous account in which Etsuko turns to her relationship with the textual addressee to transform her fragmented selfhood into a consistent narrative structure. At the beginning of her confession, Etsuko presents herself as a depressed mid-aged housewife living alone and estranged from her daughter as well her neighbors. Despite her failure to militate the self-felt guilt, the autobiographical narrative is frequently subverted through repeated unreliable memories, rather than as one coherent, essential and original entity. The performative dimension of confession "functions, then, in a different mode to the cognitive, as a verbal utterance which can not be verified and which also keeps the meaning of the action he is confessing 'open'"(Anderson, 2001: 49). This performative slippage from cognition to performativity turns out to be a failure of self-knowledge displaced by stagings of guilt, shame and confession. Obviously, the feeling that stirs Etsuko to justify herself is the guilt of her motherhood she has undertaken, which is closely related to "exhibitionism, and there is a connection between hiding oneself and self-revelation" (Anderson, 2001: 50). Thus, Keiko's suicide itself is not significant, but as a signifier of desired identity that backs up her confession. Despite its no reparation to her victim, Etsuko applies this opportunity to present her disgrace and desire to justify her crime to the addressee Niki and to her inner self. Paul de Man argues that "to confess is to overcome guilt and shame in the name of truth" (paul de Man, 1979: 279), but the truthfulness of this confessional narrative demonstrates its inclination from self-accusation to self-justification, "it does not suffice to tell all [...] is not enough to confess, one also has to excuse" (paul de Man, 1979: 280). The performantivity, according to paul de Man, does value more than the cognition of autobiographical narrative, through which the narrator Etsuko seeks the excuses to perform and stage the drama of her self-image. What she wants is not to explain away the true story she has experienced, but the desire to justify her past choices and conducts.

The autobiographical confession of this novel is permeated with pathetic memories and disillusions, which flash between the space-time distance to reflect her psychological mechanism of apologies or excuses for the infanticide complex. Stimulated by Keiko's suicide, Etsuko addresses Niki about her Nagasaki life not as self-accusation but as the arbitration of her true story, and even distorts her intentions of honesty and sincerity. The truthfulness can only be established totally through self-knowledge, deprived of the surveillance of Augustine's God, or more, so like Rousseau's *Confessions*, whose autobiography is "less an attempt to remember the past, to memorialize the life he led, than to make others recognize the inner truths about himself that he already knows" (Anderson, 2001: 45). Etsuko's past experiences can be readily regarded as the continuously disastrous reactions of nuclear bombing, in which the narrating "I" reminisces over her self-conscious misgivings resulting from her narratee's encounter with friends Sachiko and Mariko. During Niki's visit, Etsuko still struggles to accept the blame for the unhappiness and suicide of Keiko, whose phantom hovers over and haunts the survivors' current life. Niki's mission is to absolve her mother from Keiko's death, and she blames her sister's unhappiness in England on Mr. Sheringham's ignoring for most of her life. Whereas the narrated Nagasaki tale takes the form of Etsuko's confession about her abusive crimes against Keiko and seeks excuses to shed her shame and responsibility, the present narrator's story accounts for the anxiety that Etsuko and Niki suffer and offers its different and hindsight judgement of their past experiences. From a psychoanalytical perspective, Lois Tyson regards this kind of projection as "ascribing our fear, problem, or guilty desire to someone else and then condemning him or her for it, in order to deny that we have it ourselves"(Tyson, 2015: 15). Tyson thinks that this kind of regression belongs to certain mechanism of defence where a man can not only imagine it but also relive the situation he once experienced. In this case, a man can relive his or her pleasant, and most probably, painful memories, so that he can obtain the strength to deal with the current issues he is now encountering.

Rather than the coherent narration of the traditional autobiographies, the novel applies the perspective of unreliable first-person narrator, sprinkled with selective ellipses and evocative gaps for readers to piece together a sketchy picture of the guilt-stricken woman who attempts to confess past conduct to her addressee. But her attitude to confession oscillates between her determination to confront and her wish to apologize so as to erase her guilty feelings through reminiscing over her experiences in Nagasaki. The reconstructive memories deriving from Freudian psychological mechanism confirms the nature of Etsuko's confession that memory "can be an unreliable thing; often it is heavily coloured by circumstances in which one remembers, and [there is]no doubt [that] this applies to certain of the recollections I have gathered here" (PVH, 1990: 156). Wojciech Drag regards her defense mechanism as "glaring inability to confront the bombing in her narrative and her recurrent recourse to concealment, suppression and evasion" (Drag, 2014: 90) that helps to form a satisfying story for her Nagasaki life. Etsuko's imagined Nagasaki, rather than the realistic world where the narratee lived, is embedded with the experiential histories the narrator has once suffered and the selfhood she now performs in order to escape into her inner fantasy of estrangement from the outer world.

What impresses readers most is the similarity between the imagery of Etsuko and Sachiko, through which the narrator can undertake the role of detached and objective eye-witness to defend the participating conduct of the narrattee. From the start of the novel, Etsuko's narrative is readily trapped in paradoxes and controversies of recounting her autobiographical self-consciousness, and it is not a surprise to recognize that the story she tells and its emotional results repeatedly turn against the truthfulness of her confession. As Etsuko remembers, her married life in which she lives with her Japanese husband Jiro and father-in-law Ogata-San is a satisfying and serene one in opposition to Sachiko's displaced condition resulting from a similar bereavement, but readers gradually recognize the insinuations of the hostility and lack of communication between father-son and husband-wife relations. Her husband is mostly involved in his work or reading newspapers, who ignores the emotional requirements of his family members and subsequently leads to the disappointment of his father. This foreshadows the failure of the marriage and Etsuko's immigration to Britain. Like Etsuko, Ogata-San also reconstructs and rationalizes his memory about past experiences, which prefigures the impending emergence of narrator Ono in Ishiguro's next novel *An Artist of the Floating World*. Confronted with the public accusation of his wartime conduct by former student Shigeo Matsuda, the retired teacher defends his traitorous behaviour of imprisoning five co-workers and absolves himself through his patriotic and professional dignity which contributes to the Japanese nation. Like Stephen in James Joyce's *Ulysses*, Ishiguro delineates the new odyssey of Etsuko, a female Stephen, through which readers recognize her bereavement and being taken in by Ogata-San, and finally develops her intimacy with the symbolic father. While Etsuko finds it difficult to adapt to her new home and desperately escapes from Japan, Ogata-San, the paternal Bloom, suffers the hostility of his own son and seeks solace from Etsuko. As for her anxiety and misgivings of pregnancy, Mrs. Fujiwara and Sachiko repeatedly encourage her to keep delighted and positive attitudes to the impending parenthood, which countervails Etsuko's self-assurance of her positive outlook on both individual and collective future. The estrangement of familial relation deriving from the war-time devastation is attributable to the disturbing upheavals of postwar ideology, through which the young generation would like to embrace American pragmatism and democracy represented by American soldier Frank rather than the dignity of the aged Ogata-San.

The parallels of Etsuko's and Sachiko's similar family backgrounds gradually surface to readers' recognition that the present Etsuko is just the same as its would-be Sachiko, both of whom have lost their families during the war and later married into the families respectively represented by Ogata-San and Kawanda. They both suffer a lot from their tyrannical and "pharaoh" husbands, with whom they can not verbally and spiritually communicate or share the harmonious family atmosphere as a result of the prevailing hegemony of traditional patriarchy. In addition to the unorthodox manners of Sachiko, Etsuko volunteers to look after and comfort the "stray" girl Mariko while her mother flirts with her American lover, and until the last moment readers recognize that Etsuko's ideal motherhood collapses and converges with the self-serving mother to privilege her own prospects at the cost of her daughter's happiness. One episode of her confessions of uncaring motherhood near the bridge prefigures the future tragedy of Keiko, where Etsuko expresses her would-be unfulfilled promise with "a piece of old rope" (PVH, 1990: 173) held in her hand probably as a symbol of threat. The image of rope, linking the damage to Keiko and its subsequent tragedy against her initial promise, symbolically binds together several aspects of the novel, such as the narrator's guilt, Sachiko's relentlessness to her daughter's happiness, Keiko's suicide and Etsuko's haunting dream of the little girl on a wing.

The narrator is trapped in the entanglement of her confessional imagination and realistic truth, and thus integrates the story of her narratee through the deliberate connivance and trickiness of Sachiko's tragedy into her inner upheavals imposed by the historical events. The calm and reticent matter-of-fact voice of the narration, in relation to her reconstructive memories, points to Etsuko's attempts to conceal the hideous truth haunting her anxious mind and her psychological suffering. Overwhelmed by her sense of loss, Etsuko conceives of her haunting guilt as "a wound on one's own body, it is possible to develop an intimacy with the most disturbing of things" , squeezed into the remotest recess of emotion, and suffers her compulsively reenacting the image of "my daughter hanging in her room for days" (PVH, 1990: 54). Etsuko suffers the repeated images of repression, and her fear of unfulfilling the motherhood of caring for Keiko as well as the suppression of confession finally surges into the "ghost" image of her daughter that she imagines encountering. Here the image of Etsuko is compared to the Tokyo woman, a symbolic illustration of war-time legacy, which is "a projection of Etsuko's sense of guilt about her failed motherhood, thus reinforcing the traumatic strand linking Keiko's suicide with the ordeal of war" (Drag, 2014: 102).

The stories of Etsuko and Sachiko constitute the parallel structure of the motif based on pursuing their self-serving prospects through sacrificing their daughters. Readers recognize that their distinct life trajectories gradually converge into each other and finally dissolve their respective imagery. Should this be attributed to Etsuko's symptom of melancholia or the quality of constructive memories? Brian Shaffer comments that Etsuko can confess and justify her own treatment of Keiko through the outer structure of "present" narrative where Sachiko and Mariko "function less as 'real' individuals than as individuals onto whom Etsuko can project her own guilt for neglecting and abusing Keiko" (Shaffer, 1998: 21). As for the plausibility of this explanation, the Freudian concept of "melancholia" can be applied to exploring Etsuko's psychological upheavals of denial and concealment. While the subject's willingness to consciously remember is like a commitment to tracing the origins and easing the damaging anxiety, the unconscious forgetting turns out to be its resistance and even the compulsion to repeat or act out the repressed scenes of trauma defined as a complicated defense mechanism.(Freud,2006 313) Whereas the repressed emotion will ultimately come to the surface through the story of Sachiko, Etsuko insists on her reluctance to account for her past treatment of Keiko, and tends to avoid the mention of her suicide even when asked by her neighbour Mrs. Waters. Etsuko's narrative is pervaded with the intonation of "a painful past and sense of personal failure that she attempts, sometimes successfully and sometimes not, to repress" (Shaffer, 1998: 16). Whereas the sacrificing behavior of Sachiko echoes her neglect of Mariko and rejection of Japanese morality, the haunting image of Tokyo mother drowning her kid foretells of Etsuko's similar mistreatment and its consequent suicide of Keiko.

As the identity of Keiko/Mariko evolves more confusingly, Etsuko denies any links with the story of Sachiko and their mutually emotional upheavals. Although Etsuko's attitudes towards Keiko can parallel Sachiko's abusive motherhood for her daughter, one of her refutations is that her selfish "motives for leaving Japan were justifiable, and I know I always kept Keiko's interests very much at heart" (PVH, 1990: 91), which echoes Sachiko's repeated declaration of leaving for America. The imagery of Etsuko and Keiko turns out to be the protagonists of its inner story, and the decision of migration becomes the core of the mother-daughter conflict and reiteration of cultural communication. In this way Etsuko changes her role of participator into arbitrator, and integrates meaning and significance into her autobiographical narrative of reconstructing past experiences. Barry Lewis recognizes the estrangement existing between the outer and inner narratives, and attributes the unstable narration or lack of writer's voice to such competing patterns as following: (a) confused sets of memories; or (b) merging memory and fantasy; or (c) projecting her regret about bringing Keiko to Britain onto Sachiko; or (d) projecting her guilt onto the imaginary self-image (Lewis, 36). The last choice is considered as preferable, which can account for Etsuko's complicated process of psychologically reconstructing her memories to obtain transient comfort during her confession of guilt. The juxtaposition of Etsuko's double-role images provides a useful paradigm for understanding her appropriating Sachiko as a mask to perform her confession of guilty misconducts over her elder daughter that can trace back to the mother-daughter relationship in Nagasaki. As the story of Sachiko goes on, Etsuko gradually sinks into the pattern of daughter-abusing parallel through confessing her regrets of neglecting Keiko's benefits, and the guilty feeling appears stronger than ever while she sheds off her disguise. After acknowledging her selfish desire to forget, Etsuko makes it clear that her Japanese husband "for the seven years [...] a good father to her. Whatever else I convinced myself during those final days, I never pretended Keiko would not miss him" (PVH, 1990: 90). However, the whole narrative still remains a relentless and tranquil voice to compulsively reenact her repression, which may be seen as Freudian failed mourning or compulsive melancholia to willingly repeat traumatic experiences or crimes.

The Freudian talking cure process is to make patients, whose mind is just like battlefield for the above forces to wrestle with each other, conscious of the repressed memory and liberate themselves from its repetition impulse to overcome its resistance and work through the "mourning" process. (Freud, 394) Through the narrative of self-deception or self-protection, Etsuko relates her story and tends to reenact out with melancholia and turns the process into the pattern of how someone ends up talking about things they can not face directly through other people's stories. Ishiguro acknowledges that readers should regard the story of Sachiko as "highly Etsuko-ed version of this other person's story; and at the most intense point, I wanted to suggest that Etsuko had dropped this cover. It just slits out: she's now talking about herself. She's no longer bothering to put it in the third person" (Mason, 1989: 337). In this way Etsuko's narrative undertakes the "extradiegetic" role to comment Sachiko's guilt or abuse of her daughter and her own "homodiegetic" treatments of Keiko. The effort of repressing one's past life reflects the general attitude of articulating the post-war traumatic narrations, and its inclination of sensationalizing one's attitudes towards the literature of holocaust and nuclear bombing.

The process of forgetting or denial of Keiko's death and her own sufferings in Nagasaki reflect Etsuko's melancholia to force the scenes of wasteland or valleys of ashes resulting from the war-time devastation into the shadows of the distressed psyche. Instead of Freudian remembering or working through the past trauma, Etsuko chooses to forget and justify her guilt through Sachiko's story, and confirms the untruthfulness of modern confession. Just like Mrs. Fujuwala's exhortation, postwar Japanese people "should be thinking about the future", and regards "thinking about the dead" and its consequent commemoration as immature and "shame" (PVH, 1990: 25). The only mention of its miserable consequence Etsuko makes is the portrayal of her neighbourhood reconstructed after the war, where "I lived [...] and I was once told that before the war a small village had grown up on the riverbank. But then the bomb had fallen and afterwards all that remained were charred ruins" (PVH, 1990: 11). Whereas these dysfunctional "ruins" of her neighbourhood are satirically attributed to officials' delinquency, thc peace memorial is ironically represented as a muscular Greek god or a policeman conducting traffic, which deprives it of its deservedly solemn and symbolic connotation of melancholic trauma and the opportunity of genuinely working through a painful history hidden beneath the collective and national consciousness. Instead of rousing nostalgia and communally unified feelings, such public commemoration reminds people of unspeakable pain and leads to its civic division. Barry Lewis regards her denial as survivor guilt and summarizes three developing phases of this genre which include: (a) descriptions of the nonrepresentational by survivors, (b) interrogations of political and historical context and (c) allegorical warnings for future generations (Lewis, 2000: 40). The toll for death and survivor guilt persecutes Etsuko and Keiko, both of whom have been damaged or "shocked" to the extent that the former chooses compulsively playing the violin at night and the latter frequently encounters mysterious ghosts out of their traumatic experiences.

The narrative of guilty survivors is tangled with the ambience of shame, guilt and doubt, and is suspected of an intent to express the fragility and ubiquity of death mainly accounting for the emotional or psychological consequences. The present narrator conceived her confession as an alibi where the narrative "I" was steeped in public ideologies and "institutional discourses, through which people come to understand themselves and to place themselves in the world, or as Althusser terms it, through which people are interpellated as certain kinds of subjects" (Smith and Watson, 2010: 76). The writer Ishiguro, born in postwar Nagasaki and educated in Britain, applies the role of ideological narrator to describe the emotional upheaval that people are doomed to suffer. Through the role of judge or addressee of Etsuko's self-justification, Niki undertakes the precipitate function to help her mother work through the mourning process and her attachment to the lost objects, which confirms her self-assurance that Etsuko "did everything you could for her. You're the last person anyone could blame" (PVH, 1990: 176). Despite their attempts, Etsuko and Niki can't shed the haunting guilt for Keiko's unhappiness and her ultimate choice of suicide, which prefigures their continuous nightmares of ghosts and "a disturbing feeling about that room [...] a strange spell seemed to linger there even now, six years after she had left it — a spell that had grown all the stronger now that Keiko was dead" (PVH, 1990: 53). Up to this point readers may recognize that the origins of her compulsively reenacting nightmares about the innocent girl winging in the village park point clearly to a series of child murders in post war Nagasaki that connect with the image of Mariko/Keiko hanging from her bedroom ceiling.

Despite the mutual painful depression, mourning is preferred as a momentary solution to the loss of beloved objects through the regained capability of attaching to others, but melancholia only demonstrates the Freudian features of "reduction" of self-consciousness, "self-recrimination" , and "self-directed insults", which turns out to be a "pathological disposition" (Freud, 2006: 310-311). Etsuko can not reestablish the attachment to its abandoned object-cathexis of her guilt-triggering daughter, as a result of her refusing the finality of loss or even bringing back the daunting ghosts of the past to represent the haunting felt-guilt of the present. The narrator's melancholia prevents her from further reconciliation with the past and performing her successful mourning, through which to confront the traumatic remorse. As a war-time victim, Etsuko links the images of survivor guilt such as Mrs. Fujiwala and Ogata-San with its devastating origins, and suffers a disorder of psychic melancholia deprived of the capability of narrating her past experiences. Whereas Ogata-San and Mrs. Fujiwala choose to forget the past to challenge their postwar life with self-dignity, Etsuko would rather escape to England, who subsequently neglects her responsibility for Keiko. Through the reacting of past truth and traumatic memories, Etsuko attempts to restore her normal identify narrative, and diverts to account for the emotional upheavals of individuals and their new recognition of survivor guilt.

Like Ogata-San who refuses to revisit his old haunts ravaged by the war, Etsuko rejects the existence of the Tokyo woman drowning her kid and killing herself, and purposefully attributes the ghostly-appearance woman Keiko/ Mariko encounters to her visiting cousin Yasuko Kawanda suffering her own bereavement. More than once, Etsuko/Sachiko neglects the care of her daughter, but compares her to a "filthy" and "dirty" kitten that deserves only drowning and "figurative murder of her daughter" (Shaffer, 1998: 33). When actually drowning the caged kittens, Etsuko's metaphorical guilt of infanticide prefigures her actual complicity of murdering Keiko through prisoning her with negligence and abuse. As for the relation of Sachiko and Mariko, Freud raises the idea of a Sado-masochistic impulse of self-destruction, of which the individual's aggressive desire can't find its satisfactory outlet to the outer world, but only divert its direction to the inwardness (Freud, 1965: 105). The repressed desire desperately seeks its outlets in the form of phantasmal dreams, which ultimately transverse the flimsy safeguarding walls of psychological self-definition, with the aim of accusing of and rejecting itself inside the psyche.

The sadistic role of Sachiko confirms the narrator's own shame of motherhood and also her pleasure through figuratively drowning her kittens, and forces Mariko to undertake the masochistic role in taking pleasure in self-punishment. Given her hostile relation to the external world, Etsuko absorbs the historical events into her inner world through the narrated story of her encounter with Sachiko and their mutual frustrations of life to keep at bay her present guilt. As her confession goes on, Etsuko feels increasingly besieged by the addressee's or readers' doubts and sympathies and forced to confess her remorse and truth of story. Estranged from her Nagasaki family, Etsuko is now using her autobiographical confession as a form and attitude to put right the social and personal misrepresentations and misunderstandings of her motherhood. The more significant point for her is not the content of her confession, but the performance in order to achieve her self-definition or her step out of the mask and the public role in revealing the unconscious self.

Ishiguro recounts the immigration experiences of the narrator Etsuko and her friend Sachiko, through the polyphonic structure, the intertextuality parodies in the typical opera *Madame Butterfly*. Householder defines parody as "a narrative poem of moderate length, in epic meter, using epic vocabulary, and treating a light, satirical, or mock-heroic subject" , as well as "a usage of comic imitation" (Rose, 1993: 7), and utilizes the textual tension to subvert the parodied "classics" and express its euphemistic judgement. Compared with Etsuko, the image of Westernized housewife surfaces to readers' imagination, echoing the parodied geisha Cio-Cio-San. The suicide complex in the parodying text continues the self-aphasic of Cio Cio-San resulting from cultural hybridization, which parallels the similar state of living alone and suffering from the estrangement of their own families.

The orientalist scrutiny conceives of Keiko's suicide as national instinct, disregarding that the popularity of exaggerating films of shomin-geki and samurai can not confirm the suicide complex the Western people have imagined. Once people are classified as certain cultural belongings, they will be regarded as different species, such as the respective British and Japanese national ethnicities represented by Niki and Keiko. As the deception of memories is gradually divulged, readers ultimately recognize that Etsuko bring Keiko to escape to Britain, but only fails to find the safe haven for her lost soul. As a product of cultural conflicts, the name of Niki foreshadows different symbols held by Etsuko and her husband Sheringham, which parallels the identity crisis Keiko suffers and her subsequent suicide. The immigrants such as Etsuko and Keiko treat their homelands as a mixture of memory, speculation and imagination, who "are not and will never be unified culturally in the old sense, because they are inevitably the products of several interlocking histories and cultures, belonging at the same time to several homes-and thus to no one particular home" (Gilroy, 1993: 362). The oriental immigrants suffering from the conflicts of different cultures reluctantly identify with their Western tradition and even posit themselves in the predicament of anxiety and despair, which force them to respect and combine the bicultural legacies to reestablish their new self-definition.

Floating outside the culture of her migrated homeland, Keiko becomes the vagrant exile away from her imagined homeland and even excluded from her own family, "Keiko had retreated into that bed room, shutting us out of her life. She rarely came out… had no friends, and the rest of us were forbidden to entry into her room… when by some impulse Keiko ventured down into our living room, we would all feel a great tension" (PVH, 1990: 53). Readers recognize that the private space Keiko has resolutely safeguarded haunts the survivors like a curse, and the little girl swinging in Etsuko's nightmare prefigures her anxious feeling of guilt stepping from the negligence of her elder daughter's happiness. The appreciation of different culture and tradition should enhance the identification and the understanding of each other, otherwise the individuals can only lose oneself and the concomitant self-consciousness will dissipate and turn into fragment and fragility. Despite her immersing in Western culture, Keiko adheres to her oriental legacy and the identification, and she forces her self to undertake the compulsively embedded position of subordinates, while suffering from the loss of equal communication with others, and even the discrimination and estrangement from her sister and stepfather.

As the immigrant of second generation, Niki ultimately casts off her orientalist prejudice so as to reflect on the origins of her family tragedy. Confronted with alienated identification, the immigrant "Others "have never enjoyed any fruits of their integrating into the local society, for its communal culture is endowed with its unique social tradition, cultural values and ideology.

The narrative of individual identity is embedded in the everyday speech and cultural tradition we should abide by, and can only be reconstructed through recounting or remembering the traumatic experiences. As the inheritor of bicultural legacies, Niki represents the compulsive or voluntary phenomenon of postwar migration and foreshadows the currently alleged international identity-narrative of postcolonial society. The hybrid identity of Niki posits herself outside the ambience of extreme nationalism and cultural prejudice, consoling the disturbed soul of her mother. The dilapidation of courtyard insinuates the heart-breaking family relations and the conditions of Keiko's being neglected, and stimulates Niki to reflect upon the national categories her father and sister respectively represents, which endows her the impartiality to revalue her family history and the mistreatment of Etsuko towards her daughter.

Despite her sojourning in England for many years, Etsuko still likes to indulge in her reminiscing over the experiences in Nagasaki, and frequently interrogates the rationale of forsaking her former family life. Influenced by the nightmare of nuclear bombing and its subsequent postwar optimism of reconstruction, the national ideology is challenged and overwhelmed by Americanized fashion of freedom and democracy. Feeling the traditional values such as family duty and fame unbearable, Etsuko decides to embrace the Western manners and creeds, only to find herself stranded in an enclave "within nation-states of the west, leading to a 'pluralization' of national cultures and national identities" (Hall, 1992: 306). Although shedding off the traumatic memories becomes her only practical choice, Sachiko abandons her responsibility of motherhood in the name of democratic freedom and prospects of her daughter to gloss over her own self-serving willingness of escaping from Nagasaki. Despite the disappointment at her lover's behavior, Etsuko still embraces Western culture detests the tradition of her homeland, who does not awaken or regret over her abuse of Keiko until the occurrence of her suicide.

Seen from Etsuko's memorial labyrinth, the pathetic and sorrowful tragedy gradually looms, but its consequent conflicts and reconciliation of cultural values will continue to haunt others. The fragments of memory have been infused into the traumatic reenacting of realistic living status, and "what animates such appeals is not only disagreement about what happened in the past and what the past was, but uncertainty about whether the past really is past, over and concluded, or whether it continues, albeit in different forms" (Said, 1993: 3). Such individuals of diaspora encounter their confusing and temporary transformations of identity, and attempt to reestablish the new international narrative which exceeds the anger and mania of subordinates to concentrate on the private happiness and restrained emotions of secular society. The vagrants floating in foreign lands suffer the uprooted loss of cultural tradition and lacking in identification with new system of ideology deriving from the upheavals of changing morality and values.

Ishiguro posits the cultural identification and confusion of immigrants in the context of historical events, and enacts the contemporary pilgrim to integrate into other cultures through Etsuko's Freudian defense mechanism of "remembering" and "mourning" elaborated by the parodied text. Seduced by similar American soldiers, Etsuko and Cio-Cio-San react passively with distinct attitudes which provide the new oriental context for Ishiguro's identity narrative. The ethnocentric complex of *Madame Butterfly* produces comical and discordant comparison and its consequent anxiety of textual influence. Later on, the bestselling book *Memoirs of a Geisha* (1997) and its consequent adaption of movie, an alleged modern portrayal of Puccini's opera, once again confirms the occidental fascination of its oriental exoticism. Etsuko, out of parodying text, regards to migration as her only way of escaping from the current predicament resulting from her admiration of Western democracy. Despite her disgust of the obscene and laziness of her drunkard lover, Etsuko voluntarily chooses to marry into foreign land. Confronted with the dominant position of Western culture, the narrator Etsuko suffers the collective aphasia of inferiority complex, through combining her specific national characteristics and ethnocentric hierarchy.

Instead of extolling her choice of self-serving prospects, the narrating Etsuko finds herself the victim of external events, fatefully determined by the outer world of postwar Nagasaki, alone and powerless to react against her tragic trajectory. Despite her negligence of motherhood, what disturbs Etsuko most is that the mother would like to flirt with an American soldier Frank who promises to satisfy her fantasy of escaping from her sequestered situation, rather than attend to her "stray" daughter, let alone cultivating her proper manners and behaviors. The similar American soldiers Frank or Franklin act as an intertextuality of parody in relation to the opera *Madame Butterfly* by Puccini, who both seduce and later abandon the Japanese female protagonists Cio-Cio-San and Etsuko. Barry Lewis compares the "kujibik stand" episode where Mariko wants to win a basket for her kittens with the settings of "exotic costuming, its sets of flake cherry blossoms and sliding rice-paper screens"

(Lewis, 2000: 23), and emphasizes their mutual fictive quality of artifacts born out of memories and imaginations. Distinct from the innocent image of the parodied oriental otherness, Etsuko is clearly aware of her lover Frank's quality of lecherous drunkard, and regards him only as the means of escaping or avoiding her family responsibility-the care of her daughter, just like her repressed desire to confess, "I'd go to America one day, that I'd go there to become a film actress" (PVH, 1990: 109). Etsuko's desire or, in Lacan's term, "absence" of self-identity infuses into the specific objects or symbols and leads to her permanent anxiety to approximate the object-fulfilling complex.

This cultural intertextuality applies the parody of colonial and figurative signifier so as to deviate and subvert its system of overwhelming ideology, but its complicated complex of coexisting obedience and resistance produces their hesitation or stasis. Even if Etsuko is eager to escape from Nagasaki, She consciously realizes that her romantic love should be betrayed and abandoned, and feels the oscillating choice of her migration. To readers' surprise, Etsuko immediately posits her in the dilemma of flirting with American soldier to serve her selfish prospects, which contributes to her later confession of ignoring her motherhood leading to the scapegoated fate that Keiko "would't be happy over there" (PVH, 1990: 176). The narrative of autobiographical acts is so internalized personally and culturally that the narrators "seem 'natural' and 'universal' characteristics of persons", and competing for "ideological notions of personhood coexisting at any historical moment" (Smith and Watson, 2010: 77). Thus the Freudian repression of psychological instincts is influenced by the ideological civilization the one-dimensional individual lives in, which accounts for the orientalist suppression and substitution of local cultural identification for dominant ideology in opposition to its marginalization of colonial otherness. Whereas American soldiers Pinkerton and Frank similarly regard their eastern lovers as the innocent and delicate "Others", awaiting their white knights to save, the invaded "Others" Etsuko and Cio-Cio-San can only alienate their traditional morality and Cultural Values belief to reconstruct their new identity belongings. Just as the parodied Cio-Cio-San is fascinated with her lover Pinkerton and even disengages herself with her family and replaces her Shintoism for Christianity, Etsuko appreciates American democratic rights and even at all times talks of its household patterns and fashions. "The Americans came [...] They decided our schools would be like American schools, the children should learn what American children learn. And the Japanese welcomed it all" (PVH, 1990: 66). Despite the paralleled trajectory of their life choice, the contemporary "Others" Etsuko transforms into woman knight to save her American soldier from his living mires, and starts her adventurous journey to foreign land at the expense of abandoning her Japanese family and sacrificing the happiness of her daughter.

The mixture of parodied images creates the polyphonic dialogue of different textual structures. Confronted with the westernized others, Ogata-San adheres to his Confucian Values and morality, which is another parallel of the parodied image uncle Monk indulged in his obstinate Shintoism. He regards disciplines and duties of human beings as necessities of his powerful empire, and questions the suitability of American democracy defying his loyalty to the family, the superiors and the country. The marginal images of Monk and Ogata-San are witnessed as ignorant and frail laggards of their living epoch, and becomes the polyphonic structure of Western knight spirit in relation to its typical textual images of Crusoe and Friday, Rochester and Burtha in Western Classics.

The textual autobiographical narration itself possesses the symptoms of mental schizophrenia deriving from the strategies that the narrating "I" can not only govern her self-consciousness, but also applies the third-person Sachiko to act as self-referential role to explain away Etsuko's own story. Freud argues that mental handicap as the status of mental self-unawareness can only be treated through talking cure or narrating one's traumatic past, but even if the self-narrator penetrates into the truth beneath the reconstructive memories, she can only temporarily guarantee the distancing between the reasonable narrator and her unreliable narrated story at the expense of sacrificing the self-consciousness(Freud, 1965: 106). The narrator applies its visual distance to perform the mediator of narratee and readers and share information with her addressee, while the space-time distance creates the self-awareness of narrator and endows Etsuko with Sachiko's perspective to recount her own experience in Nagasaki. If readers substitute the life trajectory of Etsuko and Keiko for that of Sachiko and Mariko, the fact that the transformed Sheringham from Frank in Nagasaki dooms to estrange from his stepdaughter, and even Sachiko's treating her daughter like a dirty animal prefigures her later being abandoned and choice of suicide.

The narrator transforms into coexisting image of the narratee and the third-person Sachiko, and applies the space-time distancing to frequently make self-judgement and comments, thus underneath the Janus-faced image exists the textual narration of the narrator and the narratee which diverges the attention of readers to the polyphonic dialogue of text narrative. The fact is that either the parodied Cio-Cio-San suicides for her son or the parodying Etsuko sacrifices her daughter to marry into England, both of which become the symptoms of preconceived ideology, the narrator is forced to accept or resist. The oriental "Otherness" alleged by Euro-centrists is actually the self-portrait and artifact of imagination to define Western civilization, including the competing process of such factors as history, knowledge and hierarchy for its discourse rights. The cultural hybridization of dominant ideology and its oriental "Other" does not create the equality but collective inferiority complex, through which the parodied Cio-Cio-San blindly admires her lover's knight spirit and image of savior. She would rather question the credibility of local religion and even the nestling instinct of robin in springs than Pinkerton's flirtation, only to find her lover's emergence with his wife, and ultimately preserve the dignity through her suicide. However, the oriental woman warrior Etsuko reluctantly seduces her timid drunkard lover to marry into Britain, and ultimately fulfills her transformation of identity from marginalization to centralization at the cost of her daughter's happiness. In fact, what she finally obtains is not the elimination of national ethnology and prejudice, but the invasion and suppression of dominant culture in opposition to its estranged subordinates.

Etsuko and Cio-Cio-San in different epochs similarly rely on the justice of Western democracy as their self-guarding walls, only to find that the subjects invaded by Western ideology have estranged from their living atmosphere and replaced themselves with the objected conception they accept. As the parodied textual image, the fateful tragedy of Etsuko and her daughter derives from the orientalist preconception of self-imagination to explain away their ideological self-images, but such ideological hierarchy forces and assimilates the identity narrative of oriental "Other" in opposition to the self-consciousness and self-definition of cultural subjects. As the addressee of Etsuko's confession, Niki begins to reflect the immigrant identity of her family, and feels the prejudices and biases her father holds for the responsibility of Keiko's tragedy. The images of textual parody fulfill the dual-coding of Puccini's classical opera, not only deconstruct the Western knight spirit and innocent image of oriental woman, but also parody the comical return of central discourse journeyed by the oriental woman warrior and its international identity narrative.

The traumatic memories of oriental "Other" stimulates Ishiguro to construct his "imagined homeland", and the alleged "third space" to comb through the ideological discourse through deconstructing its unequal dialogue system and "rhetoric trap" of individual self-consciousness. While writing her confessional narrative, Nagasaki remains the psychological centre of Etsuko's universe. Despite her living abroad for several decades, she instinctively returns to her youth and past experiences to compare with her living state. The exaggerating portrayal of parodied text *Madame Butterfly* prefigures the later questioning and defying the conventions of normative autobiographical fiction to express the narrator's critical opinions. The splitting distancing of narrator and narratee endows Etsuko with a double self-image that unveils her innermost secrets of guilt and then holds together the disparate times of her life through her retrospective narrative to acquire her epiphany for initiation of her new life. Ishiguro's reflection upon the ideological defaults to prevent the reenacting of historical tragedies will provide more justifiable self-definition for individuals in multicultural conditions.

2.2 Apologies of a Floating Artist

Ishiguro continues his odyssey of transforming his own migration experiences and impressions of imagined homeland into the next autobiographical narrative of his oriental complex. As its sequel piece, *An Artist of the Floating World*, a novel that wins the Whitbread Novel Award, performs the exploration of his Japanese legacies he commenced in his debut *A Pale View of Hills*, in which the painting teacher Ogata-San who suffers his accusation of promoting Japanese militarism is now replaced with his equivalent Masuji Ono. The novel recounts the apologies of its narrator Ono, a retired Japanese artist teacher, who reminisces over his artistic career and justifies his former conducts of extreme nationalism from the perspective of current duration between October 1948 and June 1950. The narrator Ono here focuses more on the responsibilities of an artist and his emotional upheavals beneath its calm surface of his narrative, of which the motif will recur in his *The Remains of the Day* (1989) and *The Unconsoled* (1995) . In order to build their identities, the writers of autobiographical writings have the emplotment "converted into literary form" to account for their life stories. Smith and Watson comment that the genre of apology "justifies one's own deeds, beliefs and way of life" for the narrator to self-defend his culpability against "the allegations or attacks of others" (Smith and Watson, 2010: 255). Whereas the narrative of Etsuko relies on the genre of confession to construct its autobiographical writing, the dominant form of the latter is that of apology for

Ono to rationalize and justify himself of his previous behaviors.

Ono's narrative invites a structure of the apology, in which the narrator criticized by the community for his past conducts chooses to justify his misdeeds and the justice of moral choice he has advocated. However, the motivation of his performance is not the heartfelt guilt or repentance, but the success of his daughter's marriage negotiations and his own self-righteousness. Thus the apologetic narrative is supposed to satisfy his self-interests and obtain his emotional catharsis and moral conscience to remove from the public criticism. Despite similarity of their symbiotic states of Freudian mechanism, the definition of shame "affects the interactional self, and threatens the individual with 'losing face'" concerning its extraneous social relationship, but guilt infringes upon "the inner self, and can corrode self-esteem even in those situations where there is no possibility of the misdeed's disclosure" (Lewis, 2000: 46). Instead of assuring the addressee Etsuko of her innocence for Keiko's death, the narrator Ono purposefully self-defends the integrity of his artist career in the context of social and ethical circumstances, of which the real goal is not to explain away his autobiographical truth, but to rationalize or apologize his participation in the political affairs. Ishiguro comments that Ono's "position is that he's not ashamed of anything he's done; but gradually his point of view shifts and he starts owning up" (Tookey, 1996: 34), and attributes his own shame to the great desire to do something of worth or to distinguish himself from the mediocre public. The out-dated characters such as Ono and Matsuda suffer Freudian melancholia, compulsively reenact the self-image of pursuing ideals and dreams, but fail to undertake the responsibility of reflecting on their imperial complicities, "the likes of him and me, we have satisfaction of knowing that whatever we did we did at the time in the best of faith [...] this is surely preferable to never putting one's convictions to the test" (AFW, 1986: 201). Although Ono does not turn away from a full account of his career of artistic propagandist, he does conceal the stories of his son's and his wife's deaths, and of the betrayal of his former student Kuroda, probably due to his finding it too painful to dwell upon. Through the narrator's self-presentation, the writer accounts for how Ono justifies, both elegiacally and dishonestly, his artistic ideals and dignities that have been projected onto the wrong trajectory but exonerated his artistic prestige from social accusation within the postwar public ideology.

From the start of the novel, the retired artistic teacher is entangled in his trivial household routines, such as accompanying his grandson, visiting his old friends and seeking marriage negotiations for his younger daughter, but alone his anxious reflections frequently flash back to his former career, especially that of the grandeur of propagandist period. Just like what Etsuko reacts to Keiko's death, Ono similarly represses the mention of his son Kenji and wife Michiko and their death resulting from his survivor guilt and the unspeakable accusations suffering from the postwar Japanese ideology. Ono does not dwell upon the mourning of his family bereavement, except for their death during the wartime and "freak raid" (AFW, 1986: 91), so as to avoid the triggering of his humiliating shame or the judgement from the public. The sense of survivor guilt not only reminds him of the fascistic ideology he has acquiesced through his war-record paintings, but also divests him of the courage to undertake the responsibility for his family devastation. Through the historical documents of memories and imagination, Ishiguro presents with readers the portrait that concerns itself with the influence and responsibility of the artist to society as well as the way in which the present changes affect the perceptions of the past. The narrator's autobiographical apologies of his individual shames embedded in the tempestuous events posit Ono in the ambience of current public ideology to underline his deep-down upheavals of individual emotions and feelings.

The narrator Ono combines his current painful events with the past story of narratee, flashing back and forth to outline the reconstruction of mnemonic "fault-lines by sudden tremors of space, time, mood and perspective", rather than a "seamless and coherent" narrative of normal autobiography (Lewis, 2000: 61). Suffering from his haunting shame, the present narrator "I" unconsciously reveals his repressed emotions and psychological anxieties, which forces him to self-deceive and self-apologize his past behaviors through falsifying the truthfulness of historical events to rebuild his new self-imaging through emphasizing that "even if he was wrong, at least he was influential: that it is more important to have made one's mark than to have been a right-minded nonentity" (Shaffer, 1998: 59). The present narrator revalues his former role of imperial aggressiveness, questions and analogizes his self-definition of artistic achievement under the upheavals of postwar ideology, just as what Ogata-San does for his public humiliation. Just like Keiko's suicide in *A Pale View of Hills*, his younger daughter Noriko's miai episode performs the central linkage to the polyphonic structure of Bakhtin's dialogues. Ishiguro applies the stratagem of polyphonic dialogues, through which the central motif concerns Ono's progress of artistic activities and his apology of betraying former student Kuroda who gains the reputation of a political martyr.

The outer structure is permeated with the anxieties of his family life which becomes the impetus of his justifying himself from the previous shameful conducts. Through the remembrances of his autobiographical writing, Ono's story seems to "fill in gaps and elusive meanings as the novel progresses, but what occurs instead of discovering is the narrator's own version of life made more palatable in the act of telling it" (Wong, 2005: 38). The flashing back and forth of his traumatic memories and its consequent disruption of logic represents the vulnerability of individual identity shackled within social reality and ideology, not only emphasizing its oriental narrative of foreign lands, but also prefiguring the prophesy of its nationalist complex. Ishiguro is interested in the Freudian defense mechanism that "somehow takes on board some of the post-Freudian tensions in life—that comes not from buckling up, not from being unable to express yourself, but from just being pulled left, right, and centre by possible role models and urges, by a sense that you're missing out" (Shaffer, 1998: 14). The Freudian mechanism emphasizes the re-constructiveness and "deferred action" of autobiographical memories, which inclines to attach its significance and logic to the unworthy or transient past events, and distorts them to accord to the present motivation(s). The repression of mentioning the deaths of Ono's son and his wife resulting from the war he once supported indicates his traumatic state and secret impetus to keep his autobiographical memoir so as to absolve himself from the responsibility for their tragic bereavements.

Different from the present hollowness of his retired life, Ono takes pride in his past prestige of social role as a respectable artist who is admired and surrounded by his students and acolytes as a result of the collaboration of artists with the militant government. To his disappointment, his ideal of contributing to Japanese society ultimately turns out to be the misguided waste of life undermined by his contribution to the war effort. As an autobiographical apology, the present narrator privileges the re-constructiveness of memories to self-apologize himself in the guise of family benefits, rather than performs his guilt-felt confession, in order to reconstruct his self-knowledge which is no longer suitable for the current public ideology. Confronted with the public consensus that the older generation should be responsible for the war-time devastation, Ono holds the opposite opinion and rationalizes his "courage and honesty to accept what he did in the past" (AFW, 1986: 125), while his former student Shintaro chooses opportunistically to dissociate the relationship with his former virtuoso. Ishiguro, in an interview, conceives this novel as "an exploration of somebody trying to come to terms with the fact that he has somehow misused his talents unknowingly, simply because he didn't have any extraordinary power of insight into the world he lived in" (Mason, 1989: 339). The desire for wholeness of human life orients the characters like Ono to seek the existential meaning within the throes of historical events, only to find themselves stranded in a plight that they need to be exonerated from the postwar humiliation. Ono's identity which relies heavily on the outer context that involves a collapse of ascribed identity and social hierarchy leaves him floating between the past and the present to seek exculpation from fragmented memories.

Distinct from Shintaro's denial and the suicide of Jiro Miyake's company president, Ono self-apologizes for himself with his professional life of misguided principles, and feels, together with Matsuda, no need to blame himself for the futility of their well-meant efforts because they "at least acted on what we believed and did our utmost. It's just that in the end we turned out to be ordinary men. Ordinary men with no special gifts of insight" (AFW, 1986: 200). The contextualization of Ono's professional choice confirms the performance of his apology through foregrounding his idealism and concerns about the suffering of his compatriots. His later encounter with Matsuda enables him to abandon the decadent pursuit of aesthetic beauty and then turns to a moral and social function of realistic paintings. However, it is exactly due to the humanistic consciousness that Ono ultimately connects his career with nationalism and later scandalous accusations of postwar ideology. Through Ono's first-person narrative, the writer dramatizes "the connections between public history and an 'I' dependent for definition on its circumstances, suggesting that the unconfident and marginalized self of the posthumanist world view is drawn to find writerity in totalitarian politics" (Scanlan, 1993: 141).

As a relentless patriarch who attributes the tension of father-daughter relation to Noriko's embittered temperament or marriage anxiety, Ono also shows little sympathy for his former student Kuroda he once betrayed. Even while being accused of an national traitor and his lack of self-felt guilt, he feels shocked and does not understand the resentment received during his visit to Kuroda. What he feels necessary is to forbid "the young man's words to upset me unduly, but in the light of Noriko's marriage negotiations, the possibility that Kuroda was as hostile to my memory as Enchi suggested was indeed a disturbing one" (AFW, 1986: 114). As a "conscience-troubled" aging man,

Ono frequently hesitates between moral responsibility and psychological expedience and between disclosing and glossing over his haunting shame, whose narrative is "carefully designed to conceal while appearing to reveal his past culpability" (Shaffer, 1998: 43). Ono applies his self-deceptive strategy to absolve his innocent status and guarantees "certainly a satisfaction and dignity to be gained in coming to terms with the mistakes one has made in the course of one's life. In any case, there is surely no great shame in mistakes made in the best faith" (AFW, 1986: 125). Roger Horrocks even defines it as the mental healing process, in which the psyche of subjects undertakes the dubious competition between forgetting and remembering for the privacy to cling to or shed off the traumatic burden. The remembering or talking cure process can be considered as the mental operation of "liberating the repressed content of the unconscious" (Horrocks, 2001: 56), and thus integrate the traumatic incidents into the life narrative for the subjects to walk though his melancholia.

Due to his complicity of propagandist nationalism, Ono is not only blamed indirectly for the death of his son and wife, but also urged by his elder daughter setsuko to take precautionary steps to prevent the "misunderstandings" of Noriko's marriage negotiations. The current negotiation with the Saito Family, during which both parties should investigate the family fame and status of each other, forces Ono to reconsider the morality of his previous conducts. Fearing that his nationalist status might have turned into an obstacle to Noriko's miai, Ono resorts to his visiting and persuading the event witnesses of concealing his wrongdoings to guarantee their positive responses to the would-be inquiries of the Saito family. During the period of her negotiation, he writes off this personal memoir to perform the meditations and justifications about the past. Despite Setsuko's later denial of suggesting his "precautionary steps", Ono assures himself once again that it is right for his elder daughter who advises him to guarantee the miai through visiting and requesting the favors of his past acquaintances. However, the episode of debating with Jiro Miyake he suspects of leading to the failure of Noriko's previous marriage gradually first infuses into the shadow of his imagined paranoia, and then ultimately dissolves into another version of his quarreling occasions with his son-in-law Suichi. Here Ono blames the failure of Noriko's marriage negotiation on his higher family status and the anachronistic war, rather than the relevance of his past conducts. Another episode Ono chooses to self-deceive is his response to his grandson Ichiro's request of looking at his paintings because of his great fame of acting as an artist. Instead of endorsing the act of apologizing for personal complicity, Ono disagrees with the suicides that certain politicians have committed for their wrongdoings.And he proudly defends his supporting of the war of aggression, and feels no need of feeling shame for his replaced ideals and values.

Flashing back to his culmination of artist career, Ono reminisces over Mori-San's embarrassing conclusion of life that "I have devoted it to the task of capturing the unique beauty of that world, I believe I will be well satisfied. And no man will make me believe I've wasted my time" (AFW, 1986: 150-151). Its pathetic ambience sounds more like his own predicament of current discredited status to justify his own misguided life when addressing his pupils. Margaret Scanlan argues that the narrator inclines to abstract and generalize his conduct, "when he talks about other people, he frequently appears to be talking about himself. This trick, of course, is a familiar psychological defense, but in Ono's case it seems to point to a more fundamental confusion of himself with the people he discusses" (Scanlan, 1993: 145). Through twisting the perspective of his story, Ono inclines to commit the common autobiographical mistakes of weaving his own illusions to rationalize what he thinks the world should be or his own apology of the past conducts. He has neither the desire nor the capability of standing aside and observing his fate criticized in a truly objective perspective, "however accurately one may fill in the surface details of one's mirror reflection, the personality represented rarely comes near the truth as others would see it" (AFW, 1986: 67). The montage-like textual scenes Ono elaborates are more like film-editing method of dissolving to connect the two images of similarity or difference through depicting events occurring in the past but relative to the present. Barry Lewis argues that the narrative of selecting, concealing and arranging his autobiographical chronologies is "a subjective, sometimes 'confessional', device that mimics an individual's thought processes and usually involves an enigma of some kind" (Lewis, 2000: 62). The narrator's perspective traces back to the past achievements of narrated Ono, only to find that his influence and social status stretch beyond his own imagination and memories. Through divulging of his apologies, the younger daughter Noriko and ever readers recognize the fact what her father has dedicated to the artistic career becomes a self-deception glossing over his surrender to the imperialist ideology in the name of humanitarian ideals, just like Ogata-San's apology that one "shouldn't be blamed for not realizing the true consequences of your actions" (AFW, 1986: 148).

The autobiographical narrative offers a framework of Bildungsroman or educational novel for Ono to recount his artist development through contextualizing the circumstances of his consecutive stages of professional career. Traditionally, the Bildunsroman structure accounts for a young sensitive protagonist who attempts to "escape from a repressive family, schooling, and a journey into the wide world of urban life where encounters with a series of mentors, romantic involvements, and entrepreneurial ventures lead the protagonist to reevaluate assumptions" (Smith and Watson, 2010: 263). As a kid, his rebelling act against the suffocating family background marks the onset of his melancholic suppression that spurs him to transcend the limitations of bourgeois values represented by his father. The family life Ono contemns as "mediocre" prompts him to pursue the genuine ideals of paintings. The first stage is his apprenticeship at Master Takeda's that produces Japanese images to appeal to foreigners for commercial values. His artistic ambition propels him into the second stage at Mori-San's to catch up the beauty of modern utamaro, an aesthetic spirit of the Floating World thriving in Japan from the 17th to the 19th century to fit in with the European impressionism. However, Ono regards the third transformation of his artist career as the pinnacle of creating paintings for his "significant contribution to the people of our nation" (AFW, 1986: 163). The realistic pattern of paintings under the tutelage of Shigeo Matsuda lays the foundation of his prestige and also brings about the later scandalous accusation.

His involvement in the Okada-Shingen Society that brings him the culminate social honor and acolytes in the Migi-Hidari can allude to the fictitious equivalent of the real-life Nika Society, a private group of painters who allied themselves with the government control of the arts from 1935. The framework of apology helps the autobiographical narrative "assert his erstwhile significance and the value of his career in the face of the futile and dispiriting present, and lessen his guilt by presenting morally reprehensible actions as required by his fidelity to his idealist artistic principles" (Drag, 2014: 68). However, Noriko's future makes Ono admit to his involvement with the Japan's imperialist movement, which demonstrates his struggle for the present dignity of survival through his nostalgia of past accomplishments. Through the emplotment of his narrative, Ono offers his own apology for the humiliation of his "misguided" past life, and reassure himself of the belief that "no man will make me believe I have wasted my time" (AFW, 1986: 151). The urgent insistence on his artistic ideals enables him to justify his involvement in fascist war-campaigns in which his artistic values have been rooted. Nevertheless, his reconciliation with future turns into a symbolic gesture of relieving the burden of past life, and permits him to possess "another chance to make a better go of things" (AFW, 1986: 206). The deceptive quality of autobiographical writings makes him attempt to reconstruct a coherent narrative identity, but his current epiphany of hetero-normative social status and purposeful excuses of propagandist paintings confirms the paradox of his juxtaposing the individual accomplishments and the public mediocrity within a postwar political climate.

Ishiguro posits the outer structure in detailed backdrop out of his own memories and imagination to elaborate the emotional upheavals concerning Noriko's wedding between 1948 and 1950. Ono is now frightened of disclosing his wrongdoings as a war criminal because of his once sympathy for the aggressive government and betrayal of his student Kuroda. However reluctant, the emergence of Noriko's miai urges Ono to overcome the shame to concede his misguided political sympathy. In case that his past wrongdoings would cause the Saitos to cancel their wedding negotiation, Ono finally makes an apology that "much of what I did was ultimately harmful to our nation, that mine was part of an influence that resulted in untold suffering for our own people" (AFW, 1986: 123). Without mentioning any details, his public admission of involvement in Japan's propaganda art campaign becomes a disingenuous performance as a result of his alcohol-fueled perception and desire to ensure Noriko's happiness. His anxieties that his past should obstruct his daughter's future happiness force him to justify the professional career. Despite his admitting the feelings of guilt and regret, what he really emphasizes is not the remorse for his past life but the dignity of undertaking his historical responsibility. Being intent on resurrecting his artist status, Ono reveals unconsciously his predicament of reconstructing the self-portrait he envisions stemming from his gradual transformation and rationalization of the present anxiety.

Ono frequently comments upon the unreliability of his memories and concedes that his conversation with Jiro Miyake may happen between his son-in-law Suichi and himself. Just like Etsuko's self-defense confession, what Ono retells of "is all a matter of many years ago now and I cannot vouch that those were my exact word" (AFW, 1986: 69). Brian Shaffer views Ono's narrative as self-defense mechanism to apologize his past conduct, through which he "exhibits repression and projection to the extent that he lies to himself, rationalizes past activities, comments upon himself (through others), and selectively filters the past" (Shaffer, 1998: 43). In each case, Ono memorializes some specific qualities of his mentors which later make up a composite of his own self. In the end, Ono envisions a new self that is not only a loving and dutiful father and retired teacher, but also one that has been prepared by parental expectations and visions of social moral to perform the dictates of his ethical status. The defense mechanism endows Ono the psychological expedience to selectively forget and memorize things to reconstruct his identity. To explain away his current predicament, Ono attributes the untruthfulness of his accounts to anything but himself so as to absolve from his guilty feelings. Ono takes pride in his stage of national propagandist, and considers his earlier apprenticeship as materialist and decadent in relation to Japanese aggressive nationalism. The present narrator even refuses to accept the postwar progress of Americanized democracy, which exposes his "lacking in vision, opportunistic, pandering to crowds, and incapable of changing his tune [...] he is shown to mimic patriotic themes and slogans, and to be incapable of understanding why his message no longer falls on sympathetic ears" (Shaffer, 1998: 48). Although Ono regards himself as a freethinking and righteous artist, readers gradually recognize his similarity with the Hirayama boy, both of whom indiscriminately succumb to the political propaganda, rather than challenge the sway of political writings Ono claims to have done. After the war, Ono still frequents the Migi-Hidari bar alone where he once addressed his artistic ideals and enjoyed his prestige, which has now transformed into burnt-out buildings and heaps of rubble. Like the simpleton Hirayama boy, Ono's image is also fixed on the prestige and popularity he once obtained and now becomes a refugee looking oddly incongruous in postwar circumstances. Because of his failure to adjust to the changing ideology, Ono regards the prevailing Americanization of postwar society as a paradoxical entity after abandoning its traditional values by the public.

Despite the optimism of his reconstructing nation, Ono holds on to a dubious attitude towards American democracy and his own questionable patriotism. Thus he starts the writing of his memoir to apologize the righteousness of his conducts through purposefully concealing or ignoring his previous service for political ideology and its consequent devastation. In several episodes of this novel, Ono emphatically comments his complacence and his repressions of desire "deriving from the conviction that one's efforts have been justified; that hard work undertaken, the doubts overcome, have all been worthwhile; that one has achieved something of real value and distinction" (AFW, 1986: 205). His desire to defend the qualities of the artistic, moral and social contribution, in spite of its contamination of political ideology, reassures himself of his "worthwhile" ideals and career to which he has dedicated his whole life. So long as he can achieve the recognition of his professional efforts in the arts world, he would rather readily confess the mistakes he has conducted.

The two idols Ono admires of and identifies with is that of Akira Sugimura and Matsuda who symbolically represent the different stages of obsessions with his past accomplishments and contributions to the public benefits. Whereas Sugimuro and his mansion symbolize Ono's ambition to "rise above the mediocre, to be something more than ordinary, surely deserves admiration, even if in the end he fails and loses a fortune on account of his ambitions" (AFW, 1986: 134), Matsuda stands for the declining status whose dignity of efforts and ultimate failures one can pathetically find for his whole life. Ono's "mental landscape" of autobiographical self-portrait endows himself a perspective beyond his historical environment and social morality to "salvage dignity, a quality important to the writer's vision of how people accept and deal with failure in their lives" (Wong, 41). The content of reminiscence tends to reconstruct themselves to consolidate the inherent or meaningful narration, and thus turns into an imaginative reconstruction built out of his present attitude towards a serial of organized past experiences. However truthful and sincere his accounts sound, Ono can not conceal the fact that his story of the narratee caters to the present narrator. This kind of deviation from authentic material of the past, which is considered as the principle of "effort after meaning", originates from the preconceived schemata to seek his self-justification and vindication from his accusers.

Flashing back and forth the space-time distance, readers an recognize that Japan undergoes great changes from its glorious samurai imperialism to the postwar Americanized liberalization. Ishiguro recounts not only the development of Japanese paintings and its concomitant historical events, but also the realistic customs of miai traditional for both parties of the matrimonial match to encounter each other. Furthermore, the Kasuga Park hotel where the Onos and the Saitos encounter is delicately portrayed as a plethora of Japanese manner. Malcolm Bradbury conceives such details of portrayal as "a work of odd mannerism, a stylised piece of Japonaiserie" (Bradbury, 1987: 365), and as the representation of Ishiguro's own experience of screenwriter with scripting *A Profile of J. Arthur Mason* (1984) and the Shomin-Geki films of Japanese culture. Ishiguro admits that he "had Shu Ryuchi, in mind a regular actor in Ozu movies, when he created the character of Masuji Ono [...] whereas the biggest question about Ono's past is whether what he did during the war was morally wrong or not" (Groes and Lewis, 2011: 48-49). The structure of Shomin-Geki motivates his unique depiction of underlining emotional upheavals and seemingly irrelevant conversations or reminiscences, rather than its plethora of important events, attractive dramas or plots. Besides, the genre features in the monotony and melancholy of domestic life, especially the conflicts between parents and children, which is congruent with Ishiguro's earlier novels portraying the generational estrangement among family members.

This novel continues the motif of Shomin-Geki in *A Pale View of Hills*, and posits the historical events and political affairs within his trivial routines of family backgrounds. Its understatement of plot, everyday characters and slowness of pace are particularly suitable for the choice of movie adaptation. Barry Lewis argues that Ono's autobiographical narrative's editing of his tangled, fractured memories is more like the technique of filmic "congenial methods for portraying the associations and elisions of memory and speculation guiding Ono's reflections" (Lewis, 2000: 70). As one of the most common methods, the flashing back and forth of Ono's narration performs a role of linkage between the present narrator's anxiety and the narratee's story. For example, Noriko's mentioning her chance meeting with Jiro Miyake reminds Ono of his own meeting and conversation with Jiro about the suicide of the president of the latter's company one year ago which he doubts causes the later failure of Noriko's marriage negotiation. Another technique of film editing is the adaption of dissolving which "allows the filmmaker to join two scenes regardless of how separate they are in time and space" (Beedham, 2010: 30). The scene of Setsuko's arrival at Ono's house and conversation urges Ono's reminiscence to flash back to his own visit to his father's house and the burning of his paintings which will compulsively reenact during his later artist career.

Through the filmic jump cuts, Ishiguro's omitted parts of an event causes its ellipsis of the plot, and condenses Ono's Bildungsroman development into his respectively five short scenes at the Takeda studio and two episodes at Mori-San's villa. The filmic cross cut accounts for the trails of Ono's mnemonic "alternation between lines of action, but sees them as separated by time rather than space" (Beedham, 2010: 31). For example, the parallel of Migi-Hidari's previous popularity and present decline embodies Ono's discredited prestige falling from his mature career. Another of such images is the matching-up of paintings *Complacency* and *Eyes to the Horizon*, which represents his regression from the humanitarian concern to the aggressive nationalism that still haunts the history of the postwar Japanese society. Just like the haunting ghosts of Etsuko's nightmare, the reenacted image of Migi-Hidari turns out to be Ono's reincarnation of emotional upheavals to apologize the public shame he suffers.

The repetition of three scenes out of its four parts, including October 1948, April 1949 and June 1950, can "act as a girding for the rest of the narrative" (Lewis, 2000: 67), and represents Ono's repeated reenacting his melancholia and consequent efforts to conceal his past wrongdoings. The contrasting attitudes the different generations take up for themselves demonstrate the difficulty for Japanese people to formulate its communal memory with regards to the history of this war period and its relevant responsibility. The inter-generational incomprehension reflects not just Ono's lack of communication with his daughters, but also the tempestuous upheavals of public ideology. Like Niki and Ichiro, the postwar generation shows less respect and obedience than before, but approves more about Americanization of democracy and individual rights. In opposition to Ono's advocacy of Japanese tradition, the young parents Suichi and Setsuko identify more with Americanized thoughts and encourages Ichiro to admire Western heroes such as Lone Ranger and Popeye the Sailorman, rather than Samura warriors such as Lord Yoshitsune as a result of American's assumption of parental power for postwar Japanese society. Ishiguro uses these images of Japanese films to "retard and disperse the impetus of his narratives in order to reveal subtler and surprising aspects of character" (Mason, 1989: 44)[1], and expresses a mood of regret and loss more in Ono's mind rather than through his physical actions.

Ono's apologizing process squelches his shame beneath from resurfacing and gradually develops into hysterical symptom due to his intensifying resistance and compulsive repetition. Readers find that the early part of Ono's apology has the tone of absolute assurance, but when it comes to his shameful conduct, the tone of assurance gives away to melancholia and apologized expiation rather than performing his confession of ego-self. In this way, the narrator holds on to what is worthy for his past life-his familial duty and professional ideals, but he only admits to his lack of capability to predict the future effects of his past conduct that leads to the tragedy and shame of life he currently suffers. The episode of burning paintings is of central significance to link with Ono's various stages of artistic development. As a fifteen-year-old boy, Ono is expected to attend the weekly "business meeting" for his later inheriting the family business, rather than his obsession in artistic painting. His rebellious choice as an artist brings about the burning of his paintings as a punishment from his strict father. The violence of burning continues to haunt Ono in his later career, "still makes me uneasy [...] not son long ago it meant bombings and fire [...] next month it will be five years already since Michiko died" (AFW, 1986: 200). The embodiment of burning is also alluded to Ono's blemished moral and lost innocence deriving from his betrayal of unpatriotic Kuroda. The persecutory role of others compulsively recurs in his life to confirm his shame and also secret pleasure, just like his confession to his mother that his father's actions only kindle his ambition of success. Later on, Mori-San's similar treatment of burning his paintings is repeatedly projected onto his own pupil Kuroda. His self-deceptive megalomania relies on the prestige of his artistic achievement which supports and propagandizes aggressive nationalism, and elaborates such occasions of appreciation and respect as "auction of prestige" of Sugimura's mansion, recommendation letter for Shintaro's brother and even Dr. Saito's admiration to act as self-proof of his once prominent status.

Probably out of defense mechanism, Ono deliberately avoids the mention of his previous family life and mainly concerns his professional career and its concomitant prestige. At the beginning of his first instalment, the narrator attempts to attach the meaning and significance to his career and enlists his first evidence, that is, the grand mansion he has won through the "auction of prestige" (AFW, 1986: 9) as the most worthy artist, and relies on its justice and moral to reconstruct his embarrassed identity. Despite the war damage, it still remains the embodiment of the status and reputation of its possessor, which helps to justify his professional ideals and resurrect "his former self as a process of self-bereavement, as a way of mourning that lost self" (Wong, 2005: 43). Besides the mansion witnessing the transformation of Japanese society, the pleasure district, especially the Migi-Hidari restaurant Ono once enjoyed favorably, sccms like the burial site of "some abandoned funeral" (AFW, 1986: 29), only reminding readers of Ono's nostalgia for its demise. The delusion of its reestablishment that " the old district will not return again?" (AFW, 1986: 77) refers to the incarnation of the narrator's and even Japan's discredited status confronted with postwar Americanizing reality. In this way, Ono can apply his narrative to deconstruct the shameful criticism he currently suffers and walk through his mourning process to restore the moral of his past self-image.

His mnemonic fragments constitute what Ishiguro purports to portray as normal human beings who can not see beyond his own environment and stand outside the prevailing values of his time. The denial of Setsuko confirms the unreliability of autobiographical narrative and its individual reflection on the obedient collectivism against unjust the aggression of war. Because of the upheaval of ideological changes and its concomitant reflection of traditional values, the familial relation undergoes Americanized liberalization which transforms Ono into an amiable retired artist who suffers the shame his former actions have caused. His attempt to restore the writing of traditional values in the postwar turbulence of reconstruction period becomes the post-humanistic self-image of collective inferiority complex and alienation from its dominant ideology. The paranoid fantasies conceive his fragmentation of self-definition as the equivalence of collapse of modern civilization, which stimulates Ono to fulfil his ambition and contribute to social progress, but finally ends up with the accomplice of imperialist propaganda. Social morality and war insanity propitiate the present narrator into the entangling net of identity, through which readers can emphasize with Ono's efforts of dedicating to his ideal world. The autobiographical narrative portrays the emotional upheavals of the narrator and applies the space-time distance to advocate the alleged international identity, echoing Ishiguro's own complicated Japanese complex as an immigrant displaced from his imagined homeland.

The configuration of traditional ideology has once attracted such speculators as Ono and Matsuda, but the current thought begins to bitterly rebuke and abandon its historical marks and imperialist values to embrace Americanized internationalism shaking the traditional foundation of familial relation. Flashing back to the story of narratee, Kuroda accuses Ono's "China Crisis" paintings of its artistic value, and the young generation such as Jiro Miyake and Suichi regards the suicide for their regret of war guilt as the necessary action responsible for historical events and victims. With postwar democratic thoughts prevailing, his son-in-law Suichi refutes Ono's traditionalism and disclaims that the Americanized heroes have become the more ideal embodiment, which aggravates the generational misunderstanding and posits Ono in an anachronistic predicament, "if your country is at war, you do all you can in support. And there's no shame in that [...] those who fought and worked loyally for our country during the war cannot be called war criminals" (AFW, 1986: 55). The transmutation of postwar cultural thoughts stimulates Ono's helplessness at the crossroads of life and his complaint of worshiping American manners. The artistic achievements he feels proud are treated with contempt and shame, which exacerbates his predicament of relation with young generation.

Although some youths would appreciate Americanized democracy rather than traditional national and ethical valucs and reflect on the advantages of their different values, just like what Ono expects for himself, his nation "seems, whatever mistakes it may have made in the past, has now another chance to make a better go of things" (AFW, 1986: 206). The attitude of hesitation towards Ono's dubious past can be attributable to the turbulent and polemic social ideologies, which brings out his once professional achievements, only turns out to be a blemish of his reputation. The present anxiety and confusion precipitate the narrator to articulate and revise his life story "propelled by an array of different motivations: to order, understand, justify and explain their past, to reassure themselves as to their achievement, and, finally, to work through their losses" (Drag, 2014: 53-54). Although the young generation such as Kuroda are regarded as "traitor" for their rebellious spirits, they are now endowed with the hero roles to undertake the leadership to reflect on traditional ideology and reconstruct the new heterogeneous identity of nationalism.

The quality of "excuse" and self-justification determines Ono's boastful image of self-esteem. The prestige and status of nationalist artist confirms what Brian Shaffer defines as an overestimation of insignificant and functionary role, because he "will admit to being wrong as long as he can maintain the illusion of having been influential" (Shaffer, 1998: 60). The apology genre offers a pattern of emplotment that can incorporate his misdeeds into the life-narrative and justification to make sense of the past using the present knowledge of hindsight. Ono's knowledge of hindsight offers a necessity to dwell on the memories of past to recount a biased account of historical events. However, his readiness of admitting the guilt that he once conducted becomes his deliberate strategy of recovering social trust and damaged reputation. The insincerity of Ono's penitence will never happen "had circumstances not impressed upon me the prudence of doing so [...] but there is certainly a satisfaction and dignity to be gained in coming to terms with the mistakes one has made" (AFW, 1986: 124). After this dramatic performance of apologetic penitence, Ono not only secures the success of Noriko's marriage, but also obtains a superior sense of "satisfaction and dignity" which absolves himself from his guilty sense and contentedly looks forwards to the future of his family and his nation. Thus Ono applies the apologetic voice of criminal suspect to get rid of the criticism of postwar ideology and even elevate his self-esteem. Despite its self-deceptive elements, The final scene of his sitting on a bench of the dilapidated pleasure district and musing about his past and future can be attributed to the therapeutic effects of this autobiographical narrative.

The estrangement from traditional values and the admiration of Western culture in public ideology make the traditional characters such as Ono and Mastuda anxious about the prospect and future, and the formation of national identity "is not an essence but instead depends on a social context that has changed so radically as to leave characters floating in an unfamiliar world" (Scanlan, 1993: 141). Like the sisters in *A Pale View of Hills*, Sestuko and Noriko respectively represent traditional and Americanized female image according to their father's view, which constitutes the cause of family estrangement. The national complex of ordinary people conceals the hegemony of social Darwinism and plants the seeds of imperial devastation for worldwide nations, which transforms the humanistic artistry into the complicity of public ideology. Like Stevens in *The Remains of the Day*, Ono focuses more on his social status and prestige than the professional morality, which explains away that "their lives are spoiled because they don't have any extraordinary insight into life. They're not necessarily stupid, they're just ordinary" (Vorda, 1991: 152). The changes of Ono's narrative transforming from his first self-appraisal to his dissembling and even denial of the accurate circumstances of his autobiographical acts represents the symptomatic remembered "truth". His desire to enhance and exaggerate the historical role is linked to his hateful parents whose approval has never been forthcoming during his artistic career, which even causes his compulsively recurring the self-portrait of frustrations through the images of burning the paintings. The self-narrative rearranges the disjointed and disrupted memories into a coherent life story so as to fill the gap and crisis of his identification as a result of ideological upheavals. The present anxiety stems from the discrepancy between the truth Ono has lived out and the current perception of the public.

Through the narratives of his protagonists, Ishiguro demonstrates "the now forgotten, or disregarded, social context in which they acted [...] the debatable choices which they made were in accordance with the values that, at the time, were regarded as noble" (Drag, 2014: 54). Despite Ono's attempts to retell of his consistent autobiography, his symbolic apology is conceived by his daughters as a psychological paranoia, due to his ordinary artist status in no direct relation to the imperialist war. In fact, the debate over artists' services occasioned in late 1945 in "the Asahi Shimbun newspaper between Tsuguharu Fujita, who justified his service to the country, and Shigeo Miyata, who insisted that those artists who produced propaganda arts should refrain from practice for a while" (Groes and Lewis, 2011: 78). It is no doubt that the debate continued its occasional appearance in magazines around 1950 when Ono justified his no other choice but collaboration with Japanese militant government. Unlike that of Ono, the suicide of composer Mr. Naguchi who once encouraged the youths to sacrifice for the war and later recognized the wrongdoings for imperialist complex makes him confess his self-felt guilt and disillusions in relation to the war responsibility for his contribution to Japan's imperialist cause.

Suffering from his historical responsibilities, Ono tends to reconstruct his memories to adapt to postwar ideology, through his self-apologizing the wrongdoings to seek his psychological comfort. Through his self-autobiography, Ono expresses his rejection of a Buddhist-related lifestyle that is to catch the evanescent and fragile beauty of "the Floating World, the world of love, beauty and art, that endures, and that the 'real' world of action, of politics and war, turns out to be treacherous and temporary [...] the old man's longings for his past become a universal lament for lost world " (Chisholm, 1986: 162). The apology of his past conducts indicates the desire to hold on to the old customs and loyalties while participating in his postwar life. The desire for a double life or the alleged Freudian Schizophrenia offers additional impetus to his redeeming apology for the demands of present self-identification. The floating world becomes Ono's voluntary refuge to confront the cultural conflicts, and the present narrator applies image of Ono's reminiscence to reveal the legacies of imagined homeland embodying his efforts to soothe his loneliness of identity crisis. The entanglement of individual and national memories endows the narrator a new perspective to the current revolution of Americanized democratic ideology to reflect on its unique identity to cultivate the others awaiting to be saved.

The narrative of Ono invites readers to scrutinize his emotional upheavals of anxious disorders stepping from his traumatic memories, which divulges how individual consciousness distorts and revises historical accounts to gloss over the wrongdoings. The self-recognition of textual narrative stepping from reconstructing and rewriting memories becomes the psychological reincarnation of restructuring historical accounts and solving self-identification. The self-distortion of present narrator makes readers witness how Ono glosses over his guilty past, which symbolizes the continuing process of cultural transplantation, replacement and restoration to keep the status of traveller. The hopelessness or desolate optimism not only embodies the deception Ono reluctantly suffers, but also transforms into the ultimate refuge and haven to seek his spiritual comfort and resist current cultural insanity. Although the outside circumstances Ono lives do not change much, his personal anxiety and shame gradually gives way to a more cheerful attitude towards the future life.

The narrator does not offer readers the confessions of his soul in remorse or his penitential outpourings of a sinner. The overtone of his narrative is that of the apologist who justifies himself in a wasted cause in order to appeal to readers' sympathy through his struggling against the outside climate as a freethinking intellectual. The sympathetic addressee he turns to is not the younger generation influenced by postwar Americanism, but his contemporaneous beings sharing the same experiences. The narrative helps the writer create more than just record his self-image to turn against the threats of shame, despair and isolation, through which Ono can justify his "old self" he feels better and dignified to fulfill his therapeutic purpose. The narrative identity offers him a psychological bridge to soothe the rift of past and present and partially reconcile with the anxiety of exonerating himself to assert the self-esteem as an innocent artist.

2.3 Testimonies of an Imperial Butler

Ishiguro's third novel, *The Remains of the Day* (1989), is a continuation and reaction of his previous novel, *An Artist of the World*. Despite the similarities of their unreliable autobiographical narratives, the author continuously provides its new historical settings where the traditional culture has formed for the narrator to hold onto his identity, but nowadays suffers his own breaking up due to the dramatic subversion of postwar social ideology. This novel, a Booker Prize winner in 1989, recounts the narrator Stevens's current anxieties of professional duties which mainly originate from his political service and witness to Lord Darlington who conspired with the Nazis in the 1930s. Like Ono, Stevens's emphasis of political idealism reflects Ishiguro's own anxiety about "personal position at the time, having grown up in a much more politicized atmosphere compared to the one the younger generation are growing up in today [...] I became wary of political commitment" (Groes and Lewis, 2011: 250), which points to his self-referential attitudes towards how people confront their moral and emotional conducts. The strategies of self-aggrandizement and self-elevation common in autobiographical writings are employed to guard against his life regrets through justifying Darlington's and his own errors, "but in the end it is self-deceit he serves more than any proprietor of Darlington Hall" (Kamine, 1989: 22). Through Stevens's autobiographical narrative, Ishiguro establishes a textual gap between the present narrator's justification and the detailedness of his narrated events which undermines the basis of his testimonies for the ideals he has pursued.

The testimonial narrative invests Stevens with a revised life story as a participant and witness to help maintain the wheel-structured system with awkward confidence and dignity. John Beverley defines the genre of testimonio or literally translated "testimony" as "a novel or novella-length narrative in book or pamphlet (that is, printed as opposed to acoustic) form, told in the first person by a narrator who is also the real protagonist or witness of the events he or she recounts, and whose unit of narration is usually a 'life' or a significant life experience" (Beverley, 1992: 92-93). Due to the mediated process, testimony increases the possibility of deforming and convening the truth-seeking effects the form attempts to produce. It provides a textual space in which the moral ambiguity depends upon the process of setting oneself as a witness to the truth of historical events. It also raises the concerns about its suitability to represent oneself or one's community. Here, the anxieties Stevens undertakes can be revealed through the process of bearing witness. Thus readers of the text perform more like a jury member in a courtroom to judge its sincerity of intention rather than its aesthetic literariness. The embellished story offers him a self-deceptive fantasy to fulfill his ideals of professional role and diplomatic contribution to world peace through his being political "consorted" with celebrities such as Winston Churchill, Anthony Eden and Lord Halifax for matters of foreign policies. As an act of eye-witnessing, its intention out of a political context challenges the boundaries between intimacy and publicity, secrecy and disclosure, which addresses an audience whose mutual identity of collective community reinforces to "communicate the situation of a group's oppression, struggle, or imprisonment, to claim some agency in the act of narrating, and to call on readers to respond actively in judging the crisis" (Smith and Watson, 2010: 282). But the act of leaving Darlington Hall and driving into the world outside only opens Stevens up to the scrutiny of post-war public views that entails his objective witness status as a butler to defend Lord Darlington's involvement with British appeasement policy. The justice and humanity he has witnessed in the personality of Lord Darlington begin to disintegrate as he gradually reveals Darlington's dismissal of the Jewish housemaids and his subsequent meetings with fascists.

The testimonio form brings about the latent polyphony of other voices which can point to the various representational value systems, a key to reveal the fallacy of assuaging his guilt-felt anxiety. And its dominant aspect is the voice "that speaks to the reader in the form of an 'I' that demands to be recognized, that wants or needs to stake a claim on our attention [...] a desire not to be silenced or defeated, a desire to impose oneself on an institution of power, such as literature, from the position of the excluded or the marginal" (Beverley, 1992: 96). Unlike other forms of autobiographical writings, testimonio challenges the authoritative function of its "author' with that of its substituted compiler, and makes a dialogical relation or complicity between the narrator and the readers. Thus the narrator Stevens needs Miss Kenton, the former housekeeper at Darlington Hall, as his soul mate who can act as an interlocutor with a different ethic and social background to question the moral system he insists on. While Stevens chooses to comply with Darlington's dismissal of his Jewish housemaids, Kenton regards it as "a sin as any sin ever was one" (ROD, 1989: 149), and assumes the moral responsibility in her professional careers that they "should not merely decline to assist in such acts; they should also act affirmatively to promote justice in their representation of private clients" (Atkinson, 1995: 191). Unlike Stevens, Miss Kenton concedes her regret of obedient complicity and even identifies the immorality of dismissing someone based on one's racial prejudice. In her opinion, the dismissal which has harmed the innocent can also violate the principles of the professionalism incorporating humane morality as its inseparable ingredient. However, Stevens regards the wishes of his employer as the substantive factor of the professionalism and his duty that "there was nothing to be gained at all in irresponsibly displaying such personal doubts [...] his lordship, I might venture, is somewhat better placed to judge what is for the best" (ROD, 1989: 148-149). Because of this austere professional rationalism that deprives his affective connection with the outer world, Stevens rejects her romantic attachments to him and her moral reactions to Darlington's anti-Semitic complex through erasing his emotional part to guarantee his own physical and mental safety. His romantic relationship with Kenton begins with their pantry chatting, but gradually moves on towards the inevitable tragedy that reminds him of the guilt he feels towards moral responsibilities.

The conception of dignity which has forced Stevens to defer to Darlington's wishes ultimately deprives him of the moral burden, "not the burden of choosing the lesser evil with open eyes, but that of making a serious moral judgement about the right thing to do" (Atkinson, 1995: 209). The compiler and witness of Lord Darlington's political life, Stevens, is also a typical butler who can combine the contradictions and complicity between aristocratic and public society. His account of their relation develops with the layout of his testimonio, of which the problem Stevens encounters is that he has to make his choice about whether he should endorse Darlington's values or should correct them according to his own social status and background. Thus this novel is not only a narrative about Lord Darlington, but also Stevens's contextualization of his political sympathies. From the narrative's inception, the figure of Darlington is transformed into an empty signifier to make up for the meaning of Stevens's own life choice. The self-defense intention of autobiographical narrative enables Stevens to highlight his "lordship's good judgement" (ROD, 1989: 225) so that he can conceal his own complicity as a participant and witness. Ishiguro claims that the challenge his narrator has to overcome is "all about having the right values in the first place and somehow having the strength of character to stick to them" (Shaffer and Wong, 2008: 170-188). The notion of his aggrandizing the traditional aristocrat to the status of humanistic ideals is mainly maintained within the "civilized" gentlemen that require the general public to accept his professional dignity and overcome his political disengagement. Despite the possibilities of misrepresentation and distortion, the argument of the author of this book is that Stevens's narrative seemingly rejects the voices of individual particularities and even identification of an "other" so as to lay the overtone for his defensive rationalization.

However, the testimonial representation does not go ahead in one way, but ramifies all around the author's actual attitudes towards historical events. Stevens is obviously aware that he is not only exploiting his interlocutor Miss Kenton to have their romantic story as the counterpoint to his currently failed and restless life deriving from his previous complicity, but also attempting to influence the intentional addressee for the political task of the social group Darlington belongs to. Moreover, the authorial power can not be possessed by the compiler alone, who recognizes that his account will later be used against the people like himself. Although Darlington performs the determining factor influencing their common life, the textual voices are composed by Stevens and depend on his intentions to elaborate the relation of the narrator, the subject and the readers. Sklodowska comments that discourse of a witness cannot be a reflection of his or her experience, but rather a refraction determined by the vicissitudes of memory, intention and ideology. The intention and the ideology of the author-editor further superimposes the original text, creating more ambiguities, silences, and absences in the process of selecting and editing the material in a way consonant with norms of literary form. What makes testimonio different from other autobiographical forms is its urgency of narrating the political situation as one understood as the authenticity that possesses determinate effects on the reader through foregrounding its political and moral responsibilities the individuals should undertake.

The meaning of testimonio consists not in the uniqueness of the individual but in its ability to stand for the experience of the community, which is different from the autobiographical forms such as confession, apology and memoir, probably stemming from its lack of authorial function. Thus the genre of testimonio "represents an affirmation of the individual subject, even of individual growth and transformation, but in connection with a group or class situation marked by marginalization, oppression and struggle" (Beverley, 1992: 103). If Stevens performs as the "writer" of his own story rather than acts as a witness and member of his social class or community, his narration would have turned into an autobiographical writing. Marc Poree comments that the testimonial "presence of verbs like to vouch, to warrant, to advocate, combined with Stevens's self-presentation of himself as a witness in a witness box, swearing to tell the truth, and nothing but the truth" (Poree, 1999: 83), which demonstrates his commitment to Darlington's political ideals of diplomatic communication. Whereas autobiography confirms and even self-elevates the narrator's status or social situation, testimonio stands for the urgency of moral or political changes which will later influence the readers' attitudes or value systems. Like Ono, Stevens recollects his involvement with fascism in the 1930s and locates his current identity on the basis of traditional culture that has been disintegrating.

The narrator consciously recognizes the doubtfulness of his memories and elevates the valuation of his butler status and its concomitant ideals at the expense of his happiness of private and family life. Margaret Scanlan points out his nostalgic epiphany he encountered "the evening his father died, when he had kept away from the deathbed for all but a few minutes to pass his tray and attempt to placate a hypochondriacal guest complaining about his infected blisters. Ignoring the tears that suggest the survival of some inner emotional self, he recalls only his success at keeping up the role" (Scanlan, 1993: 151). Ishiguro continues his reconsideration about how to deal with the misguided career which has undermined the basis and purpose of the narrator's life. The gap between the narrated memories and the present narrative dismantles the reliability of Stevens's witness through presenting "Lord Darlington as a great humanist, but also tells us about Darlington's dismissal of the Jewish housemaids, Darlington's meetings with fascists, and his own denials of Darlington" (Beedham, 2010: 48), and throws the reader's doubtfulness on his "greatness" of this humanized aristocrat. Different from Farraday's ideas, Stevens regards socio-political construction as the essential stereotype of Englishness characterized by its big houses and allows Ishiguro to devise his new myth of England with his own ideals and expectations of what Englishness should be. At the beginning of his diary, Stevens compares the greatness of English landscapes to the dignity of his butler status, "the calmness of that beauty, its sense of restraint. It is as though the land knows of its own beauty, of its own greatness, and feels no need to shout it" (ROD, 1989: 28-29). The image of Englishness, according to Stevens, has more relation with the mythical ideas existing in nostalgic heritage than with his direct experience as a result of his two-decade confinement within Darlington Hall.

The landscape is abstractly transformed into an image of sublimity or dignity of Englishness that can acts as an journey of self-discovery to construct his estranged life into a justified narrative through connecting his own ideals and expectations with that of historical celebrities. The paradox it indicates points to the performance of his own identity that equates ignoring the death of his father or his romantic relationship to Miss Kenton with a great success of professional idealism. Here Stevens reassures his addressee that he is able to endorse his professional dignity even at the expense of his sorrow of family bereavement or marital happiness. However, his encounter with the villager Harry Smith challenges the pretended gentleness he imitates from Lord Darlington, which finally leads to being humiliated for his lack of own opinions about current events. Despite the controversial opinion that egalitarian ideal of freedom and dignity should not extend to the colonies, Stevens still finds himself altered by his conversations with Smith and begins unwillingly to heed the voices of ordinary people. Although Stevens repeatedly admits his ordinariness and inadequacy, his paradoxical epiphany can not conceal his position of collusion and witness in autobiographical narrative. Parallel to his public status, Stevens "enacts his memories as an ongoing act of repression, repeating in recall the same erasure of emotion that characterised the relationship itself, and cunningly allowing one aspect to emerge in order better to camouflage the other" (Guth, 1999: 131). Despite its ambiguous comments and deliberate absence, the clues overflowing from his memories build up the main plot including the four turnings which determine his current status as a witness of historical and political events.

The narrator, as well as the readers, can not understand the meaning of his choice during his professional pursuit until the end of his travel diary permeated with emotional enigmas, gaps and dislocations. The four different scenes repeatedly examine his emotional repression invaded by publicly professional self-images. Through recalling how he gradually alienates and forces Miss Kenton into the arms of other persons, Stevens attempts to sincerely perform the role as a witness to Darlington's political career. Instead of restoring his romantic relation with the former housekeeper, Stevens admits his purpose of this journey is to persuade Kenton of returning to Darlington Hall and salvage his damaged self-respect "responsible for a series of small errors in the carrying out of my duties" (ROD, 1989: 5). The repetitions of his suppression about private self-images help him recreate its meaning of autobiographical narrative on which the construction is based. The tragedy Stevens suffers after the whole life of dedication and self-denial turns out to be a discovery too late for him to subvert "the individual self he thought had no value, the ability to love a woman, to sit on a common bench and watch the sun go down without ritual or ceremony attached, without ennobling purpose or grand rhetorical flourish" (Guth, 1999: 136). Unlike traditionally unreliable narration, the narrator confirms the untruthfulness of his memories and its self-referential structure through which the implied author expects the readers to focus on Stevens's mental processes as a case of political testimonio.

The form of testimonio enables Stevens to distance himself from the authority of emotional or morale judgments. For example, he has always been admiring his father's professional ideals until the moment that he realizes "that if one looks at the matter objectively, on has to concede that my father lacked various attributes one may normally expect in a great butler" (ROD, 1989: 34). The choice of pronoun "one" rather than "I" become his defensive symptoms of suppressed feelings as a result of sacrificing his private self-fulfillment. From the start, Stevens worries about how his words and actions as a witness should be estimated and judged by his anonymous addressee who might be either another domestic servant or an imagined image like himself working in Great Houses like Darlington Hall. The addressee Stevens imagines for his testimonio reflects his current anxieties that "the likes of you and I will never be in a position to comprehend the great affairs of today's world" (ROD, 1989: 201), let alone to adjust to the current reality daunted by the charges of Darlington. Furthermore, Stevens even attaches the professional perfection to his journey to visit Miss Kenton in order to conceal his expectation of restoring the once lost romantic love. The discrepancy between his narration and the voices of other persons such as Miss Kenton and Darlington is probably attributed to his repression of any non-professional judgments in the name of his cherished dignity.

The significant episode of turning points he regards as leading to his ultimate tragedy is that he attempts to comfort Miss Kenton upon hearing the death of her aunt, only to end up with his relentless censure of her neglected duties. Apart from the scene of his response to the death of his father, Stevens performs similarly, after knowing the news of Kenton's engagement, to attempt to transform his emotional loss into professional triumphs. The mourning process that substitutes his lost objects with newly imagined ones offers Stevens courage to confront and even reconstruct his life story. The narrator not only doubts the accuracy of his memories, but also sometimes figures out his mistakes. Through its travel narrative, the author has always been pulling Stevens into the nostalgic past, and regards his narrative as "a re-examination and justification of his life as Lord Darlington's butler and of the values that to a large degree determined and constructed that life" (Wall, 1994: 31). The morale values Stevens upholds nevertheless reveal the true attitudes Ishiguro cherishes towards the historical events that trouble his narrator and the resolution he tries to avoid. Stevens sometimes admits that despite thc accusation of Darlington's egoism or else arrogance, "his lordship was persuaded to overcome his more retiring side only through a deep sense of moral duty [...] that he was a truly good man at heart, a gentleman through and through, and one I am today proud to have given my best years of service to" (ROD, 1989: 61). The digressed remembrance enables him to justify his past value system as a witness and participant of Darlington's political activities. For example, the self-aggrandizement of his political role is reflected by the "greatness" of Hayes Society criteria to which he manages to live up and finally realizes through his "small, but significant contribution towards the easing of relations between Lord Halifax and Herr Ribbentrop" (ROD, 1989: 136), that is, his silver polishing skills have positive influence upon the solution of international affairs due to its humanizing value his profession has imposed. Kathleen Wall comments that even though Stevens "knows that Lord Darlington's career has been a 'waste', he merely reveals here his tendency to compartmentalize his knowledge into bearable segments and, further, the strength of his drive to protect himself from any contradictions that will undermine the values on which he has constructed his life" (Wall, 1994: 32). The current accusation of Darlington urges Stevens to flashback into his past life to justify the dignity he has applied to guide his professional life. However, his conversation with Smith who advocates egalitarian dignity that is not the privilege of gentlemen, but "something everyman and woman in this country can strive for and get" (ROD, 1989: 186) finally pierces through his last fortress of defending Darlington's political prestige.

The discrepancy of their respective conception of dignity disturbs Stevens's peaceful mind and his continuous justification for his employer and propels him to excavate the causes of dismissing two Jewish housemaids. In opposition to Stevens's blind belief, Harry Smith elaborates his own opinion of dignity that confirms "Darlington's failures and must recognise that he cannot justify his own life by praising the man he served. Stevens's questioning of Lord Darlington suggests his questioning of himself" (Beedham, 2010: 54). Although Stevens construes how Darlington has been duped by the Nazis through privileging his qualities of humanistic gentleness, the readers can still recognize his thinking progresses of autobiographical life surrounding the historical events in which Darlington has been involved. At the beginning of his diary, the narrator confidently expresses his pride and satisfaction as a witness and participant of Darlington's political career. The atmosphere of postwar democracy and accusation of Darlington makes Stevens reflect on his employer's misguided career and mistakes. However, even at the end the narrator still refuses to concede his own mistakes, which endows him with no other identity than a witness of historical events. The reassessment of his professional career at the expense of his romantic love and family life probably originates from "the huge investment he has made in a certain image of himself and of his place in life" (Wall, 1994: 36). The pivotal scene that daunts Stevens most is his standing outside Kenton's parlour hesitating about whether of knocking at her door or just leaving for his service for an international meeting. The response to Kenton's engagement after several decades still "has for some reason remained with me vividly through the years" (ROD, 1989: 212), and serves as a turning point of foreshadowing the tragedy of both his professional and family life to come. However, his intimate rclation with Kenton has to surrender to the significance of the political meeting between the politicians in Darlington Hall. The moment in his memories has "seemed a significant period [...] of course, I was required to hurry upstairs to serve some of the most distinguished gentlemen of the land and I cannot imagine I would have delayed unduly" (ROD, 1989: 227). Instead of his romantic attachment to lose, Stevens regards her scheduled departure only as a professional loss Darlington Hall has to suffer but cannot render the whole dreams forever irredeemable. The loss of his professional dream becomes the only melancholic symptom that makes him unable to recognize the disillusion of restoring Kenton's status of former housekeeper. The melancholic attachment to lost objects, in Freudian terms, is due to the confusion of the patients who are "aware of the loss which has given rise to his, but only in the sense that he knows whom he has lost but not what he has lost in him" (Freud, 2006: 312). Stevens's insistence on the significance of Kenton's status as a housekeeper testifies his mental mechanism of melancholia about the anachronistic professional ideals on which he has constructed the identities of Darlingotn and himself.

The scene of the turning point that results in Kenton's departure not just sets up the reminiscent tone of regret over the loss of her professional ideals, but also his regret and disappointment for the missed opportunity of their romantic relation. Thus it could be regarded as his dilemma entangled in the conflicts of personal and professional sphere, "to sacrifice the possibility of personal fulfillment (represented by Miss Kenton) for the sake of professional duty and prestige (represented by Darlington), but ensuing events reveal that he is about to lose them both" (Drag, 2014: 47). However, the diplomatic meeting Stevens leaves for his service turns out to be Darlington's political efforts of alliance with Hitler government, and ultimately spurs a nationwide criticism of his treasonous activities. To retort the postwar dominant accusations, Stevens begins his theoretical definition of a "great butler", his professional ethos that can be seen as a justification of Darlington's justice through his perspective of a witness. The quality of his dignity he proudly invests in his service is to have applied "his talents to serving a great gentleman — and through the latter to serving humanity" (ROD, 1989: 117). Furthermore, he even boasts once again his "privilege of practising one's profession" and fortunately accomplishes "a contribution to the course of history" (ROD, 1989: 139) through supporting his employer's misguided politics. The intended testimonio becomes his only means of defending his professional dignity and self-respect damaged by his choice of holding upon his employer to judge its value and morality. In order to confirm his ethical morale of sacrifices, he chooses to alienate from the post-war democratic ideology and builds his identity upon his trust in Darlington's moral status through refusing the charges of his alleged anti-Semitism and Nazism.

Although the background of Suez Crisis that occupied newspaper headlines remains deliberately concealed, the disparity of political ideas Harry Smith upholds reveals the democratic tendency the British public advocate. Stevens's avoidance of mentioning this crisis reveals Ishiguro's consistent concerns of morale and humanity through foregrounding private experiences of the ordinary people to reflect large historical events. The Suez crisis, which has forced the Prime Minister Anthony Eden to resign under the condemnation of war and American pressurc, provides the contextualization of historical events to understand the complexities of the international affairs and Darlington's humanity and benevolence of political activities. Like Eden, Darlington has been, according to Senator Lewis, "decent, honest, well meaning" (ROD, 1989: 102), and should not be simply characterized as the pro-Fascist politician suffering from the postwar accusations. The aristocratic politician who disparages the opinions of the populace pushes his nation into the role of complicity with the Nazis. The similarity between the roles of both politicians is that "the story that Stevens tells about Darlington, the story of an expert perceiving himself above democracy and being led by that perception to betray the nation, parallels Eden's story" (Beedham, 2010: 91). Unlike Eden who resorts to the use of force to handle international affairs, Lord Darlington relies on diplomacy and international cooperation to contribute the worldwide peace which seems anachronistic against the aggression of the Nazis. John P. McCombe comments that Stevens's testimonio "highlights and juxtaposes two discourses of appeasement, one concerning a genuine threat in post-Weimar Germany and the other serving as a farcical justification for a British military action oppose by much of the wold community in the mid-1950s" (McCombe, 2002: 94). In fact, the policy of Eden government receives approval among the rural villagers in Tavistock who attempt to confirm their Prime Minister's humanistic personalities. During the departure of Mr. Farraday from his Darlington Hall, the Eisenhower government abandons its longtime ally with Britain, which stirs its similar allusion to American attitudes towards Versailles Treaty the senator Lewis upheld.

The accusation of American foreign policy, according to the Frenchman Dupont, who attended Darlington's international meeting, confirms "American 'duplicity' during the Suez affair connects with the 'deceitful' thinking of the American senator, Lewis, whose desire to relax the terms of the Versailles Treaty is related to the repayment of American war loans" (McCombe, 2002: 82). The ethos of social appeasement emerges popularly among the members of upper aristocracy represented by British economist John Maynard Keynes who warns that the reparation of Versailles Treaty should result in devastating crisis and conflict in Germany. It is of no surprise that Darlington should feel anxious about the rights of German people growing out of a liberal reflex that leads towards his appeasement. However, the similar failure of different crisis solutions cannot conceal the pursuit of British imperialist power concerning the process of government policy-making by the secret compromises of elite aristocrats.

The disparagement of Americanism Darlington demonstrated in the international meeting of March 1923 continues in Stevens's preference of English greatness and gentleness over American behaviors revealed in his responses to Farraday's hobby of bantering. Despite his avoidance of mentioning the Suez crisis, the bias against Americanism among the public might have probably been seeded since the divergent attitudes towards Versailles Treaty. There is no surprise to see that Stevens still lives in his anachronistic era when Mrs. Jane

Symons's *The Wonder of England* advocated the greatness of its landscape as the Englishness of national values that distinguishes England from other countries. In order to connect the greatness of England with national identity, Stevens resorts to the typical profession of butlers which can define his own professionalism as "a dignity in keeping with his position" (ROD, 1989: 33). He regards the country house like Darlington Hall as the symbols of Englishness and his serving as an "insider" as the contribution to the imperial machine. Ishiguro states in an interview that "this green, pleasant place of leafy lanes and grand country houses and butlers and tea on the lawn, cricket — this vision of England that actually does place a large role in the political imagination of a lot of people [...] I felt it was a perfectly reasonable mission on my part to set out to slightly redefine that mythical, cozy England, to say that there is a shadowy side to it" (Shaffer and Wong, 2008: 46). The historical context Stevens recalls from his mine of memories is partly tempted by his self-interests of excusing the behaviors Darlington and even himself have undertaken to disconnect the notion of the idealized national past with its political reality.

In opposition to Smith's definition, Stevens strictly confines the rights of freedom to the elite class and excludes the public like himself. That the discourse of professional values dominates over his sentimental feelings probably originates from his desire to defend himself from acting as the role of witness. James M. Lang comments that the narrator "struggles to reconcile his own private memories of Lord Darlington (and what seemed to Stevens, in historical context, as Darlington's noble and virtuous — intentions) with the subsequent public vilification of Darlington after the war" (Lang, 2000:

145). The conflict between his own experience and the official accounts of historical events contributes to the confusion and anxiety of political identity. The contextualization of its historical events makes Darlington's and Stevens's choice of moral value acceptable acting as a means of retorting the current scandalous assumption they are suffering. The extensive accounts of Darlington's noble humanity and concerns about the "great suffering he had himself witnessed in Germany" (ROD, 1989: 92) offer a new judgement for the "desire to see goodness and justice prevail" which is approved by "warm and sustained applause" (ROD, 1989: 103) among politicians and diplomats of different countries. Stevens' narrative which reflects the glimpses of ordinary and dispossessed persons produces such conflicting mindsets of historical accounts that affect the feelings of the readers about Darlington's and his complicity with the Nazis caught up between emotional sympathy and repugnance. As a political testimonio, Stevens's narrative alienates itself from his political judgement and background of Suez crisis and upholds the judgement that the cause of Darlington's tragedy is his moral duty to do justice for others, whose good intentions cause him to have been caught up in a web of someone else's greed and advantage.

The retrospective flashing common in autobiographical narrative endows the narrator and even the readers with the outcome of their activities which Stevens readily refuses to accept as a witness who is unable to predict their impending trajectory. The unreliable narration Stevens frequently confirms reflects his current anxiety of justifying Darlington's political career and the tendency the implied author invites the readers to interact with the historical text.

The memory problems Stevens encounters produces the lack of certainty and even unease in readers anxious for the truthfulness the narrator has recounted. The memorial fragility insinuates the state of his own doubt and trouble of recollecting events that happened several decades ago, as Stevens sometimes admits that "I cannot recall precisely what I said" (ROD, 1989: 167), or "I am not at all certain now as to the actual circumstances" (ROD, 1989: 212). The biographical account that is full of purposeful forgetfulness or remembrance, according to Lillian Furst, "reflects the oscillation between transience and persistence [...] disconcertingly from one period to another, drifting associatively in a discontinuous movement that is the literary correlative of a mental stream of consciousness" (Furst, 2007: 538). The disparity between historical events and his remembrance establishes an ironic distance between the biased or dishonest narrator and the implied author to communicate through the voices of other persons' witnessing. Despite the changeability of his transient memories, Stevens seems to show off his confidence in persistent remembrance of professional experiences. The archaeological memories waiting to evacuate deliberately foreground Darlington's political activities, especially the international conference in 1923, which continuously daunts Stevens's moral judgement. As a political witness, Stevens purposefully exaggerates his role of importance through polishing the silver to relax the tension between Halifax and Ribbentrop for their diplomatic meeting. Despite his well-intended attempts for defeated Germany, Lord Darlington's association with right-wing celebrities such as Lady Astor, Lord Halifax and Oswald Mosley (ROD, 1989: 134-137) highlights Stevens's ideological bias, and more probably, the status of justifying the politician he has served.

Through juxtaposing the glory and decline of Darlington Hall, Ishiguro presents the changes of national identity represented by dignity and greatness to redefine the individual ethos of anachronistic politicians. Unlike the greatness of white England, the nostalgic imagery Stevens produces confirms a hierarchical society in which the public should rely upon the elites for their ethical insights. As a conservative politician, Darlington claims to show humanistic sympathy for the postwar Nazis on behalf of the British nation, and regards its sanction as barbarous, "unbecoming to go on hating an enemy like this once a conflict is over. Once you've got a man on the canvas, that ought to be the end of it" (ROD, 1989: 87). Furthermore, the ethical ideals Stevens readily emphasizes in his political testimonio turn out to be the final enclave that the privileged such as Darlington and Mr. Spencer claim to possess their entitlement and rights to govern the public as a response to their fascist attitude toward British parliamentary democracy. The status of accomplice deprives him of the capability of understanding Lord Darlington's political activities accused of his roles in the policy of British reconciliation to Hitler government.

The development of autobiographical narrative, including two haunting scenes of turning points, elaborates Darlington's admirable qualities of character such as humanistic instincts and sympathy for defeated enemies, and then justifies his moral falling from innocence stemming from good intentions in order to reconcile Stevens' perception of Darlington as a witness with his condemnation suffering from the public. While Darlington is hailed as the great hero and diplomat of dedicating to the worldwide peace, Stevens even applies his contrasting image Senator Lewis to allude to the postwar Americanized individualism, and ultimately obtains his philosophical epiphany that "Lord Darlington is holding on to a lost historical ideal, one in which men of power can settle their international affairs with informal and honest deliberations" (Lang, 2000: 157). However, the contextualization Stevens attempts to construct cannot either excuse or rationalize the fact of Darlington's complicity with the Fascist diplomat Herr Ribbentrop and the dismissals of his Jewish housemaids.

The readers, as well as Stevens himself, have the reason to doubt the truthfulness of his texture of memory undermined by his desire to exonerate Darlington and even himself. The mythical England Ishiguro contextualizes foregrounds "a cautionary subtext that criticizes and warns against the dangerous social and moral regression enacted by the Thatcherite celebration of Englishness and Victorian moral values and its refusal to acknowledge the nation's darker life of the mind" (Groe and Lewis, 2011: 119). The Victorian morale values Stevens fits into seem already anachronistic to fight back the dominating Americanism in opposition to the benevolent paternalism Darlington has been standing for. The opposition of morale systems between the postwar new society and Stevens' imagined world makes him a biased witness to historical events to justify his ideal of faithful servant at the expense of his personal fulfillment. The typical image of Victorian dignity his father has established has offered its justification of sacrificing individual conscience and feelings to the authority of Victorian social hierarchy. For example, the legendary story his father retells, in which the admirable butler working in India calmly shoots a tiger to protect his employer's banquet, provides an image of prototype for the father and son to achieve.

Stevens connects the story with the pathetic but dignifying experience his father has once undertaken in which he has to serve a notorious general who should be responsible for the death of his brother, and then enables him to excuse his absence from his father's deathbed and later giving up his romantic love. The stories Stevens retells of becomes a form of self-advertisement for his autonomous but egoist identity acting in the service of justifying Lord Darlington's morality.

The mission Stevens finds to compensate for his personal loss is to fulfill his professional ideal of "furthering the progress of humanity" and "contribution to the future well-being of the empire" (ROD, 1989: 114) through serving a gentleman like Lord Darlington. However, his accidental conversation with Smith who advocates the postwar democratic vision of speaking and fighting for oneself gradually shakes up his confidence in the values of dignity and self-effacement. O'Brien comments that Stevens "violates the terms not only of the narrative of romance, but also of the narrative of history, whose consummation may be read in the vision of democracy described by Harry Smith" (O'Brien, 1996: 795). The anachronistic loyalty causes the misattribution of political complicity that "takes the form of misinterpretation. His devotion to Lord Darlington is such that he fundamentally misinterprets his secret negotiations with the Germans" (Furst, 2007: 542-543). The priority of his professional career provides a self-defending means to justify his sacrificed personal happiness through his lack of intelligence and political loyalty. Furthermore, his relationship with Kenton is also included into his political ideals, which emphasizes her competence as a housekeeper of Darlington Hall for both Darlington and Farraday. The journey to visit her turns out to be a "self-schema that privileges certain aspects to the exclusion of others. His perception of Miss Kenton is as biased as his attitude to Lord Darlington; in both instances he projects a unidimensional image" (Furst, 2007: 547). The professional attitude Stevens inherited from the stories of butlers his father told not only stirs Kenton's curiosity, "Why, Mr. Stevens, why, why, why do you always have to pretend?" (ROD, 1989: 154), but also denies the final fulfillment of his professional and even personal life. The interpretation of Kenton's letter becomes Stevens' own exaggeration he wants to judge for the moral self-justification of political complicity, which enables to adopt "a more positive outlook" to his political career through serving "those great gentlemen at the hub of this world" (ROD, 1989: 244). The Procedural performance of his dignity urges him to depreciate personal feelings within his work, that is, to limit his relation with Kenton and even with his father to justify his professional identity even while Kenton concedes her fancy of an alternative marriage during their meeting in Little Compton.

The contextualization of postwar Suez crisis as the motivation of autobiographical narrative reflects Ishiguro's continuous "interest in exploring the ways in which history intrudes upon individual lives and invalidates the ideals and values which were formerly held as worthy" (Drag, 2014: 36). Stevens finds it essential to justify Darlington's political ambitions and pursuits accused by the radical shift of social values, and resist the dominant "backshadowing" judgement of historical events from the perspective of the present. The strategy of backsighting helps him pinpoint the ignored connections between different events and turning points for his personal and professional defeats. Stevens dismisses the accusation of Darlington as "a great deal of nonsense" (ROD, 1989: 63) and justifies the dismissal of two jewish housemaids as "entirely untypical" and "extremely minor" incidents due to the influence of Sir Oswald Mosley (1896-1980) and his notorious fascist party of the "blackshirts". Like Darlington who later admits his mistake, Stevens also feels "great concern, great concern indeed" (ROD, 1989: 153) about the decision of the dismissal incident. The episode becomes the only occasion Stevens alienates himself from his commitment to maintaining Darlington's reputation. The mistaken judgement leads to Stevens' gradual doubts about the appropriation of his total trust in Darlington's judgement and "lays the blame on his master and turns vindication upside down" (Poree, 1999: 83). Despite his self-defensive intention, Stevens absolves his employer of the anti-Semitic blame through foregrounding his moral and humanistic personality on which the professional ideals have been constructed.

After his encounter with Miss Kenton, as well as his introspective epiphany, Stevens confesses that Lord Darlington "wasn't a bad man at all. And at least he had the privilege of being able to say at the end of his life that he make his own mistakes. His lordship was a courageous man. He chose a certain path in life, it proved to be a misguided one" (ROD, 1989: 243). The journey to Western England partly shakes him out of his self-deception and self-confidence of his professional ideals and turns into a pathetic portrait of someone, like Darlington, who has misspent the whole life on the misguided and even foolish political career. The autobiographical testimonio helps Stevens apply the structure to keep at bay the blame of Darlington's political life and maintain the conviction of his respectability. However, his narrative concerns more about the self-justification rather than contextualizing the truthfulness of historical circumstance. Although

Stevens "does shed new light on the circumstances of the ethical choices taken by Darlington (and others like him) by emphasizing certain motives which have been overlooked in the unanimous and unconditional condemnation of his conduct" (Drag, 2014: 66), his narrative nonetheless falls into the paradox of disingenuousness and self-deception common in the genre of autobiographical writings. The desire for existential meaning in his telling of past stories enforces his professional ideals onto the later crucial life decisions that result in a defensive attitude towards the humiliation of Darlington's and his own misguided life-efforts. However, his attempt to seek absolution for Darlington and himself may act as a release of guilt and responsibility shackled to their past iniquity and offer him an opportunity to enjoy what remains for his life. This kind of life narrative retrospectively rearranges his life stories that keep his personal views and emotions at bay in order to defend the future results of what Darlington has been doing. It seems that what matters is not the historical truth, but the capacity and the necessity for remembering and forgetting.

The changes of social and political values epitomized by the transfer of Darlington Hall from British aristocrat Lord Darlington to American businessman Mr. Farraday deepens Stevens' sense of alienation from an anachronistic era he tries to justify. Despite his struggling efforts, he still finds himself unable to adjust to the Americanized pragmatic and egalitarian reality beneath Mr. Farraday's lighthearted and straightforward bantering. His ultimate epiphany that regards Farraday's hobby of bantering as "the key to human warmth" (ROD, 1989: 245) reveals his reluctance of surrendering his code of dignity to the Americanized professionalism, represented by Lewis and Farraday to disparage the structures of social hierarchy. Like Ono, Stevens ultimately attempts to connect the "human warmth" to his "dignity" of obedience and begins to recognize his alienated identity achieved through his "internalizing the attitudes of their social systems, they change from being objects of pity to being cautionary figures warning against the banality of complicity" (Groes and Lewis, 2011: 116). Toward the end, Stevens regards the American bantering positively and struggles to confine his lost objects to the past for the transfer of his attachment to new objects, that is, to walk out of the melancholic process. Despite its playful and liberating features, the skills of bantering Stevens struggles to obtain cannot erase the power existing in the system of social hierarchy and conceal his failed avoidance of absolute alienation, even if he has sacrificed personal freedom and individual fulfillment. The prototypical stories of great butlers Stevens has been appreciating confirms the professional ideals entrenched in the previous era and allows him the primary motivation to accomplish his visit to Miss Kenton as a means of confirming the justice of his professional ideals.

2.4 Memoirs of a Dislocated Detective

The novel *When We Were Orphans* (2000) continues its exploration of its saviour-type detective Christopher Banks, who like Ryder in *The Unconsoled* (1995) reconciles his personal ambitions with the public expectations of redeeming the crisis of civilization to dismiss the sorrows of their life. Ishiguro concerns more about Banks' accounts of contextual life he has witnessed to personalize the historical events as an observer or participant for his coming to terms with the past, whether personal or public. Here my attempt is not to differentiate memoirs from autobiography, but regards it as a distinctive form of writing practice, just like apology, testimonio and diary categorized within autobiographical writings, to contextualize the memoirist's memories within historicity. Through his personal reminiscence, this novel offers a haunting account of personal and historical accounts as the true stuff of old Shanghai in the 1930s through investigating the mysterious disappearance of his parents. Thus what the story Banks retells involves more of "the time in which the life is lived and the significant others of the memoirist's world" (Jolly, 2001: 595), which grants more detailed portraits of his times and places in relation to the psychological insights of his former protagonists. Ishiguro in his interview claims that he has "other reasons for choosing that kind of cozy detective story as a thing to parody or pastiche. I was quite keen to look at that view of how you deal with evil" (Shaffer and Wong, 2008: 158). As an internationalist novel, the form of memoir presents the controversial self-hood of the narrator through its dialogical format of different cultural traditions. The main purpose here is to distinguish the verifiable truth from Banks' inventive imagination, and shed light on historical events, people around him and his experiences in a politically personalized context.

The memoir-narrator Banks performs his roles of eyewitness, participant and histor to account for his past historical life infused with individual vision of morality and awareness of historical hindsight. Lee Quinby comments that "memoirs promote an 'I' that is explicitly constituted in the reports of the utterances and proceedings of others [...] therefore operate in resistance to the modern era's dominant construction of individualized selfhood, which follows the dictum to, above all else, know thy interior self" (Quinby, 1992: 299). Unlike its self-representation of conventional autobiographic genre, *When We Were Orphans* reconstructs a new form of subjectivity that refuses the normalizing individuality of modern times through subverting its narrator Banks's selfhood, morality and even poetic consciousness. The narrative centers around the contextual border of fact and fiction to reflect upon the historical truth which originates from Banks's observation and other sources of information that can personalize the public realm of historical events. Helen Buss even regards it as a mode of autobiographical writings for writers who are more "concerned with the human subject always historicized by the 'times' rather than a construction of subjectivity that is a self-actualizing discrete entity" (Buss, 1997: 204). The memoirs are not just an exclusive record of political events, but also associate itself with the "invisible presences" seen as indispensable determinants of subjectivity through which the narrator Banks can illuminate the "times" of his ideographic selfhood in history and his relation to the historicity of other characters.

The narrator enacts his past events through creating the illusion that incites readers to experience the narrated events once again. But the illusion that derives from the creative fictionalization can not be regarded as a neutral account of historical truth, but as a unique pattern of personalized historicity. One of these significant "illusions" the readers should not ignore is his idealized mother who is too close, too central a burden for him to evaluate neutrally and objectively. Banks presents his childhood as doubly displaced because of Chinese hostile atmosphere in Shanghai and the British ethnocentric prejudice he suffers from both of his cultural heritages. The embarrassing confusion he felt as a child stirs in him a fantasy of house-servant Ling Tien's wizardry which can turn severed hands into spiders (WWW, 2000: 96). However, he also lives in fear of being classified as lacking in quality of gentlemanly Englishness among his British patriots who regard him as "a mongrel" for his embarrassed status. Michael Gorra points out the motivation and estrangement of Banks's Englishness "will remain for him a form of learned behaviour, in which he compounds the simulacrum of a character from both the gestures of the people around him and his reading in *The Wind in the Willows* or Sherlock Holmes" (Gorra, 2000: 12). The estrangement from both cultural identities still haunts him even in adulthood, which turns into ritual of exorcism to drive the fears away through resolving the case of his parents' disappearance. The subjectivity Banks attempts to construct must be examined in a drastically political context, that is, the Golden Age of detective fiction in the 1930s when people "went through the trauma of modern warfare and realized that the bad things in life cannot emanate just from some clever evil character" (Shaffer and Wong, 2008: 192). Ishiguro sketches an imagined world in which Banks represents a naive and innocent part of readers who experience the empathy emotion of escaping into a world of better time and space. The world of order and justice that sustains Banks's and Sara Hemmings's nostalgia ultimately turns into a kind of poignant escapism, an unattainable "world better than this world we discover when we grow. We remember and wish good world come back again. So very important " (Quinby, 1992: 263). This sentiment of their nostalgia stimulates both of them to play a role in maintaining the idealized world and provides readers with a framework for dealing with its slow disclosure of truth. However, the genre of detective fiction is closely associated with social hierarchy and its poignancy for social order and idealism. Michel Foucault claims that social mechanism of appliance dominates over the individuals to function smoothly through "proliferating, innovating, annexing, creating and penetrating bodies in an increasingly detailed way, and controlling populations in an increasingly comprehensive way" (Foucault, 1980: 106). This novel is perfectly portrayed out of this mindset, of which Banks's career as a detective and his ambition of combating evils in war-ridden twentieth century remind readers of the figure of Sherlock Holmes. The frustration that Banks encounters becomes readers' expectations which stimulate the suspended engagement with the text. As an essential characteristic of memoirs, Banks's entanglement with public history and its devastating influence upon his private life confirm what Marcus Billson defines the tripartite role of "rhetorical stances-the eyewitness, the participant and the histor" (Billson, 1977: 271). Here Ishiguro locates his imagination of family life in an actual contextualization of old Shanghai and testifies to the truth of Banks's family life, that is, its tripartite role of acting as a witness to his parents' refusal of modern subjectivity and as participant of his family's myth trapped in the contextualization of the historical reality he created.

The memoir form asserts the reconstruction of Banks's individual subjectivity through arousing and then rejecting the generic expectations of his detective storyline. When he offers readers the story of his parents, he revises the victim-hood story into his own personal essay to negotiate the traps of political ideology. Francis Hart comments that contemporary memoirs' solution to public/private identity crisis is to "retreat to the 'privacy' of my anonymous, indistinguishable room where, unable to 'opt for us,' I relax with the public intimacics of television and occasionally talk to myself" (Hart, 1979: 210). In fact, the narrator establishes his narrative identity through his interaction with the life stories of significant "others" that can combine the public discourse and personal life, as Banks does by rewriting himself into the outer historical accounts. Banks transcends beyond the role of passive witness to his mother's tragedy and transforms into a participant to reconstruct the myth of his parents. As for his role of histor, the narrator contextualize his personal subjectivity in its public realm in which the fantasy of individual dignity his mother passes onto him makes him "live in your enchanted world for ever. But it's impossible. In the end it has to shatter. It is a miracle it survived so long for you" (WWW, 2000: 294). Banks organizes his memoirs around the case of his parents to emphasize the larger historical context of his professional preoccupations as a proper understanding of a given event or period.

The pathetic overtone of detective fiction the Golden Age readers appreciated is probably due to their response to the detestation of the First World War and the nostalgic idealization of an Edwardian world as their imagined home. W. H. Auden comments that the Golden Age "detective is to restore the state of grace in which the aesthetic and the ethical are as one [...] the detective, must be either the official representative of the ethical or the exceptional individual who is himself in a state of grace" (Auden, 1998: 21). In the world of Banks's life, the public need a superhero like him to guide and savour the society through restoring the order that once existed before the Great War. Compared with Holmes, Banks's memoir seems more restricted and despairing, because it can denote a more settled nostalgia for Golden Age and even a response to the destabilizing results of the two world wars. Furthermore, the elite society like Mr Sir Cecil Medhurst and Grayson of Shanghai's international community welcomes the evil-fighting detective and readily celebrates his great achievement of redeeming the collapsing civilization through "solving the case. Which vital clues finally led to your parents, that sort of thing" (WWW, 2000: 178). Like Stevens in *The Remains of the Day*, Banks tries to live up to the demands of public society to shape but to be shaped by the social mechanism, which leads to the "main character's unerring ability to miss the call of freedom, in the blindness that his sense of obligation imposes upon him" (Gorra, 2000: 12). While crossing the war zone of Shanghai, his ironic complex of human-savour culminates in the episode of breaking into the house where his kidnapped parents should have lived, only to find inside three Chinese corpses and a shocked little girl whose parents have been shell-killed. The ethical responsibility stimulates Banks to undertake the detective role to examine the disastrous scenario with his magnifying glass to identify "whoever did all this, whoever did this ghastly thing, they won't escape justice [...] I'm just the person you want. I'll see to it they don't get away" (WWW, 2000: 272). Rather than confront the war-torn world outside, Banks transforms the irrationality and brutality of war into his childlike illusion so that he can preserve his unique status of reshaping and healing the brutal reality that impinges upon the protecting bubble of idealism.

The story of Banks that is situated mainly within the drastic changes of

1930s actually reflects the life of his grandfather and father who lived in "old Shanghai" during the 1920s and the 1930s where different foreign communities coexisted together. Ishiguro concedes that the international community of Shanghai is "put together in this book from my association with that city [...] I learned about it through my father. There were a lot of photos that he had in an album" (Shaffer and Wong, 2008: 190). Even though his real-life father might not conform to the characterization, readers can still feel the tendency of believing in the extra-textual stereotype of his real family life projected unto the consciousness of the writer. The enclave of old Shanghai is painted as one of his flawed idealism, in which his family's picture of "the carefully tended 'English' lawn, the afternoon shadows cast by the row of elms separating my garden and Akira's and the house itself, a huge white edifice with numerous wings and trellised balconies" (WWW, 2000: 51), constitute his cherished childhood nostalgia of solace and serene halo. Through depicting the disappearance of his parents, Banks portrays the intensity of dominating power structure, in which his mother Diana Banks becomes an important site of battleground between the alliance of social system and its rebellion of individual morality. His recollections give readers a more extensive account of childhood experiences that sketches out how Banks's subjectivity is later formed as an idealist detective. Ishiguro explains that Banks's nostalgic childhood vision originates from his "own memories of being young. The children playing in *When We Were Orphans* are drawn from memories about how I used to play imaginary games with my friends when I was a little boy" (Groes and Lewis, 2011: 256). The importance of nostalgia can trace its roots in his early childhood living in Nagasaki before his family's migration into England that permanently severed the ties with his grandparents and a world of innocent childhood. According to different attitudes towards the past, the nostalgic complex can be classified as reflective and restorative one, which is analogous to the Freudian terms of mourning and melancholia. Instead of accepting the former as an irony or playfulness of the irretrievable, Banks lives up to the principles of the latter to restore order to the messy and cruel world, and is ultimately "anxious to regain, relive, and transmit it so that it will be preserved in all of its depth and wonder [...] a unique contribution to our understanding of the past" (Billson, 1977: 268). His refusal of accepting the truth of his parents' loss gradually transforms into a naive belief in his superheroic power of solving the conflicts within his family. However, the family's prosperity relies upon the misconduct of the imperial trade firm Morganbrook and Byatt, for which his father works as a professional servant.

The ideological mechanism represented by the opium-trade firm exerts a great impact upon the individuals, and brings "prolonged exposure to the contradictory messages from parents and other relations in childhood that leads to the condition of schizophrenia" (Groes and Lewis, 2011: 190). Like Stevens and Kenton in *The Remains of the Day*, Ishiguro continues his fascination with the exploration of how private life responds to the domination of public values. The opium trade the firm involves causes so immense a suffering to the Chinese nation that Diana Banks feels exasperated and accuses the inspector of their British crimes of importing Indian opium into China responsible for the untold misery and degradation of the whole nation. In fact, the crimes of exploiting trade can track back to the Opium War in 1839, and finally becomes an accustomed phenomenon of mass addiction in Shanghai where the young Banks reminisces that "seeing each day, from the carriage that took me to school, the Chinese men doorways along Nanking Road, sprawled in the morning sun" (WWW, 2000: 60-61). The episode of Diana's argument with the inspector of the opium-trade firm provides the socio-political background that determines the vision of Banks's childhood into adulthood. Thus the resistance of his family to the repressive ideology subverts the mythologizing image of persecution as benevolence and cultivation, of which its colonization should not "need to be invalidated as the figment of a paranoid imagination, it should be experienced as kindness" (Laing, 1967: 49). In rebelling against the mechanism of alliance, the mother's idealism perpetuates through his child's inheriting conduct against the repressive imperialism that maintains their kinship ties.

From childhood, the political atmosphere of family relation emitting from the public realm of imperial ethnocentrism has prescribed the role of his personal development. Although Banks concedes the influence of his familial arguments and has "never concerned myself unduly with them. In any case, it was only in the smallest ways that they ever impinged upon my life" (WWW, 2000: 71), readers can obviously recognize his efforts of glossing over the emotional upheavals and psychological loss. Indeed, the repeated arguments set the trajectory of his later tragedy suffering from his schizophrenic state forever into adulthood. The prediction of the family originates from the status of his father as an accomplice of his employer that brings the suffering from religious and ethical conscience. The child Banks, who is exposed to the dilemma of his parents, attributes it to his own fault and manages to solve the question through resorting to Uncle Philip, who has once been his mother's colleague, for a solution of his "wondering. How do you suppose one might become more English?" (WWW, 2000: 76) The prolonged exposure to political mechanism ultimately internalizes the relationship of him into an imagined vision of schizophrenic childhood to exclude the development of identity into maturation. Barry Lewis notes that Banks's childlike "obsession of solving the mystery of his parents' disappearance drives his adult enquiries, and brings him to the point of madness" (Lewis, 2000: 7). His sense of responsibility that originates from the strained relationship of his parents gradually inflates into his childhood illusion of redeeming the world from its wartime disaster through the deluded powers of his status of detective.

The disappearance case serves as a source of cause and effect, within the recalled and constructed memoirs that demonstrate what subjectivity is representative and what is subjected to his present anxieties of self-elevation. Furthermore, the disappearance of his parents which engages the attention of the best detectives in old Shanghai becomes Banks's self-inflated conviction in his later empowering position of a detective to keep alive the lost objects. Banks's melancholic attachment, according to David Eng and David Kazanjian, serves as his "ongoing and open relationship with the past - bringing its ghosts and spectres [...] into the present" (Eng and Kazanjian, 2003: 3-4). The games he plays with Akira reflect the responsibility of a illusionist whose Holmes-like story lines should conclude with a magnificent ceremony held in Jessfield Park, "In many ways, it's where I've continued to live all my life. It's only now I've started to make my journey from it" (WWW, 2000: 227). The recollections of his childhood is the paralleling with and continuation of his maturation in England, during which he imitates the manners of Englishness to dismiss his anxieties of displacement. Interwoven with the detective fiction by Conan Doyle, Banks patches together his new identity of narrative to protect his childhood illusion of desperately solving his family problem. The Holmesian complex transforms the disparagement of his school friends into an ideal image of his detective status with a magnifying glass at hand to investigate the cases such as the Mannering Case and the Trevor Richardson affair, only to end up with a melancholic orphan fixed permanently onto his childhood. The introjection of Holmes-like figure gives rise to a modern version of the detective Banks who is subjected to his family tragedy caused by public ideology.

The strident nationalism Banks and his mother rebel against ultimately leads to the breakout of the Chinese People's War of Resistance against Japanese Aggression which an Japanese compares to its imperial ambitions the nineteenth-century England once advocated. The ensuing life in England, that is, the period of his boarding school and university stage, and detective career in London, does not provide him a homely atmosphere, "never really felt at home there. The international Settlement. That will always be my home" (WWW, 2000: 257). He has to convince himself that he has successfully "blended perfectly into English school life" through his imitating a mannerism popular among school boys, that is, when underlining their remarks he is "tucking the right hand into a waistcoat pocket and moving the left shoulder up and down" (WWW, 2000: 7). The mechanism of constraint, according to Foucault, functions through "the practices of alliance, particularly the confession and penance, it now operates through and within the domains of medicine, education, police surveillance and psychiatry" (Quinby, 1992: 302).

The narrative of Banks is a discourse of rebellion against the subjectification of a detective following the demands of social mechanism. Despite its difficulty and even tragedy, the resistance becomes the only link of parent-child relation within its example of family dynamic the mother has set up. Whereas his father worked for a British firm named Morganbrook and Byatt (revised from the original name "Butterfield and Swire" as a result of defamatory tattoo of Britain's colonial past) that sold opium to the Chinese, the exploitative practices of the firm on which the prosperity of his family depends situated the mother in an embarrassed position that daunted her religious and ethical principles. Her verbal protests had gradually transformed into an anti-opium campaign that converted many wives like her to accuse their husbands of service for the notorious firm.

The conflicts within his family push the child into a swirl of political values where Banks is later doomed to regain the approval of his mother through his "trying to find her, trying to save the world from ruin" (WWW, 2000: 306). Devoid of the professional ideals, the father awkwardly accepts his complicity in the imperialist machinery that is "dedicated to the continuance of European rule, the exploitation of natural resources, and the spread of European culture as an accompaniment to the continued subordination of native peoples" (Punter, 2000: 2). The denouement of Banks's detective story does not restore the expected order and peace to the war-ravaged society, only to offer him a pathetic epiphany about his life-long truth-seeking anxiety. His mother's humane integrity aroused not just the humiliation of her husband who later eloped with his lover and died of typhoid, but also stimulated the retaliation of Wang Ku, a Chinese warlord who kidnapped and humiliated her as a concubine to subjugate "her 'spirit' - highly attractive [...] as he would a wild mare" (WWW, 2000: 291). The truth of his mother's disappearance, hidden underneath the sexuality and desire, is readily alluded to the imperialist power and nationalism dominating in old Shanghai.

The ideal of her campaign, according to Uncle Philip's explanation, is to subvert the alliance of the dominating ideology that "actually wanted the Chinese to be useless. They liked the Chinese to be in chaos, drug-addicted, unable to govern themselves properly. That way, the country could be run virtually like a colony" (WWW, 2000: 288). Here the opium trade becomes a battlefield between political and ethical principles respectively upheld by warlord Wang Ku and Utopian-fighter Diana Banks. The ethical responsibility connects Diana Banks with the double deployment of social alliance and sexuality. On the one hand, she resists the female role the patriarchal society has prescribed for her, and even humiliates her husband and her colleague Uncle Philip through her devoted campaign of fellow-Christians. On the other hand, the feminist suffers from the constraint of sexuality considered by Foucault as "a hermeneutics of desire", through which the "truth of their being" can be retrieved in their desire for the human subjectivity to reconstruct. His mother's example encourages Banks to break the mechanism of social alliance that applies the public discourse to invade the personal subjectivity. The construction of his mother's tragedy is made plausible through Banks' persuasive conviction in his professional idealism trapped in his obsession with the genre of Golden Age detective story. While the story of his parents is retold by Uncle Philip as a metaphorical warning, it symbolizes the first disobedience of personal subjectivity against its public discourse. Unlike the linear storyline that foregrounds its cause, the truth of his parents' case appears at the end of the novel, which empowers Banks acting as the role of witness, participant and histor to disobey the requirements of the warning represented by ideology of repressive social system.

The memoirist narrates three historical periods he performs both as a protagonist-participant actor who experiences the events and as a witness narrator who recalls his past. Ishiguro regards the surrealistic Shanghai section in the novel as "a picture of what the world might look like if it ran according to the less rational emotional logic that we often carry within us" (Shaffer and Wong, 2008: 157). Thus Banks' narrative transgresses the boundary lines of its retrospective and present point of view that subverts the traditional discourse of authentic reporting of historical events to metaphorically adjust something wrong in the past. The desire of sexuality, as Uncle Philip concedes, stimulates him to have aided the kidnap of her and "lived vicariously through Wang. It was almost as though I'd conquered her too. I gave myself pleasure, many many times, imagining for myself what was happening to her" (WWW, 2000: 296). The hysterization imposed by patriarchal society deprives her of the last autonomous subjectivity and all of her concerns for the opium campaign, only to find the suffering of the double muteness on her and even pathological babbling as amnesiac creature in a mental asylum of Hong Kong. The sense of autobiographical self that advocates the autonomy and righteousness here gives away to its interconnectedness with and subjectivity to the political or cultural historicity of an ensemble subjectivity.

The deployment of coexisting past and present time presents the paradox of selfhood between the narrating "I" and its narrated object that acknowledges his own alterity of otherness interconnected with the narrations of others. The narrative identity relies heavily upon the retelling of its narrator's traumatic memories of his childhood and family, "struggling to recall something [...] ingrained in my mind [...] that with each passing year, my life in Shanghai will grow less distinct, until one day that will remain will be a few muddled images" (WWW, 2000: 67). Furthermore, the only two witnesses of his childhood experience are Uncle Philip and Colonel Chamberlain, who respectively overturns his conviction in the idealized "home" of Shanghai and validity of his professional career. Whereas the former, who once escorted Banks to London from Shanghai, insinuates his self-deception about the excitement of "life aboard the ship, as well as by the prospect of the future that lay before me" (WWW, 2000: 27), the latter cruelly pierces through the bubble of his whole life through laying bare the truth of his parents' disappearance. The only corroboration Banks can obtain is his own memories which appear potentially erroneous or conflict with each other, that is, he has severed all the relationships to the trustful witnesses of his idealized past. Probably through his emphasizing the reconstructive nature of remembering, Banks may "wish to divert the readers' attention from the graver 'sins of memory' that undermine the validity of his representation of the past" (Drag, 2014: 159). *When We Were Orphans* rejects the autobiographical "self-elevation" that traditionally chronicles the life of its protagonist, and challenges the objectification and subjection normalized in its ideological context. In stead of performing a consistent and continuous "mourning" process, Banks's memoirs constitute an ensemble subjectivity permeated with textual conflicts and confusions to obstruct the empathy of readers.

Banks' sense of selfhood consists in the stories he retells of their sources, either related by Uncle Philip or from his firsthand experiences. The autobiographical self, according to Helen Buss, always possesses "the potential-because of the memoirist's preoccupation with historicity-of 'confrontation' with accepted versions of subjectivity" (Buss, 1997: 206). Basically, the stories of his three women, that is, his mother, adopted daughter and girlfriend, contribute a lot to rewriting his narrative identity through resisting the mechanism of patriarchal society. The fate of their common "orphanhood" interconnects Jennifer, Sarah and Banks, who share together "a sense of mission" for their seeking out both the literal and metaphorical "shadows of vanished parents", which, as Ishiguro claims, should have served as "the protective bubble" of childhood to ultimately maturate into the idealism of human conscience. However, the cause of sacrificing family happiness for his professional ideal remains confusing or beyond the comprehension of readers. In infiltrating into the construction of their stories, Banks sets up his role of tripartite narrator to weave the reality of his own life with the "times" he has grown in, of which readers can examine the various possibilities and traps for these rebels to undertake. The original episode that arouses his ambition is the case of children murder he investigates in Village of Coring, Somerset, when encouraged by a police inspector to "go this day to where the heart of the serpent lies and slay the thing once and for all" (WWW, 2000: 136). Furthermore, his cleric friend Canon Moorly urges Banks to promptly undertake the role to identify "the source of all our current anxieties [...] spread its poison over the years ever further across the world, right through our civilisation" (WWW, 2000: 138). Yet the determining factor that speeds up his choice to investigate the disappearance case of his parents is his chance Sarah encounter with , who challenges him to depart for Shanghai and overcome "a pathetic conspiracy of denial; a denial of responsibility which has turned in on itself and gone sour, manifesting itself in the sort of pompous defensiveness" (WWW, 2000: 162) to slay what the inspector calls the "serpent" of human society. Like Stevens, Banks invests his case-solving narration with an infantile ideal of profession to gloss over his discontinuous and stranded identity of narrative.

The Shanghai section of Banks' narrative focuses on the devastating eruption of international conflicts in 1937, which is also his life record of handling with his parents' case as well as the impending disaster of worldwide war. The British public as well as politicians, such as Sir Cecil, all believe that the crisis in Shanghai has become the heart of the political swirl that urges Banks to undertake the mission of saving the whole world from its "brink of catastrophe. What would people think of me if I abandoned them all at this stage?" (WWW, 2000: 212) Here the narrator invites the common identification or empathy from readers with his professional idealism at the expense of his family duty. After abandoning his normal life living with his adopted daughter Jennifer, Banks leaves for Shanghai and joins the elite society represented by the outstanding couple Sir Cecil and Sarah who naively await their saviour to come, that is, to follow his "authorial instructions" and witness the war-crisis to be solved.

Like Banks' mother, Sarah sacrifices her marriage and even her life to the contribution of civilization. She selects the retired diplomat Sir Cecil as the one who can deserve her love as well as her mission of fighting against the worldwide evils in old Shanghai. However, the latter regards his newly wedded wife as just a harlot, which finally pushes her into the arms of Banks. The lack of childhood warmth and sheltering motivates her searching for communal connection or at least "a little home" of Banks' love and companionship. Despite their planning of eloping to South America, Banks ultimately recognizes her romantic contact and their prospect of "home" as an escapism from his professional responsibilities for others. The illusion of a ready-made home Sarah promises lifts off the "heavy burden" from his back and situates him out into "the light and fresh air after being trapped in a dark chamber" (WWW, 2000: 212). Banks dismisses the fear and desire of himself, on which relies his future life mirrored in Sir Cecil who has escaped from his diplomatic responsibility. Even if this assumption of future life comes true, it will only turn into the repetitive tragedy of his father or Sir Cecil who made the similar decision of abandoning the family and ethical duties.

The life stories of the three women respectively contribute to the structure of resistance to the power of patriarchal mechanism to perpetuate a subjectivity that can reverse the forces of repressive ideology. Banks' schizophrenic obsession with his professional ideals unfortunately evolves into his impotent resistance to the power of social mechanism represented by political and economic institutions. Despite his specious success of being a detective, the mechanism of social alliance pushes all the rebels of the novel such as Diana and Sarah, into the abyss of hell. The hostile ideology Banks rejects unfortunately leads to a sense of displacement and yearning for a "home" that can console his emptiness and fate as orphans. The desire of belonging is representative of the displaced plight that forces them "to face the world as orphans, chasing through long years the shadows of vanished parents. There is nothing for it but to try and see through out missions to the end" (WWW, 2000: 313). Here the image of parenthood exceeds his familial dependency and becomes a professional idealism and crime-fighting aspiration for the communal complex. At the end of the novel, the "orphaned" father and daughter cling together to await the prospect of their imagined "home" and new life entangled within the aftermath of devastating war and ghosts of their missing parents.

Banks' struggling to substitute Shanghai with his present "home" in London perhaps can be "considered as a mark of the completion of his process of mourning, defined as a stage when, after severing its ties to the lost object, the ego regains the capacity to attach itself to other objects" (Drag, 2014: 152-153). But his London myth that signifies a strange place of today full of foreigners drifting through has been deprived of its idealizing symptom, which subverts his conviction of self-definition for the ensuing existence without its former nostalgic aura of childhood. The displacement reveals so exiled a living state that Ishiguro "had no clear role, no society or country to speak for or write about [...] I think this did push me necessarily into trying to write in an international way" (Shaffer and Wong, 2008: 58). Ishiguro needs the memoir form to recall the historical context where Banks's parents lived and died or disappeared in a repressive society that threatens its members' survival and deprives them of the conscientious principles. As a novel concerned with historical events, the state of Banks' loneliness and homelessness prefigures the fates of numerous migrants and orphans through historicizing this imagined story into the authentic contextualization of the painful historical episode. And the historical analysis of its repressive ideology that is imposed on the public becomes an unique perspective, as well as its reflection upon the inherent limitations of the impending autonomous subjectivity.

2.5 Bildungsroman of a Subaltern Schoolgirl

The novel *Never Let Me Go* (2005) appears to be an exploration of allegorical self-portraits of marginal clones that receives the shortlist honor of the 2006 Arthur C. Clarke Award, but it actually borrows its science-fiction genre to reflect upon the fate of human beings. Ishiguro mainly focuses upon the fortunes of its narrator Kathy and her intimate friends Ruth and Tommy through their common school experiences at Hailsham and the Cottages of an alternate England in the late 1990s. Despite their pathetic destinies of "carers" and "donors" of vital organs for human inhabitants, their semblance of an ordinary human condition invites the readers' empathy that "you have to shield children from what you know and drip-feed information to them [...] controlling the bubble of innocence around a child, regulating it. All children have to be deceived if they are to grow up without trauma" (Adams, 2005: 17). Ishiguro condenses the life expectancy of the clones like Kathy into the duration of around thirty years for its protagonist's formation of "self" and reconciliation with social roles that parallels the readers' experiences of Bildung roman as school and college students.

Never Let Me Go, like Ishiguro's other novels, features his first-person narrator Kathy who is now thirty-one years old and forced to abandon her role as a carer and confront her "completion" of human existence. As a result, Kathy begins to sift through her memories about her schooldays, friendships and career as a carer to "realise now just how much of what occurred later came out of our time at Hailsham, and that's why I want first to go over these earlier memories quite carefully" (NLMG, 2005: 37). The definition of Bildunsroman, according to Wilhelm Dilthey, can be applied to a story of a youthful protagonist like Kathy that recounts how "he enters into life, searches for kindred souls, encounters friendships, and love, and how he engages in a struggle with the hard reality of life, and thus maturing as a result of the multiplicity of life experiences, he finds himself and becomes aware of his purpose in the world" (Jolly, 2001: 105). Here the genre emphasizes the accommodation of its narrator into the social ideology that confines his freedom of determining his own lifestyle and destination within the settings of fictional contemporary England. The protagonist should internalize oneself into the mechanism of social ideology in which his trajectory is always a progression from the quixotic idealism of youth toward the systematized logic of adulthood. The Hailsham institution, on which Kathy's nostalgia of childhood rests, belongs to the philosophy of utilitarianism that perceives of human beings as the functional cogs of social machine. The maturation of its narrator Kathy from an innocent youth into an institutionalized tool of society and its dominant values becomes the principal aspect of this genre that features how the repressive social system reproduces the essential citizens for its own benefits rather than a positive development of its individuals.

Kathy's narrative involves different strata of life experiences associated with specific places and times in which she grows up and performs her ultimate epiphany as a Hailsham student. Furthermore, the genre involves the maturation of its narrator deriving from her positive interaction with outer environment which repressively integrates the development of its individuals into the public discourse of social system. One essential aspect of Bildungsroman is its internal tension of "contradictory demands on the protagonist to develop fully his individuality and Kathy harmonize his development with the goals of the greater community" (Jolly, 2001: 106). Kathy's narrative restores the Goethean form of Bildungsroman represented by Wilhelm Meister's Apprenticeship (1795-1796), which deals with a struggling integration of a disenfranchised minority into a larger hierarchical order. However reluctant Kathy feels, the sacrifice of individuality to obtaining a sense of harmony with the existing social mechanism becomes her ultimate destiny to accept and document the oppressive control of individual subjectivity. Kathy's pride in her caring job that makes a difference to a donor's life and its being appreciated by her superior authority arouses the reader's judgement of its social morality. The exploration of its political aesthetics reveals the utopian/dystopian aspects of future framed within the constraints of our present historical reality. Darko Suvin comments that the genre of science fiction "focuses on the variable and future bearing elements from the empirical environment [...] Where the myth claims to explain once and for all the essence of phenomena, SF first posits them as problems and then explores where they lead" (Suvin, 1979: 7). Despite his engagement with cultural and ethical concerns, Ishiguro regards this novel as an allegory that can spur a humanistic resistance to a repressive reality entailing social changes to exceed beyond the present historicity.

Never Let Me Go features the maturation of these youths wandering on the borders of their adult world, alongside its ethical and cultural institutions represented by Hailsham. In contrast to its typical form of conventional Bildungsroman, Ishiguro not just imbues his writing with a sense of nostalgia for his missing childhood spent in Nagasaki, but also underlines the reluctance of and resistance to the social roles the clones are expected to accept. Adulthood, while inevitable, is a disenchanted space overrun by logic, science, and capitalism. Not only is maturity dispiriting, but, if accepted passively, it imprisons and even annihilates the soul. The narrator Kathy chooses her enchantment of childhood when she grew up in Hailsham that is considered as the ideal space to escape the repressive reality of existence. The contrast between her enchanting childhood and dispiriting adulthood confirms Ishiguro's statement about his motivation of applying the form of science fiction as an allegory of human existence to retell of "that kind of hinterland period between being an adolescent and being an adult in post-student times. To some extent I'm sketching from life-but that's not the same as creating autobiographical characters" (Groes and Lewis, 2011: 256). The alternative landscape of the 1990s England offers a logic fantasy of the repressive existence imposed by a scientific society that entices the readers' anxiety about the ethical foundation for social and cultural life.

The structure of Bildungsroman bestows Ishiguro with a new perspective of parallel consciousness to reflect upon the cause and consequence of adulthood in relation to the fulfillment of childhood. Jane Bennet criticizes of the human relations of post-modern life that "There was once a time when Nature was purposive, God was active in the details of human affairs [...] this premodern world gave way to forces of scientific and instrumental rationality, secularism, individualism, and the bureaucratic state-all of which, combined, disenchant the world" (Bennett, 2001: 7). The professional idealism cultivated throughout their childhood has penetrated into their rationale and private realms of human life within its repressive bureaucracy. The reality of their adulthood, according to their guardian Miss Lucy, deprives of their opportunity of human happiness that the clones have "got to know and know properly. None of you will go to America, none of you will be film stars. And none of you will be working in supermarkets as I heard some of you planning the other day. Your lives are set out for you" (NLMG, 2005: 80). Despite its science-fiction premise, the unexpected reality almost resembles the future most of human readers have dreamed of but ultimately failed to realize. The disenchantment Kathy suffers in her adulthood offers an excuse of her escape into the nostalgia of ideal childhood as a result of her remorse for the dominant apathy and parochialism of scientific ethos. The remedy to the predication of maturation, according to Jane Bennett, is that "to be enchanted is to be struck and shaken by the extraordinary that lives amid the familiar and the everyday" (Bennett, 2001: 4). However, the emphasis of "the extraordinary" existing amid "the familiar" of ordinary social life cannot get rid of the ethical principles established by Goethe's bildungsroman Weltanschauung of combining the individual selfhood and social morality.

Kathy's struggling to perform "human" role of daily existence and reject the pessimism of her disenchanted destination within a repressive society confirms the readers' perception of postmodern disillusion. The childhood world in which the youths at Hailsham have fostered their dreams of future human roles as film stars and football athletes opens the possibility of wonderfulness for daily life of human beings. However, the adulthood world becomes a repressive arena where childhood dreams have been surrendered to a social system of scientific and moral ideology. Like the traditional models of Bildungsroman, such as Wilhelm Meister, Ishiguro portrays the gradual transformation of creative youths into the "dignified" adults deprived of any humanistic and meaningful life. But unlike the models mentioned above, Kathy's disenchantment originates more from a repressive system and its withered sense of societal ethics that threaten her individual self-identification. Through addressing her allegory predicament of human existence, Ishiguro undermines the rules of traditional Bildungsroman narrative that foregrounds the idealistic innocence of a youth and his willingness to undertake an ethical responsibility of his familial or social role. Kathy's maturation connects the cruel reality with her idealized enchantment of childhood at Hailsham leading to a parallel world where creative capabilities like paintings, poetry and music are underlined as proofs of their existent souls.

Presiding over this "Other" world is Madame who establishes this benevolent institution to provide the semblance of ordinary human existence for these cloned students. Just as the symbolic meaning of the novel title reveals, the song *Never Let Me Go* by Judy Bridgewater, to which Kathy dances with a pillow held close to her breast, makes Madame upset and sob, because she regards the episode as an impending substitution of a crueler and harsher world for "the old kind world, one that she knew in her heart could not remain, and she was holding it and pleading, never to let her go" (NLMG, 2005: 267). Kathy's education in traditional Bildungsroman sense should never be fulfilled unless she escapes the confines of Lacanian "real" and comprehend the principles of cultural ideology that allows her a marginal status of post-modern and technology-dominating society. The Lacanian projection of the Other-world becomes her symbolic rejection of surrendering to the realistic responsibility and all-round maturation. The alternative world that Kathy encounters is an allegorical dystopia of post-modern epoch familiar with the present readers in which the distorted reality is assembled into a Lacanian mirror of human existence. Kathy's melancholic longing for her Hailsham childhood becomes an invaluable foundation of her identity and a refuge of human morality for her to resist the bleakness of adult world where "Hailsham with me, safely in my head, and that'll be something no one can take away" (NLMG, 2005: 281). The album *Songs After Dark* which symbolizes the absence of Lacanian desire connects Kathy with her memories of schooldays at Hailsham and the Cottages as a reminder of their ultimate destinies.

To the readers' surprise, the cover picture of the cassette in which Judy's "her elbows up on the bar and there's a cigarette burning in her hand" (NLMG, 2005: 67) entices her reflection on the taboo of smoking at Hailsham. The prohibition of smoking is carried out in name of protecting their organs from damage, and thus cut off from any book or magazine such as Sherlock Holmes for its provoking episodes of smoking. Furthermore, the rumors of these pupils that regard Norfolk as "England's 'lost corner', where all the lost property found in the country ended up" can be traced back to the Geography lessons of Miss Emily that purposefully encourages their spread to console the anxieties, of which the loss should end up regaining becomes "accepted fact virtually throughout our entire year" (NLMG, 2005: 65). The deceptive cultivation the pupils are forced to feed on alludes to the construction and projection of the cultural values of social reality that conceals the truth of raising the closes as no more than educated cattle who are deprived of the thought of escape and resistance. In a word, their sense of impending destiny is gradually integrated into their daily activities and mind of thoughts through repeatedly emphasizing forbidden smoking and health checking. As a pedagogic machine, Hailsham deprives the clones of their possible contact with the outside world and gradually transforms them into the products of ideological system through their being "told and not told. You've been told, but none of you really understand, and I dare say, some people are quite happy to leave it that way" (NLMG, 2005: 79). The education of their maturation in this parallel world is never her personal desire but the reflection of social desire for them that is determined by the dominant culture.

The loss and regaining of the cassette connects together the relationships among Kathy, Ruth and Tommy, and "if I happen to get the tape out and look at it, it brings back memories of that afternoon in Norfolk every bit as much as it does our Hailsham Days" (NLMG, 2005: 171). The first substitution for the original one is the tape *Twenty Classic Dance Tunes*, which is the compensation of Cathy's complicit favour for Ruth's making up her intimate relation with their teacher Miss Geraldine through showing off her secretly newly-acquired pencil case. Despite their innocuous vanity, the pencil case episode establishes for Cathy the foundation of their mutual friendship and "especially Ruth has gone, it's become one of my most precious possessions" (NLMG, 2005: 75). The objects they've acquired at the Sales can be seen as the artefact of human culture, but have gradually been transformed into the reserve of new memories that should isolate them from the outside cruelty. However, the replacement coming from Tommy's piece of the Bridgewater tape during their visiting Cromer in Norfolk enhances their friendship but surprisingly estranges Ruthy's intimacy, which symbolizes their equation of emotional values with human beings. Furthermore, Ruth's betrayal of Kathy's secret love affairs and comments on Tommy's childish paintings of animals placates a big wedge between their friendship and ultimately causes their splitting apart of intimate relationship. Unlike Stevens and Banks in previous novels, Kathy cannot completely understand her plight of identity, let alone the meanings of human life such as friendship, love and death that define the nature of our human world. Thus the idealization of Hailsham world is only an illusory image of symbolic projection from the distorted reality of cunning pedagogic machine that manipulates the education and information to control their actions and destinies through misinterpreting their experiencing as the aesthetic dignity and human responsibility.

The ignorance of their real identity the Hailsham pupils are forced to suffer is "more painfully and ironically exploited in the sense that Kathy H. and her friends are deliberately kept in the dark about what they truly are" (Groes and Lewis, 2011: 216). Kathy's nostalgia of looking back into the magic mirror of childhood should never symbolize a return of the authentic reality but a symbolic reflection of the school-cum-concentration confines of social adulthood that acts as an individual soul-annihilating mechanism. The pedagogic system impedes the maturation of their humanist personality and encourages them to regard the symbolic shadows of idealized Hailsham as the version of real outside society. Despite their literary education, the clones cannot equate themselves with those who are experiencing the cultural tradition of human life. Only during her confrontation with Madame and Miss Emily does Kathy realize that her "mental map" of their identity turns out to be "either unnecessary or completely wrong" (NLMG, 2005: 247). Like the rumored relation of "Lost Corner" and Norfolk mentioned above, Tommy's supposition that the couples in real love can obtain a deferral of donations derives from the exhibition of gallery, of which Miss Emily underlines the things "like pictures, poetry, all that kinds of stuff, she said they revealed what you were like inside. She said they revealed your soul" (NLMG, 2005: 173). This scene reminds Kathy of their visit to Cromer for the sightseeing of Ruth's "possible" mother, whose open-plan office they have found comes not from the realistic ground of social life but from the advertisements of magazines hoarding at the Cottage to echo their dreams of future inculcated at Hailsham. The Hailsham students often fantasize their source of origins and future life through searching for the "possibles" in magazines until the cruel reality pierces through the bubble of their connection with human histories or identities.

Confined within the mirror of childhood memories, the three best friends lament over the lost enchantment at Hailsham, that is, they should not anticipate the possibility of their being cloned from respectable people but "modelled from trash. Junkies, prostitutes, winos, tramps. Convicts, maybe, just so long as they aren't psychos" (NLMG, 2005: 164). The bleak world of adulthood, which is analogous to the modernist imagery of *The Waste Land* (1922), becomes the opposite of Kathy's idealized Hailsham where "everything I'd ever lost since my childhood had washed up [...] a tiny figure would appear on the horizon across the field, and gradually get larger until I'd see it was Tommy [...] and though the tears rolled down my face, I wasn't sobbing or out of control" (NLMG, 2005: 282). Here the reader can obviously feel the progression of the Bildungsroman, of which Kathy suffers the loss of her innocent childhood, fantasy and possibility of human life. The individual "true" selfhood the "guardians" inculcate into their mind that excellence in art and responsibility of "donations" express a possession of human soul in a culture of utilitarianism endows them with the only approach to the redemption, integrity and dignity. Justyna Kociatkiewicz defines the anti-bildungsroman as "a subjugation, a defeat, a frustration of the individual by the society", rather than "the substance of Bildung itself, of formation viewed on the one hand as a necessary and beneficial compromise between public and private" (Kociatkiewicz, 2008: 22). Through foregrounding the ideal state of Hailsham childhood, Ishiguro overturns the pattern of traditional Bildungsroman and its moral subjugation to social mechanism to elaborate his anxieties about historical or metaphorical thoughts of social progress at the expense of ethic and moral regression.

Despite the background of scientific utopia, readers can symbolically connect Kathy's life story with the way we human beings have lived. Kathy's elaboration of her schooldays at Hailsham and her friendship with Ruth and Tommy foregrounds Ishiguro's interest in human attitudes towards their cruel fate and human dignity. Since the modern Enlightenment, the divide between science and culture exacerbates the dangers of technological development that is, "taking over and dehumanizing man, placing him in a context of artificial substances and gadgets rather than live nature, in an unaesthetically standardized environment where means had subsumed ends, where industrial labor requirements entailed the mechanization of human beings" (Tarnas, 1991: 364). Instead of providing morale judgement over the cloning technology, Ishiguro underscores the role of mechanic discourse that subjugates individuals as the subjects of dominant ideology.

Whereas the frame of narrative follows the thirty-one-year-old carer to reflect upon her childhood of boarding school, the inner narrative acts as an idealistic nostalgia spent at Hailsham.Kathy's longing for her idealized childhood serves as a melancholic type of return to the past that has been irrevocably lost. But the maturation the clones like Kathy have undergone endows them with an emotional consolation that signifies their mental transition from the state of melancholia to that of mourning within the framework of Bildungsrom. Ishiguro compares Hailsham to a figurative "manifestation of the way all children are separated off from the adult world, and are drip-fed little pieces of information about the world that awaits them, often with generous doses of deception" (Shaffer and Wong, 2008: 199). As the reality-devastating adulthood threatens the innocence of children like Kathy, the Hailsham guardians undertake the role of setting things right. Unlike his previous novels such as *An Artist of the Floating World* or *The Remains of the Day*, Ishiguro employs an innovative technique of parallel consciousness different from his previous prototypical unreliable narration, through which the narrator simultaneously observes the estrangement between the world of her childhood and adulthood. The narrator who mediates the poles of enchantment and disenchantment constructs two versions of reality to account for the contrast of its ethical vigor.

The disenchantment of adulthood thus reduces them to the organs and bodies of scientific universe and then determines their passive acceptance of their tragic fate rather than positively fulfilling the desire of human life. The acquiescence of their predetermined process of fateful life explains how the social consciousness of Bildungsroman dominates the relation between the individual and his dependent context. Ishiguro is worried about the human "sense that it was comfortable for her to resign herself to what everybody else had done already. That it feels normal to her, that it's her duty" (Shaffer and Wong, 2008: 215). Kathy's calm acceptance of performing both as a carer and an organ-donor reveals the mechanistic reification the ideological machine of Hailsham imposes upon the worldview of these clones that "when the time came, you'd be able just to unzip a bit of yourself, a kidney or something would slide out, and you'd hand it over" (NLMG, 2005: 86). However, the passivity of their individual empowerment and autonomy is determined by reification of the Hailsham machine where they have grown up. The instrumentalist value that is deprived of its human morality constructs an unbridgeable barrier of regarding them as genetic underclass for the benefits of the donation programme.

Their compatibility with the outsider is social system enables them to willingly conceptualize a self-sacrifice human dignity, of which "the most improbable practices are therefore excluded, as unthinkable, by a kind of immediate submission to order that inclines agents to make a virtue of necessity, that is, to refuse what is anyway denied and to will the inevitable" (Bourdieu, 1990: 54). Their lack of individual autonomy originates from the Hailsham machine where its boarding students are inculcated the well-meant information about the cruel adult world to protect their innocent childhood from outside contamination and harm. The education the clones have received is akin to that of normal boarding school where Kathy and her schoolmates gradually understand their identity and dire destiny that awaits them. Thus the social norms and values gradually internalize the subclass in a structure of consciousness that submits them to the established forms of hierarchy system. Within the limits of their predetermined fate, the clones attempt to endow their life with significant meanings of human dignity through complying with the principles of Hailsham duty. Reminiscent of her tragic fate, Ruth is content with being "a pretty decent carer. But five years felt about enough for me. I was like you, Tommy. I was pretty much ready when I became a donor. It felt right. After all, it's what we're supposed to be doing" (NLMG, 2005: 223). The identification with Hailsham allows Kathy no other possible future than to follow her precedent models such as Ruth and Tommy. Her ultimate choice of sacrificing herself to the benefits of human non-clones reveals the symbolic violation of childhood enchantment and sense of individuality that are damaged by an invisible force of ideological violence. Kathy's constant questioning about her humanity alludes to the existent rumors about Madame's Art Gallery and deferral of donations at Hailsham that consists in her personal maturation through coming to terms with the reality of their destiny and transforming the repression of social mechanism into a stoic and ethical attitude of human life.

The artistic creativity and utilitarian responsibility Kathy considers as reflections of their humanistic souls turn out to be the well-meant deceptions they are inculcated within the symbolic enclave of adulthood disenchantment. As the imagined enclave of adulthood disenchantment, Ishiguro placates the alternative setting in the recent England that symbolically alludes to our own society, but absolutely estranges from ours. Furthermore, the Hailsham students receive their artistic education and even experience human emotions or dilemmas such as love and death, which distinguishes them no more than the ordinary art students. Following the Bildungsroman of Kathy's narration, the readers feel how the clones deal with their outer realities and "the relationship we have with our world. Immersed in a fantastic 'secondary world' which parallels ours, we are impelled to make sense of it, even if we have no clues other than the words on the page" (Groes and Lewis, 2011: 244). Whereas the "secondary" world is mechanized into its suppression of individual autonomy, the clones' personality demonstrates her human capability of genuine love and originality even if within the cruelty of adult world. The analogue to which the reader feel about his own existential anxiety reminds us more of the life choice that is prescribed by our own parents or other hierarchy authorities rather than just a fantasy of scientific dystopia.

However, Kathy does not demonstrate any anxiety about her own and others' death but the willingness of performing a qualified carer and donor. Her reaction to the cruelty of adulthood suggests that the professional responsibility inculcated within the Hailsham bureaucracy has infiltrated into the rationale of these individual lives, and that the acceptance of their destined donation is predetermined within human society. Here Ishiguro borrows the trope of "middle-class boarding school novel, with its beguiling motivational assumption that the world is just and that effort will be rewarded, and infuses it with a dark, late-twentieth-century punk or slacker version of 'no-future'" (Robbins, 2007: 293). It is no wonder that the clones identify themselves with the role of commodities in a society of capital materialism, whose value of existential living depends upon their zipped-up bags of organs to donate for their original "possibles". The fact that Kathy accepts her limited expectations of life leads to her later suppressed agitation at the social injustice underlying the whole system represented by Hailsham. Kathy paints an idyllic myth of childhood Eden that provides high principles of education and homely atmosphere at Hailsham where the aspiring system of recognition and rewards sets the tone for their future outlook and sensitivity. Her detailed account of everyday school life, with its emphasis on artistic creativity, friendship and campus romance is much indebted to the framework of boarding-school novel.

Despite the rumors of their destinies, Hailsham seems more like an asylum of childlike happiness and innocence that inculcates the sense of belonging and community the students feel about their achievements as a carer or donor of maintaining Hailsham professional idealism. Kathy acknowledges that the childhood years she's spent at Hailsham, "tend to blur into each other as a kind of golden time, and when I think about them at all, even the not-so-great things, I can't help feeling a sort of glow" (NLMG, 2005: 76). Furthermore, the older students Kathy encounters at the Cottages, including Tommy and Ruth, acting as a couple, tend to imitate the role models and even linguistic models they watch from the TV programmes to remake up their desirable self-image and sense of belonging within a homely community for them to be "holding on to each other because that was the only way to stop us being swept away into the night" (NLMG, 2005: 269). The contradiction between Hailsham's emphasis of human education and their denial of human rights provides for them an illusion of limited meaningful and rewarding life associated with outer human society. The delusion that the cloned students have pursued affirms human existence within this dark territory. Unlike Miss Lucy's pessimistic views of their life, Kathy regards Tommy's paintings as "trash" and "ridicule" to force themselves not only to recognize the cruelty of disenchanted adulthood but to integrate into the aspirating mobility of ideological system. Bruce Robbins comments that the clones' resignation originates more from "the ideology of the welfare state, which gives a grateful semblance of meaning and legitimacy to the stopgap efforts of every day" (Robbins, 2007: 294). The complicity of larger bureaucratic machine gradually suppresses the "agitation" of these clones with the deceptive expectations of a dignified life, but only temporarily suspends their desperation about the social injustice. Kathy's resolution to confront Madame with her and Tommy's plea for her confirmation of "rumours about Hailsham students and deferrals" (NLMG, 2005: 247) represents their forceful expression of individual autonomy and sense of freedom until Tommy's image of furious screams at his destined reality ultimately defies the deceptive enchantment of idealized childhood. The only challenge Kathy ever pursues is to submit to the system of rumored "deferral" the clones like her can obtain through demonstrating their genuine creativity. Unlike Tommy's final estrangement from Hailsham, Kathy maintains her attachment after the loss of Ruth and Tommy only as a reminder of her nostalgic childhood to retrieve her self-definition and consolation within a larger social context.

The deceptive system diverts their anger and resistance from the cruelty and injustice of adulthood and subsequently substitutes with minor restitution and rewards for their resignation. The deception within Hailsham, according to Madame's rationale, "kept things from you, lied to you [...] sheltered you during those years, and we gave you your childhoods [...] You built your lives on what we gave you. You wouldn't be who you are today if we'd not protected you" (NLMG, 2005: 263). Kathy's attachment to idealistic childhood originates from her dream of maintaining a more innocent and benevolent sanctuary of memories to confront the current cruelty of adult world. Whereas the spiritual stuff of human life such as art, love and creativity brings forth its existential meaning, the logic of scientific-capitalist discourse within its adult world only glimpses "something provisional and not definitive, and therefore death for him is meaningless occurrence. And because death is meaningless, the civilized life sch is meaningless" (Weber, 140). Instead of advocating the acceptance and subjugation with their social ideology, Kathy's idealization of Hailsham childhood foregrounds an alternative possibility of human destination permeated with signs of dignity and morality. The tragedy of Hailsham students can be paralleled as the metaphor of existential predicament human beings have to suffer during their childhood. Whereas the adulthood deprives them of its meaning and value of individual autonomy, the nostalgia of childhood provides the spiritual sanctuary to set right the cruelty of bureaucratic society and confirms the ethics of enchantment as a result of its engagement with the totality of human life. Kathy finally acknowledges the limits of human existence and cruelty, and comes to terms with the reality of her adulthood. Though the progression of a child into adulthood is often assumed as a positive development, this kind of world has given way to the forces of scientific modernization and post-modernization.Through articulating the frustration of the soul-pursuit that accompanies the adulthood, Ishiguro overvalues this childhood departing from the genre's historical or cultural ideology. It is right through retelling of the most valuable experiences of her life that Kathy can recognize her meaning of human existense and even resists the story of self-identification imposed by social mechanism.Kathy's identification with Hailsham that offers them friendship, love and compassion rather than the apathy of the public ultimately provides her a sense of belonging and makes them become whom they should become within the social nature of human beings.

Chapter Three An Autobiography of Naipaul's Fiction

As the winner of the Nobel Prize for Literature in 2001, Vidiadhar Surajpasad Naipaul is seen as one of the world's most admired and contentious writers. Just like Ishiguro and Rushdie, V. S. Naipaul also draws from his experiences of childhood and youth as an inspiration for his earlier novels. Since his first novel *The Mystic Masseur* in 1957, Naipaul has begun his career of being a writer who travels as a self-portrayed colonial from rural Trinidad to upper-class England to explore the struggles of the destitute and the displaced of Trinidadian society. Whereas the novel *A House for Mr. Biswas* (1961) traces the childhood, adolescence and maturity of its protagonist, that is, the genre of bildungroman fiction, to reflect the specific nostalgia of and tribute to his father. The novel *The Enigma of Arrival* (1987) depicts his own sterile experiences of migration within the realities of England. A recurring topic in the Nobel Laureate's writings is the predicament of migration experience as a result of three cultures of his heritage, that is, an expatriate community derived from the encounters of Imperial Britain, India and the Caribbean.

3.1 An Epic of Trinidadian Pastoral

As is know to all, the major details of the novel *A House for Mr. Biswas* are based upon V. S. Naipaul's own and his father's life stories, in which Mohun

Biswas, an aspiring writer and journalist, is the reiteration of his father Seepersad Naipaul, and Anand, evidently the author himself. Unlike the conditions of pastoral village Naipaul's family lived, Mr. Biswas creates from the swamps and arid fields for himself an illusion, of which an ordered and comfortable landscape should exist to correspond with the descriptions of his English books. Naipaul's writings, like other immigrant writers, tend to combine his personal concepts and ideas with the forms and themes borrowed from abroad, that is, transposing a Western narrative tradition to the expressions of the locale. The imagery of "pastoral" village recurs in most of his novels, such as *Miguel Street* (1959), *The Mimic Men* (1967) and *The Enigma of Arrival* (1987). And later in *The Magic Seeds* (2004), the narrator Willie finally comes to his epiphany that "This pastoral vision contained the idea that the peasant labored and was oppressed. What this pastoral vision didn't contain was the idea that the village [...] was full of criminals, as limited and vicious and brutal as the setting"(Naipaul, 2004:124-125). Naipaul's novels are so pervaded with pastoral imagery that their form of pastoral fiction which relates to shepherds and Arcadia can't be even looked, because his paternal grandparents also arrived from India to labour in sugar plantation village of Trinidad.

To appreciate Naipaul's literary output, the history of West Indies can't be ignored, which is discovered by Christoper Columbus in 1492. Later in his search for El Dorado, its founder Sir Walter Raleigh set up the original version of pastoral in Trinidad, which turns out to be not the discovery of innocence but that of human indifference and rapacity. Resulting from the abolition of slave trade, the European planters began to indenture labors of India, which gradually evolves into a creole society including whites, colored people and blacks. This epic of pastoral chronicles the life of Mohun Biswas who, born as an Indian migrant, moves from the pastoral village to the clamorous city where his literary aspiration ultimately comes to its fulfillment. His name, as the Indian pundit explains, is also that of Lord Krishna who is an avatar of Vishnu. According to the Indian epic *Mahabharata*, Krishna slewed giant serpents, wooed his bride and ultimately conquered the city controlled by the tyrant king.

But the modern Mohun can never live up the such achievements, that is, defending his own family and choosing his bride, not to mention conquering the city of Port of Spain. His transformation from a Brahmin of Indian pastoral into a secularized city-dweller and later an unsuccessful journalist becomes a modern parody of the overlapping epic hero. Here, the definition of pastoral can exceed to any writing that involves elements of innocence and nature, or concerns about landscapes and countryside. Just as paul Alpers claims, "there are as many versions of pastoral as there are critics who write about it"(Alpers, 1982: 437). Biswas recounts of his own epic as a witness to the pastoral version of Trinidad. Unlike traditional forms of pastoral by Virgil and Theocritus, this epic carries no witness of Mr Biswas's birth and early years, not to mention his father's and grandparents' trajectory of social life, because the home of his childhood has been pulled down and replaced with oil field. Biswas can not look back to his nostalgia of childhood which is devoid of its historicity as an anti-pastoral of spatio-temporal location in Trinidad. Like Krishna's village lover Radha, Biswas's wife Shama is also a symbol of pastoral life, of whom Biswas waits "not only for love, but for the world to yield its sweetness and romance. He deferred all his pleasure in life until that day [...] he went to Hanuman House at Arwacas, and saw Shama"(HB, 2011: 80). The modern Radha expects to share various emotions of life stage, because, according to Hindu belief, life is a cycle that includes "joy at a birth or a marriage, distress during illness and hardship, grief at a death. Life, to be full, had to be this established pattern of sensation"(HB, 2011: 165). In his eyes, Shama stands for the idealistic reincarnation of pastoral life within which exists the constant fixity, that is, people have a tradition to follow, a religion to appease themselves and even a way of life to undertake, so that Biswas can triumph over and reap the fruit of serenity and acceptance. Yet, there is a process of comedown since their encounter.

Whereas Shama can not underpin the romantic ideal of pastoral heroine, Biswas performs far less from being a courageous and amorous hero. Consequently, his marriage life turns out to be a replication of childhood, like a returning to the village life such as stomach upsets, arguments, sulking, unappetizing food and illogical behaviors, that is, filled with boredom and futility. Besides, the hero is trapped in the atmosphere of villagers' hostility, to keep away from the fears, "Every night he bolted himself in his room. As soon as he was still he felt the stillness around him and he had to make movements to destroy the stillness, to challenge the alertness of the room and the objects in it"(HB, 2011: 238-239). His anxiety and weariness in the vacant field of Green Vale, together with the painstaking he has undertaken at Hanuman House, precipitates his descent into the void. The sense of nothingness convinces him of the necessity of building his own house, an adventure of transforming his life as a diasporic colonial. Biswas's first attempt of building a house turns out to be a depleted structure, which gradually encroaches his resources as well as his emotional attachment until it ultimately collapses during a storm night. However, his subsequent behavior of buying a house in Port of Spain, owing to its mortgage and big loans, heralds the predicament of his individual pursuit as opposed to the Trinidadian realities. No matter how austere the house feels like, the Biswas's lives "would be ordered, their memories coherent. The mind, while it is sound, is merciful [...] when the memories had lost the power to hurt, with pain or joy, they would fall into place and give back the past"(HB, 2011: 614-615). His yearning for a domestic space reflects not only his personal pursuit of coherent and meaningful identity, but also "the traumatic ambivalences of a personal, psychic history to the wider disjunctions of political existence"(Bhabha, 1994: 11). At the end of his adventurous journey, Biswas begins to accept his wife's judgement and to respect her optimism and sees her as his soul company and a symbolic incarnation of conventional pastoral, which possesses a reborn loyalty within family members. The virtues of epic heroes, such as loyalty and courage and love, are ultimately possessed by both the husband and wife to struggle against the outside enemy which exists, in the disguise of neighbors of childhood, the Tulsis House and even the Trinidad Sentinel, to stand for the reality of anti-pastoral society.

There is another enemy he intends to rebel against, that is, the preordained life by birth or fate, of which he can only become a peasant, just as his two brothers Pratap and Prasad do, to rent or buy a few acres where he can plant his own canes. However, the trajectory of his life is disrupted by the portent of his possessing "six-fingered, and born in the wrong way"(HB, 2011: 11), for which an evil spirit is supposed to come and bring misfortunes for the family. It is due to the curse of Oedipal fate leading to the drowning of his father that pushes him into the predicament of being a stranger in his own family and eventually encourages his choosing a different life, "I am going to get a job on my own. And I am going to get my own house too. I am finished with this"(HB, 2011: 66). After receiving some knowledge of primary schooling and a training of pundit, the young hero begins his picaresque journey, that is, of a sign-painting career. But this little education has already excited his curiosity to explore the unknown and new world opened up by knowledge of books, that is, his heroic journey is not only to recognize the value of a house, but also enjoy the process of struggling to offer meaning and dignity to human life. In his search for freedom and fulfillment, the inspiration Biswas draws from British literature ater offers an order and certainty to supersede the chaotic existence.

Here, two aspects of the pastoral fiction needs attention, that is, the thematic content and its conventional pattern. In a strict sense, the pattern of pastoral involves the shepherd, the young Mohun who tends carelessly a calf, and the landscapes of Arwacas countryside where the adults labour in sugar estates named "Felicity". Naipaul admits that this novel has borrowed much from his father's pastorals of Indian village in which he has examined "every new bit, every little variation"(Naipaul, 1984: 30) of the leftover drafts and stories, and later transformed them into the epic of his father. Like Krishna, Mohun Biswas also brings misfortunes to his family, and even causes his father Raghu's death. But unlike the pastoral spirit that foregrounds the value of not wealth but bravery, his family neighbors like Dhari and Lakhan carry out the action of "forking, rocking the implement in the earth, tearing the roots that kept the earth firm"(HB, 2011: 34), only to search for the money Raghu has supposedly hidden. The conventional pastoral upholds communal conceptions of property and strongly forbids its members to pursue wealth and power. Thus what connects the relationships of Indian community is not the positive values but material interests and blood ties that conceal the crimes and dilemmas of the anti-pastoral scenery. Besides, it also relates to a thematic pattern of escape or retreat from the forces of modernity.

Whereas the retreat from the city life of the Tulsis into the illusion of pastoral symbolizes its last attempted resistance against the social modernity, Mr. Biswas obviously belongs to the former, that is, an escape of an innocent, which is in parallel with Rasselas, the narrator of Samuel Johnson's novel *Rasselas, Prince of Abyssinia* (1759). The bringing in of the promised sheep without shepherds to tend and other various communal schemes all presage the Tulsis's performance of an "idyllic project", which arouses the contempt of both Biswas and Anand. As for the Tulsi children, they can be fed and punished commonly by mothers and widows for their misdemeanors, but receive their identical gifts for Christmas in case they should possess the sense of jealousy and superiority to suppress such thing as individual personality. Paul Bové regards individuation as a process of forming the whole psychological self, in which "we are most regulated by the ruling disciplines of language, sexuality, economics, culture, and psychology"(Bové, 1995: 58). But the regulated personality, according to Foucault's ideas, is not just subjugated to the dominant ideology, but also offers the possibility of resisting its power.

Biswas sees Hanuman House as a refuge of traditionalism and pastoral life which arouses not only a sense of cohesion and solidarity but also a feeling of anonymity and indignity as a social individual of human beings. The roles assigned are fixed on either the age-category or job-division. Whereas Seth and Padma are respected for their age, the brothers-in-law such as Hari are highly placated for his identity of family priest. Generally speaking, the Tulsi husbands can only undertake the roles of marrying the daughters and serve the commercial interests of family. Married into the monolith of conventional pastoral, Biswas disapproves of its religious belief and practices, and refuses the jobs assigned to him except those that value his human worth and dignity. To rebel against the boredom of pastoral life, Biswas applies the method of contempt and even invective to ridicule the life in Hanuman House, "one concrete monkey-god outside the house and two living ones inside. They could just call this place the monkey house"(HB, 2011: 123). But his rebellion and even himself are simply considered by the Tulsis as a licensed buffoon and comic clown and gradually tolerate his witty jokes. Furthermore, he speaks creole English while others speak Hindi, ridicules Hari of his religious faith, and disregards the family arrangements that attempt to suppress his thoughts of individualism. The behaviours that oppose the Tulsis' expectations offer him satisfaction of resisting his state of anonymity and of asserting his human dignity. Despite all his unheroic qualities, our modern hero's achievement, as Kenneth Ramchand argues, "lies in the attempt made with faith and ever-returning courage to interpose a human institution (the family) and a humanized object (the house) between himself and a universe threatening annihilation on every side"(Ramchand, 1976: 79). The individualism he upholds offends and even undermines the conformity that conceals the hypocrisy and contradiction of Hanuman House.

In the chaos and desolation of pastoral life, Anand inherits his father's satiric attitude, "a pose, and imitation of his father. But satire led to contempt, and at Shorthills contempt, quick, deep, inclusive, became part of his nature. It led to inadequacies, to self-awareness and a lasting loneliness"(HB, 2011: 436). Anand, the portrait of Naipaul himself, recasts the memories of his childhood and family in the pastoral tradition, so that he can reverse or disown the model or forebears to create his own version, "I don't see myself fitting into the Trinidad way of life. I think I shall die if I had to spend the rest of my life in Trinidad" (Naipaul, 2007: 277). The community of Trinidad is surrounded with dull green land which the sun scorched every day, which is the opposite of the traditional pastoral pervaded with the tranquility of shepherds and shepherdesses and cooling wind. The plantation society, which views negro-slaves and indentured laborers as animals and emphasizes only their docility, turns out to be an anti-pastoral full of various oppressions and crimes resulting from their pursuing of wealth and power.

In Naipaul's world, what alienates the residents from the surroundings is not just the man-made buildings, such as the Scottish baronial castle and Whitehall hung with tapestries depicting shepherds and dummy fireplaces, but also the system of schooling that never talks of his homeland. As Naipaul notes in his essay *Words on their Own*, "all literatures are foreign. Trinidad was small, remote and unimportant, and we knew we could not hope to read in books of the life we saw about us"(Naipaul,1964:472). The rupture between the education and social realities pushes Mr. Biswas, and even the author himself into a disappointment. However, education is still an important process for one's growth and maturity. Born as a brahmin, Mr. Biswas is expected to take on a profession of a priest. He is firstly sent to study regular knowledge of British education system, and then forced to receive traditional Brahminical training. However, neither of these episodes can satisfy him, because the estrangement of education from Trinidadian society determines his rupture of knowledge, in particular, his understanding of literature.

Different from his parents, Biswas becomes neither superstitious of Indian religion nor truly accepts the lessons he should accept at school. The knowledge of schooling makes him doubtful about certain rules and traditions of his Indian clan, and also arouses his alienation despite his attempts of evoking the images behind the words of school books. The reading of English novels alienates Biswas more from his living realities, of which Trinidad is only a tentative place, a dream to escape from. Mr. Biswas would rather see "himself in many Samuel Smiles heroes [...] and he contented himself with reading about the Samuel Smiles heroes in their magic land [...] in a land where romance was possible"(HB, 2011: 78). Biswas indulges himself in the fantasies of escaping from the reality of living conditions into the intoxicating and romantic worlds he can dream of, that is, the fantasies of Samuel Smiles heroes, along with Bell's *Standard Elocutionist* and Marcus Aurelius, have transported him to another world of "magic land". He manages to make sense of foreign novels so that "he discovered the solace of Dickens. Without difficulty he transferred characters and settings to people and places that he knew [...] he was given strength to bear"(HB, 2011: 394), at least to escape from the reality of his native island. However, the material of books prompts him to be a signwriter and later a journalist who would rather imaginatively create stories than report them accurately.

His first real job, as a sign painter, is the reincarnation of his literary instincts by the knowledge of his schooling and novels he reads. Devoid of its cultural realities, the decorations he has created of the shop at The Chase, of which he has "painted cool, ordered forest scenes, with gracefully curving grass, cultivated trees ringed with friendly serpents, the flowers bright with perfect flowers"(HB, 2011: 189-190), reflects his inability of accounting for the living conditions of Trinidad, as a result of his alienation from the empirical culture he is taught to admire. The job he undertakes is to work as a freelance journalist of the Trinidad Sentinel. It is right because of this paper that offers him a chance of possessing his own house and endows him with a sense of dignity and individuality. The paper is revealed not just as a means of transmitting the news, but also as an agency to create its own national image within Trinidadian society. For Biswas, the qualities of being a mimic colonial reflect the aims of this paper that "he could turn out presentable imitation [...] he added something of his own [...] the facetiousness that came to him as soon as he put pen to paper, and the fantasy he had hitherto dissipated in quarrels with Shama and in invective against the Tulsis"(HB, 2011: 340). In a sense, Biswas's adventurous epic to conquer the fortification of imperial language is similar to his ancestors, who immigrated as indentured labors into a land of fantasies. The fantasy, according to Arjun

Appadurai, "allows people to consider migration, resist state violence, seek social redress and design new forms of civic association and collaboration, often across boundaries"(Appadurai, 2000: 6). While incorporating the oriental values of individuality, Biswas begins a process of rejecting his roots, represented by the metaphor of Hanuman House from which he can drift away and imagine other worlds and a different life. In order to create his own romances of pastoral, Biswas has taken a course of story writing from the Ideal School of Journalism, and begun his exercise writing of articles on the four seasons, only to finish these articles with the help of the brochure.

But why does he fail to finish the assignments of creating an article? The realities of Trinidad forbid his imagination of another place of pastoral to placate his romance of "escape", to say exactly, no place to retreat as his refuge. That is, neither India nor Britain can provide for him the vision of pastoral to ask for help, just like other residents who "continually talked of going back to India [...] afraid of the unknown, afraid to leave the familiar temporariness"(HB, 2011: 201), stranded between the reality of creole society and their nostalgia of homelands. Therefore, the stories have never been finished, and the hero, a self-portrait of himself, was still "trapped into marriage, burdened with a family, his youth gone, meets a young girl [...] Beyond the meeting the stories never went"(HB, 2011: 363). The desire of colonized subjects to conquer English language and equally resist its dominant presence makes Biswas keep up his sanity against racial oppression. Mr. Biswas has always suffered the anxieties of uprootedness, and stranded between the uncertainties of either cultural creolization or retaining the traditional faiths. His lack of cultural identification ultimately deprives his Brahminic training at Pundit Jairam's house of any sanctuary and reduces it to an empty ritual without religious faith. As for the process of creolisation, the three generations of Mr. Biswas's family, together with the whole Indian community, have undergone psychological, religious and cultural changes so as to adapt themselves to the norms and values assigned by the imperial power of Britain.

As time goes on, the dominant culture has affected and changed the identity of residents living in this creole society. It is not until the third generation represented by Anand and Savi that begins to assemble into the dominant ideology of British empire, and even forget how to speak the native language of Hindi. Whereas the first generation of Indian migrants, such as Mrs. Tulsi, Seth, Tara and Ajodha, etc. follows voluntarily the traditional rules and customs, the second and third generation represented by Biswas and Shekhar begin to show indifference to and even rebellion against such traditions. While Dehuti, Biswas's sister, eloped with her aunt Tara's yard boy who belongs to the low caste, her mother Bipti feels reproached for its "not only showing ingratitude to Tara and bringing disgrace to her"(HB, 2011: 56). Another example is the rebellion of Shekhar, Mrs. Tulsi's eldest son, who expresses his disapproval about the traditional customs of marriage, and after marriage leaves home for good and uses Western names of Mira, Leela and Lena for his three daughters as an act of restructuring his cultural identification. The mode of thought has begun to diverge since the Indians' migration, and ultimately transformed into the different divisions between the traditionalists and the reformists of Hinduism. Although Biswas is a Brahmin supposed to be a pundit, he shows no passions for the religion and even resentment for the rituals and holly trees.

After his marriage into the Tulsi family, he even mocks and teases their worship rituals and becomes an Aryanist who claims that "caste was unimportant, that Hinduism should accept converts, that idols should be abolished, that women should be educated, preaching against all the doctrines the orthodox Tulsis held dear"(HB, 2011: 117). It can be see that the influence of religion and caste has always been diminishing as the Western thought encroaches the soils of Indian traditions represented by Hanuman House. Compared with their father, Anand and Savi already feel no sense of doubt and alienation between the knowledge of schooling and the realities of Trinidad, that is, they can not take their traditions and religion seriously and begin to identify with the dominant culture of Western ideology. But the Western culture that elevates Biswas as a civilized man also prompts him into a void that is surrounded by "grief for a happy life never enjoyed and now lost [...] and forced himself to cry for all his lost happiness"(HB, 2011: 279-280). In addition to his rebellion and escape, the constant anxiety Biswas has undergone is to search for a house of his own he has spent his whole life pursuing, which is not the predicament of his own situation but that of the whole West Indian society wandering to find their anchorage. Looking backward, he feels that "he had lived nowhere but in the houses of the Tulsis, at Hanuman House in Arwaças, in the decaying wooden house at Shorthills, in the clumsy concrete house in Port of Spain. And now at the end he found himself in his own house"(HB, 2011: 2). Suffering from the destruction of *The Chase*, and *Green Vale*, Biswas retreats and surrenders into the traditionalism of Hanuman House. Generally speaking, this house is often symbolized as the power of hindering his individual ambitions and achievements. Stranded in a void, his feeling of nothingness awaits its new transformation, from its countryside and communalism of the Tulsis to the city of Port of Spain and its environment of individualism.

The pastoral life Biswas leaves behind is far from the elegance of Arcadia, but some sort of "counterfeit, a series of cheating accidents. Real life, and its especial sweetness, awaits; he was still beginning"(HB, 2011: 318). His great anguish at Green Vale has eventually reaped its rewards. The house he has bought and rebuilt on Sikkim Street exceeds its superficial value, that is, a real reward for his insights of being true of himself as a frustrated sign-painter, journalist and writer. In other words, the vision of his house is paralleled with his ambition of creating a world of art and romance. During his house-building at Green Vale, his tension of relationship with his mother has been alleviated, and ultimately revolved until his obtaining the new house. When seeing his mother cultivate near his house at Shorthills, "seeing the black, forked earth, the marks of the spade, the indentations of the fork prongs"(HB, 2011: 511), Biswas feels a grief for lost love, with which he can see how absurd and unforgivable his attitude to his mother turns out to be. The anxiety within the mother-and-son relationship evolves into a literary experience, and allegory of heroic "journey he had made a long time before. He was tired; she made him rest. He was hungry; she gave him food. He had nowhere to go; she welcomed him"(HB, 2011: 511). The scenes of mother-son relationship has excited and relieved himself, and thus prompted him to share his literary instincts of creating a poem of his mother's love. The vision of house symbolizes a beacon of freedom and also a place to set down his foot, so that he can search for his own position in the flux of history and his uniqueness of social identity to keep away from the state of rootlessness and alienation. In a sense, Biswas can be called a failure, that is, he has neither completely paid off the house he pursued, not fulfilled his ambition of romance. But he has ultimately secured his human dignity as an epic hero trapped in the modern reality of boredom.

The uncertainties Biswas suffers from his confusion of cultural identities, according to Madhu Benoit, transform himself into another man "caught up in three cultures, and in the process, dispossessed of all three. Unable to integrate culturally in Trinidad where he lives, rejecting Hindu culture which he dislikes [...] equally unable to identify with British culture"(Benoit, 2007: 41)[11]. The creolization of Trinidadian cultures has not only affected Biswas himself, but the whole family of Hanuman House. The force of Westernization and urbanization causes the religious ambiguity and even combination with other religions, eventually undermines the solidarity and prosperity of the Tulsis. The thought of individualism has long been existing in the Tulsi pastoral, only to be suppressed by the dominant traditional values. Resulting from Mrs. Tulsi's long absence, the struggle of power between Seth and other brothers-in-law further disintegrate the cohesion. In fact, Mrs. Tulsi ultimately abandons the headquarter of Hanuman House and moves the Tulsi clan to Port of Spain, which symbolizes the beginning of its collapse of the Tulsidom. What's more, Hari's death leads to the eventual collapse of Hanuman House, because his presence has always symbolized the religion and tradition of Indian community, and also Biswas's suppression of individual personality.

Though the values of pastoral begin to die away, the residents like Biswas's sister Dehuti can still look to the Tulsis for cultural stability and familiar life-patterns. Besides, some older Indians still meet in the evenings and talk idly of returning to their mother land. In a rootless society like Trinidad, what has left for them to do is nothing more than an imitation of the colonial master culture, that is, either Indian or English culture, because they have no other alternative choices. Despite their long time of living away from India, many indentured immigrants and their heirs have not completely erased their cultural Indianness and sense of identification. That is, many people still uphold the emotional linage with India and regard themselves as the involuntary exiles. The Dickensian sketches of the Caribbean society have exposed the bitter self-denial of its inhabitants. The nightmarish vision of Indian community, according to Baidik Bhattacharya, becomes "intimately connected with the belatedness [...] this delay in history is not simply the land disallowed within the larger theater of cultural modernity, but a land whose late arrival is painstakingly dramatized as a caricature of a model"(Bhattacharya, 2011: 36). The chaos of cultural heritages can inevitably lead to the mimic behaviors of the colonials and their subsequent self-denial the latecomers of European modernity have suffered. The mechanism of repression inevitably leads to personal dilemma that is immanent in the unhomely space of the postcolonial diaspora.

3.2 An Enigma of Migration Experience

In his novel *The Enigma of Arrival* (1987), Naipaul reflects on of his life in an England village in the 1970s. The middle-life narrator, who is factually identical to Naipaul himself, presents the thoughts and experiences of the younger self when he first moved into his Wiltshire cottage, whereas the present perception of the adult narrator interacts with and is also determined by recalling his colonial childhood he can never shed off. Naipaul inherits a sensibility from his experience of migration so dislocated and disjointed that even as a child he became so desperate to flee from the native homeland Trinidad and would never come back to live again. The supposed Eden he chooses is England, the imperial centre he has always imagined to function as his spiritual and cultural home.

This memoir does not mention his wife patricia or even his friends except for a few neighbors with whom he was hardly befriended. The only scene he mentions of his family the final section that recounts his return to Trinidad for the funeral of his sister Sati in 1984. In a strict sense, this book is not concerned about his personal life, or his contact with the world outside, but inwardness of a solitary immigrant who is ashamed of his cultural background and striving to embrace a "superior" culture. The narrator, like Naipaul, as a descendant of Indian immigrant to Trinidad, has established a career of writer after his graduation from Oxford. Now living in a valley of England, he frequently walks around and meditates on his own life story and the changes of his Wiltshire neighborhood. As Naipaul admits, the writer or narrator "is scrupulously myself [...] this book, I do it in my own person. It's closer to the truth, and I blend that in with my fiction"(Gussow, 1987: 16). The "truth" in his memoir can not be applied to the conventional frames as a result of either his literary delicacy or avoiding personal embarrassments. That is, his marriage with Patricia Hale is not satisfactory, largely resulting from the husband's burdensome neglect and, even worse, an infidel relationship with his lover Margaret reflected in his previous novel *A Bend in the River* (1979).

Furthermore, their original marriage also demonstrates Naipaul's reluctance, which is obvious in such behaviors as his refusal of notifying his family or buying a wedding ring. According to Patrick French, his biographer, Naipaul once wrote that "I shouldn't have married Pat [...] The relationship [...] was more than half a lie. Based really on need"(French, 2008: 156). Another reason of prompting the author to exclude his wife or friends from outside the neighborhood is of the choice of literary form. As is know to all, no one still sees forms of autobiography as truth of the author's accounts of life stories, and critics can now also comprehend the delicacy of literary form the writer applies to avoid the substantial obstacles that stand between the subjective 'I' and self-understanding. It can be see that at least what Naipaul recounts of his Wiltshire life is partially true, although its transparency of autobiographical truthfulness can not be innocently taken for granted. Due to its hybrid qualities of fiction and autobiography, this novel can be taken as auto-fiction or autography. As for the notion of "autography", H. Porter Abbot suggests that "Historical truth or falsity are important only insofar as they express the identity of the author. As it is always symptomatic, autography, unlike factual writing, is in this regard always true. And unlike fiction, which may or may not achieve an organic integrity of design, autography cannot fail to be organic and integrated"(Abbot, 1988: 613). According to French's biography, many of the characters in this novel can be traced to the portraits of the real people or historical events. But what concerns Naipaul more is to address his subjective consciousness or identity, "I should make the writer be myself - let that be true and within that set the fictional composite picture because you can't use real people to hang philosophical ideas about flux and change"(Niven, 1997: 163). Naipaul is still awkward or unwilling to write introspectively in his autobiography about his past except the memory of its link with his father or India. From what he says, it can be supposed that if the author has written honestly from his own perspective, then the issue of truth-telling and self-recognization should be resolved, that is, the confidential first-person discourse is qualified to disclose his emotional life and inner feelings.

Despite the suppression and concealment of some aspects of his personality, Naipaul still presents readers an immigrant colonial of Trinidad, "all my time in England I still had that nervousness in a new place, that rawness of response, still felt myself to be in other man's country, felt my strangeness, my solitude"(EA, 1988: 8). Naipaul manages to reaffirm his roots of identity, but reveals the predicament of his displacement resulting from his being stranded between Indian traditions and the culture of mother country. This is why countless immigrants possess the desire of migration from the margins to the centre. The symbolic appropriation of British culture in mimicry represents their desire for self-approval. As for the colonized people, according to Frantz Fanon, "The more the colonized has assimilated the cultural values of the metropolis, the more he will have escaped the bush. The more he rejects his blackness and the bush, the whiter he will become"(Fanon, 2008: 3). The internalized values he upholds prompts him to repossess the meaning of cultural identity through breaking away from "the bush" of Trinidad and also enjoy the power and social status of being a cosmopolitan elite.

After many years of life in England, Naipaul confesses that "in that far-off island whose human history I had been discovering and writing about, I had dreamed of coming to England [...] I had taken to England all the rawness of my colonial's nerves, and those nerves had more or less remained"(EA, 1988: 101). In England, his "nerves" of adjusting to the living settings manifest themselves as an acute paranoid of traumatic psyche whose only outlet is to stay hidden in the camouflage of mimicry. Although the behaviour of self-interrogation somehow deconstructs the structural hegemony of colonial identity, but also represents a symbol of subjective disavowal against the meaning and belonging of the colonials. Frantz Fanon further points out that the anxiety of cultural mimicry pinpoints the systemic structure of Oriental hierarchy, "From the moment the black man accepts the split imposed by the Europeans, there is no longer any respite; and from that moment on isn't it understandable that he will try to elevate himself to the white man's level"(Fanon, 2008: 63). Here mimicry can only be seen as complicit to perpetuate the racial myth that endorses the colonial social system. Naipaul undertakes the life of mimic man, "in the ancient heart of England, a place where I was truly an alien, I found I was given a second chance, a new life, richer and fuller than any I had had anywhere else. And in that place, where at the beginning I had looked only for remoteness and a place to hide [...] I healed. The life around me changed. I changed"(EA, 1988: 103). The disorder of Trinidad Naipaul once escaped from has been internalized into his identificatory disavowal of colonial historicity. But his life in England turns out to be a paradox of exile, because he lacks the identification of specific community. According to Raymond Williams, the cosmopolitan vagrant or exile like Naipaul are those people "who, deprived of a settled way of living or of a faith, or having rejected those which were inherited, find virtue in a kind of improvised living, and in an assertion of independence"(Williams, 1975: 289). Wandering in a village of England, Naipaul feels himself an oddity, something like an upheaval in the course of English history, that is, the fact of being an immigrant from the former colony of another hemisphere prevents him from seeing the historical fragmentation of the central imperial civilization.

Though living among ruins and dereliction, the narrator creates a postcolonial link with the Edwardian past, a reminder of its once imperial culture and power. Like the poems of wanderings by William Wordsworth, Naipaul's portraits of his neighbors such as his landlord Jack and his father-in-law seem more like Wordsworthian figures, "bent, exaggeratedly bent, going gravely about Lake District solitude"(EA, 1988: 16). The scene of surrounding historical remnants and ruins, together with the relics of other human efforts and lives, reminds readers of the decay of Margaret's cottage portrayed in the poem *The Ruined Cottage* (1797). The village, surrounded by the remnant of an old peasantry, survives the industrial revolution and modernization, now becomes an antiquity, a kind of historical life, associated to the old English country customs in King Lear, and helps the narrator to establish his new identification, "with the literary eye, or with the aid of literature [...] to indulge my linguistic or historical fantasies; and enabled me, at the same time, to shed the nerves of being a stranger in England"(EA, 1988: 18-19). His identity as an immigrant causes much tension with his sense of being a writer, whose emptiness can only be compensated with the idea of literature. Through observing the gradual decay of Jack's garden, Naipaul deconstructs the idealized notion of England which is the fictional dreamland he had once believed in Trinidad, but becomes the anti-pastoral England Wordsworth explored as that of homelessness, exile and loss.

More importantly, his practice of wanderings can be traced to the melancholic meditations of the romantics, which emerged both as a mode of pastime and literary expressions of rebellions against industrial modernization. Anna Jorngarden points out that romanticism's solitary wanderings and emotions "would be critiqued by subsequent generations as nothing more than self-absorbed emotional masturbation [...] an attempt to liberate the subject from a society seen as increasingly constrictive and stifling"(Jorngarden, 2018: 212). Naipaul's literary mind enables him to perceive the colonial insecurities, because he possesses no traces of history and thus can not attach historicity to Trinidad as he does to Jack or his landlord. He sees Jack as as man who is genuine and rooted, and even a remnant of the past, but the truth is that his connection to the village is no more secure and authentic than the narrator. Jack is also a newcomer and has "created his own life, his own world, almost his own continent [...] a reminder of the brevity of the cycles of growth and creation"(EA, 1988: 93), but his sickness and death, together with its subsequent influence upon his garden, gradually subverts the narrator's fantasy of perfection, which reminds him of the constancy of change. The image of his garden is not a continuation of British tradition but an artistic product designed by the landlord. The similar background of newly-migrated identity between Jack and Naipaul brings his involuntary memories back to Trinidad where Mr. Biswas, who is the reincarnation of his father, has also built a house and garden for his assertion of individual autonomy.

Jack's garden manifests itself not just as a reminder of imperial wealth and power that is obtained with the spread of the empire in the nineteenth century, but also an image of England Jack has imagined from his readings of English literature. The garden, together with the landlord's life trajectory, also echoes the imperial decay embodied by his untended mansion. After the champagne-fueled life of the 1920s and the 1930s, the still young socialite began to suffer from malaise and retreated into the solitude of his Wiltshire village. Jack's garden in this village has been located on the spot of many vanished hamlets, and this transformation can be either the beginning or the ending of the historical process. The cottage where Naipaul now lives represents a historical line of imperial colonization, along which the migration "within the British Empire, from India to Trinidad had given me the English language as my own, and a particular kind of education. This had partly seeded my wish to be a writer in a particular mode, and had committed me the literary career I had been following"(EA, 1988: 52). As a symbol of imperial confidence and power, the manor has been threatened by the arrival of former colonial and its subsequent damage of dominant social hierarchy. Naipaul juxtaposes his migrant experience with his solitude of dwelling in England to raise a critical assessment of Thatcherite version of post-imperial culture and society. In fact, just before his moving into the Wiltshire village, Naipaul has just finished his work *The loss of El Dorado* (1969), written about a Trinidadian city Port of Spain. During the two years of searching for traces of a history about the eradication of the natives and consequent cruelty of slavery, he develops a new feeling that "reading the documents of my island in London, by the antiquity of the place to which I belonged [...] as part of the globe, seeing it sharing in the antiquity of the earth"(EA, 1988: 157). Through his literary perspective, Naipaul endows Trinidad with a sense of historicity that he originally sees as the uniqueness of England.

Faced with the temporariness of history, no one can still possess the idea of being successors and inheritors, so that Naipaul can be elevated from the melancholy of homelessness and outsider living in the village. The truth that all his neighbors of the village are newcomers like himself who don't belong here provides him the chance of "a second life [...] like a rebirth to me"(EA, 1988: 172) to make a home as many new people of this village do. Resulting from the rise and fall of the imperial history, the binary of colonizers and colonials begins to fuse together, acting as a relationship of economic interdependence between the periphery and the centre. He feels no longer the victim of imperial history, but the inheritor of cosmopolitan civilization, whose meditation is "not of imperial decline. Rather, I wondered at the historical chain that had brought us together — he in his house, I in his cottage, the wild garden his taste (as I was told) and also mine"(EA, 1988: 53). The symbolic space they share at the heart of empire suggests the empowerment of the former colonized who shares empathy and taste with the colonizers. As a middle-life cosmopolitan writer, Naipaul begins to celebrate his rooting of bicultural heritages, that is, his native Trinidad and adopted Britain.

But the different heritages Naipaul juxtaposes form a cycle of historical life, in which the collapse of imperialism heralds the birth of postcolonialism. The coincidence of the narrator's journey to England and the landlord's beginning of a recluse life, according to Fawzia Mustafa, can be seen as a historical irony the narrator "reads into his entry, as a former colonial, into his landlord's domain, empire's very heart [...] a rewriting of the imperial configuration"(Mustafa, 1995: 172-173). For the whole decade of the 1970s, Naipaul has been writing his novel *A Bend in the River* (1979), which focuses on his expatriate anxiety of the political chaos after the independence of a former colony in Central Africa. Naipaul admits that this novel is largely based upon his own relationship with long-time lover Margaret, and thus "projected the solitude and emptiness and menace of my Africa onto the land around me [...] something of the Africa of my story adhered to the land I saw"(EA, 1988: 170). As a colonial, the narrator is a man-made product of colonial background, resulting from the age of decolonization taking place in the second half of the twentieth century. But the reflection of historical decolonization not only changes the oriental elites who perform as the descendant of the colonial power, but also reveal the narrator's controversial attitude of postcolonial identification and orientalist rejection, that is, the sketch of civilized Western shopkeeper is staged as the opposition of dirty Indians, wizened Chinese and shameless black concubines. Naipaul stages the connection between an artist's formation of identity and the historical predicament of the periphery, which is regarded as "a great shaking up of old cultures and old ideas. And just as my own journey had brought about a change in me [...] so restlessness and the need for a new idea of the self had driven many other people"(EA, 1988: 159). Here Naipaul narrates his first journey from Trinidad to England in the 1950s, especially his intellectual struggle to become a metropolitan writer. In the section of "Journey", the narrator sets himself into two parts: the adult author and the adolescent self. While the latter attempts to conceal his feeling of alienation on arriving in London and also that of inferiority resulting from his Trinidadian heritage, the former always stands out to commend that the younger self fails to recognize many things worthy of noting down as the stuff of his writings. The narrator believes that if hc can retell the traumatic experience of migration, he can reintegrate the split selfhood and thus begin to regard the change of his personality as the motif of his writings. According to Simon Beecroft, "the writer is 'made' by his experiences of 'world and cultures' but he is also 'made' in books and out of texts", and thus transforms into the status of both "producer and product"(Beecroft, 2000: 84). To obtain the synthesis of writer and man, the younger narratee deliberately avoids the experiences of his Indian inferiority and thus produces what he witnesses as metropolitan style of writings. The narrator points out the fault his younger self had made, that the topic of race is then "too close to my disturbance, my vulnerability, the separation of my two selves. That was not the kind of personality the writer wished to assume; that was not the material he dealt in"(EA, 1988: 124). To become a successful writer, the younger narratee should, first of all, overcome his sense of colonial-Hindu self and recognizes the fact that he is not just an artist to reflect on the world but also a cultural product.

The surging of decolonization begins to reshape the habits of Anglophone readers and even elevates the motif of racial identity as an exotic product for metropolitan readers. The retelling of his traumatic migration marks not only the struggle of repairing his split personality, but also his psychological maturation through fitting the proper experiences into proper literary forms. Naipaul presents his own influence from modernist ideas about art and the artist, such as *South*

Wind (1917) by Norman Douglas, which nevertheless contributes the strategic exoticism to fulfill his cultural or political purpose. The approach of narrating how to write a novel is no doubt a form of metafiction. According to Patricia Waugh, it is "fictional writing which self-consciously and systematically draws attention to its status as artifact in order to pose questions about the relationship between fiction and reality"(Waugh, 1984: 2). Its feature of self-reference can not only explain the structure of the narrative, but also reveal how the textual material interacts with the realistic world. The narrator explains the inspiration of writing this novel when living in Wiltshire village in 1969. Shortly after being rejected of his would-be Booker-winning novel *In a Free State* (1971), Naipaul came across a painting by Giorgio de Chirico, which is entitled as *The Enigma of Arrival*. This incident prompts the narrator to account for a story that concerns not only the meta-fictional imagination, but also his own aspects of life. Later the story of the traveler has "become more personal: my journey, the writer's journey, the writer defined by his writing discoveries, his way of seeing, rather than by his personal adventures, writer and man separating at the beginning of the journey and then coming together again"(EA, 1988: 343-344). Through the process of metafictional writing, the narrator has ultimately obtained the effects of classical Bildungsroman, that is, a transformation of identity from an Indian immigrant suffering from Indian inferiority into a cosmopolitan traveler and writer.

The bicultural heritage prompts him to return over and again to the memories of childhood, that is, Naipaul explores his motif of contemporary Indians, Islams and Caribbeans, from the oriental perspective he adopts from his adopted homeland to reflect the predicament of homelessness and loneliness. In his Nobel Lecture, Naipaul unfolds his motivation of traveling as a writer that "I had to clear up my world, elucidate it, for myself [...] get the true feel of the history of the colony [...] I had to travel to India [...] Africa, South America, the Muslim World [...] and the purpose comes from my childhood: to make me more at ease with myself"(Naipaul, 2003: 191). The fact is that his long journey of life does not provide anything like home, except the struggling way of recognizing how to be a traveling exile. He moves frequently and often sojourns comfortably among unfamiliar books and surroundings, where he has traveled across the interiors of India, Africa, South America and also crossed North America. As a literary traveler and writer, his journey is to pursue a balance of identity, which can only be reconciled between the margin and the centre. The centre, according to Bruce King, "is now the creation and discovery of the self than external in an ideal society"(King, 2003: 136)[26]. The behavior of looking-inwardness is seen by the narrator as a solution to problems of alienation and marginalization in the process of identity-formation. The narrator describes his process of inventing an authorial personae entailed by cosmopolitan literary markets while concealing his own ethics that is, his own colonial-Hindu self to adjust to the canon of literary traditions.Whereas the Indian community of Trinidad offers no sense of a continuous historicity and national pride, his rural life in Wilsford Manor also provides no cohesive connection to project an identity and a future upon himself. While locating his childhood of Trinidad as the measurement for his later migration experiences, Naipaul realizes that his sojourn in England has not satisfied his desire of feeling at home, only ends up to be a reincarnation of the continuity of his traumatic childhood.

The vision of an outsider has always been his concerns about how to attenuate the feelings of homelessness, and furthermore, to construct his cosmopolitan identity rooted in his relationship with the rural England channeling through rural India and Trinidad. The funeral of his sister Sati, along with its accompanying Hindu rituals, prompts Naipaul to rekindle his emotional linkage with his Trinidadian familial bond and society. Despite the fact that generations of imperial education have separated Trinidadians from the past and history, people like Naipaul still choose to live "according to rituals we didn't always understand and yet were unwilling to dishonor because that would cut us off from the past, the sacred earth, the gods"(EA, 1988: 351). Ultimately, Naipaul begins to recognize the value of relationship between his tranquil life in Wiltshire and his pastoral past of Trinidad, and to write his auto-fiction of migration experience as a way of walking out his trauma of childhood.

Chapter Four Strangers in Nocturne Dreams

This collection of short stories continues the similar thematization which has been recurring from Ishiguro's beginning of creations. In Nocturnes, Ishiguro has exhibited the images of his universal characters mainly from Britain or Middle Europe, and even America, through the treatment of their spiritual or psychological traumas. The bittersweet memories his characters represent are fraught with an air of stillness and regret that is tempered now and then by moments of farce or surrealism. Through reading *Nocturnes*, readers are reminded the similar familiarity of his first-person narrators or protagonists who ironically reveal but also purposely conceal the inconsistency of their nostalgia and the present realities, which becomes an allegory of the pursuing self-identities human beings intend to elude in the foregrounding predicament of human conditions.

Just like the artists of his novels who tend to reconstruct their subjective reality or recreate their nostalgia in order to recap the predicaments of their present, Ishiguro regards his choice of writing as "a kind of consolation or therapy [...] you can somehow recorder it or try and come to terms with it by [...] creating your own world and own version of it"(Vorda and Herzinger, 1991: 152), which can compensate for the misfortune of his first career choice to achieve his fame and fortune of being a singer and songwriter. Like *An Artist of the Floating World* (1986) and *The Unconsoled* (1995), this collection continues to focus on the enigmatic dilemmas of artists, which somehow echoes such protagonists as Ono and Ryder whose ambitions are to contribute to social justice or humanity. Similarly, the characters in Nocturnes inexpressively confess their ultimate fears and desires of life confronting the inconsolable realities, which betokens the repression of their past traumas and even future demands of the ideal professionalism.

4.1 An Allegory of Diasporic Existence

The everyday boredom of these protagonists' life has been unfolded through their reluctance to face the frustrated ideals or dreams of being talented musicians, which becomes some kind of allegory of the emotional experiences of human beings. All the stories of *Nocturnes* mainly focus on the theme of unrealized potential or talent, imbued with some elements of regret. For most of the main characters in *Nocturnes*, music has always been representing an ideal self that has little to do with reality. However what binds together these stories is the conflict between what music promises and what life delivers.

As the title *Nocturnes* indicates, each story of the collection has concentrated on its music and musicians, together with nightfall as its background, which nevertheless contributes to a heartbreaking "story circle" of similar manners and behaviors. Like his other novels, Ishiguro re-exhibits such a predicament these groaning protagonists really intend to forget, only to escape into such a kind of pathetic music which "has been refined and developed so that it provides an enhanced mode of communication beyond the petty power of words – spoken or written"(Gilroy, 1993: 76). As people have always expected, this book continues the narration of unreliable first-person viewpoint which is tensely controlled by the narrators' psychological reality, through which the similar tone or atmosphere of empathy has been created because of the recurring characters and unnamed circumstances. Besides the first-person narration, the narratee of these stories is assumed to have shared the similar identities with the implied author, which betokens the attributes of the allegory "about how to make a particular setting actually take off into the realm of metaphors so that people don't think it is just about Japan or Britain, but also give it that sort of ability to take off as metaphor and parable"(Shaffer and Wong, 2008: 75).

Through the continuity of his ever unreliable memories and first-person narration, this collection *Nocturnes* presents Ishiguro's thematic concerns about people's dignity, and becomes "a figurative narrative or description, conveying a veiled moral meaning"(Drabble, 2005: 18). Despite the bittersweet or comic undertones in *Come Rain or Come Shine* and *Nocturne*, the main fundamental emotion that it reveals betokens the author's basic concerns about common humanity, such as this virtuosic American woman Eloise McCormack in "Cellists", who has chosen never to realise her music potential, instead of tarnishing her talent with professional imperfection. Whether you agree or not, what is assured is that Ishiguro continues his similar exploration of universal theme, through which this allegory of human life has been foregrounded as such stories reveal his concerns about "some little pride or dignity [...] the human capacity to accept what must seem like a limited and cruel fate"(Moore, 2005: np).

What surprises readers is that such musicians like Tony Gardner, Tilo and

Sonja present their reluctance to accept their humble destinies which indicate the obvious difference between gifted "them" and mediocre "us". That is to say, such frustrated musicians in this book have always been expected to achieve their potential goals they have set up for themselves, which properly demonstrates what Paul de Man defines the performance of rhetoric that "radically suspends logic and opens up vertiginous possibilities of referential aberration"(De Man, 1979: 10). However, these stories have been developed through the first-person narrators conversing with the counterpart narratee who is also a fellow of talented musicians or one relying on music to escape. Despite some elements of absurdity or surrealism, the story "*Nocturne*" goes on with the sensitive and croony nostalgia music, in which the narrator Steve, a frustrated but gifted saxophonist, recounts his ludicrous experience with Lindy Gardner who has suffered three facial surgeries to become much more marketable. In fact, the anxiety they have both suffered exists in the human condition of missed opportunities, which turns out to be "an act of understanding, which is always accompanied by a state-of-mind, or, in other words, which has a mood"(Heidegger, 1996: 296).

Besides the sympathy this allegory has stirred, the similar plights these protagonists encounter precipitate readers to reflect on their own choices of life or careers. That is to say, they seem to passively accept their fates without any grumble, which foregrounds the stoicism when facing frustrations and regrets of life. In spite of her awareness of "stupidity of this position"(NOCT, 2009: 91), Sonja still claims that the young singer and songwriter in "Malvern Hills" seems "much more like Tilo. If disappointments do come, you will still carry on . You will say, just as he does, I am so lucky"(NOCT, 2009: 123). Therefore, the invitations of the narrators lead readers up into an insufficient comprehension of such stories, which somehow brings up some kind of "slow readers, caught between our anticipations and the consequences of the signifier"(Britzman, 2006: 307). And then these main protagonists, such as Steve and Lindy Gardner, both reveal some passive and reluctant acceptance of their ambiguous fates, which means they almost rest their fame and fortune on the would-be facial surgery for their popularity of entertainment market, echoing a reminder of some readers' similar situations of pursuing their respective successes. However, this kind of discrepancy between reality and ideal has contributed a lot to the basic structure of this allegoric metaphor which is "precisely the figure that depends on a certain degree of correspondence between 'inside' and 'outside' properties" (De Man, 1979: 150).

Furthermore, the psychological realism Ishiguro has illustrated in his novels has always been concerned about the "wound" of narrators, which becomes "useful to look at my work as more abstract, like the work of a Beckett or a Kafka […] I've struggled to encourage people to read my books on a more metaphorical level"(Moore, 2005: np). What moves readers to tears is that Ishiguro leaves more to the perception of readers, through which readers feel like holding more insights than these characters and glimpsing more patterns of their life or essence of life itself. More importantly, what represents Ishiguro's conception of who we are exists here in an "impersonal yet thoroughgoing alienation", which nevertheless formulates "a pervasive, indeterminate anxiety, a fundamental or founding mood that Heidegger at other times also read as joy, melancholy, and profound boredom"(Krell, 1992: 45).

In other words, this kind of epiphany about life reality exists in people's assumption of its necessity to avoid their other-than human identities, which becomes some kind forgetting of the plight they have encountered to "persuade people to make the effort to learn and actually face what is often a difficult and complicated procedure–how to conduct human relationships and not mind getting hurt and upset–we have to be tricked to think there is a payoff" (Shaffer and Wong, 2008: 219). For Lindy and Steve, their facial surgery can only be some way of escaping from the cruel society, in which life turns out to be "so much bigger than just loving someone [...] I'm going to go out there anyway and give it a go"(NOCT, 2009: 183). Similarly, Steve also shares the same illusion of her wife's "doing it all for me, to make it possible for me to get this surgery. And when the bandages came off, and I had a new face, she'd come back and it'd be all right"(NOCT, 2009: 183). What Ishiguro seems to demonstrate is how the illusion of fulfilling happiness has somehow turned into the only approach of deserving their human dignities, which represents that such musicians like Steve have to "sweat and heave and break my balls to come up with something worthwhile, something beautiful"(NOCT, 2009: 166). What unites these characters is that they have all been indulging in their own various fears and desires, which leads to their final resorting to some "class of the frightening which leads back to what is known of old and long familiar"(Freud, 1955: 220). That is, it is right the struggling of reluctantly accepting their own fates that leads these characters to forget the social reality and even makes human beings much more humanistic.

What's more, the awareness of social reality, according to Heidegger's conception, is one of human-only features which have been presented through the narration of such characters as Janeck and Steve. Just like the novel *Never Let Me go*, this circle of stories is also an elegiac meditation on mortality and lost innocence, that is, a portrait of adolescence can lead to disillusionment, rebellion, or acceptance of a preordained fate. As for Lindy Gardner who has big plans and dreams since her childhood, she chooses to find out and rely on some husbands who can bring her fame and wealth, which finally leads to two marriages and divorces, despite her romantic love relationship with Mr Gardner. To our surprise, Mr. and Mrs. Gardner both intend to sacrifice their love and matrimony in order to continue their own dreams of pursuing either musical fame or familial fortune. Through the marriage and divorce of Tony and Lindy, Ishiguro blends his musical and literary conceptions into the integration of idealism and reality, through which readers begin to wonder whether the stardom of "looking at magazines of movie stars instead of studying [...] Rich, beautiful, travelled all over the world"(NOCT, 2009: 19) represents the meaning and pursuit of human life. What's more, the secular success of social individuals has unconsciously influenced such people as Emily and Charlie so that the couple is "obviously going through some sort of crisis. She must be as upset as you are"(NOCT, 2009: 46), which somehow confirms further the tone and atmosphere of these nocturnes.

Therefore, the opening story "Crooner" presents some atmosphere of melancholy, in which Janeck begins to realize the predicament the ageing American husband and wife have been facing in their familial relationship. Instead of bringing happiness and matrimony back to Mrs. Gardner, Tony's serenade, which has once been the only comfort to Janeck's beleaguered single mother, now only leads to Lindy's "sobbing" inside her hotel room before her upcoming divorce, and touched her by the heart through his romantic serenade. Just as Heidegger comments, the threat of facticity does not possess "the character of a definite detrimentality which concerns what is threatened with a definite regard to a particular factical potentiality for being. What angst is about is completely indefinite"(Heidegger, 1996: 174). With the similar tone of other stories in *Nocturnes*, Janeck becomes some typical narrator of Ishiguro, recounting his autobiography and experience with the unreliable first-person narration which has let on more than his original intention. Through the foreignness and strangeness of human facticity, the ambitious and determined musicians of *Nocturnes* seem to formulate the question of human self-reflexivity, in which human existence has always been "primordially strange and foreign, we do not even know what 'man' is [...] and we remain strangers to ourselves" (Nelson, 2008: 137). In other words, a reading of such realistic boredom turns out to be the reevaluation of human temporality and philosophical poverty, which is to be considered essentially human through performing the autobiographical self-identification of the first-person narrators.

As an allegory of human condition, these stories of Nocturnes present us the essential figures that are "thus bound up with a crisis of perception and of phenomenality, but concomitantly with a mortal danger to the subject, to the 'integrity' of its body and thus to its very identity"(Weber, 2004: 233). As for Raymond in *Come Rain or Come Shine*, the narrator "I" reminisces about his hopeless career of being one itinerant teacher, which involves Emily's referring him as “Prince of Whiners”(NOCT, 2009: 56) and ripping out the offending page of her diary. What seems farcical and even tragic is that Raymond ridiculously impersonates a dog and concocts a properly doggy smell in order to smooth over the matrimony rift between his husband-and-wife friends. In other words, Raymond has been living a destroyed life concerning “going round in bloody circles trying to find a bloody roof to keep over your head”(NOCT, 2009: 49), and desperately attempting to establish some kind of “link, however tenuous, between their lives in England and mine out here”(NOCT, 2009: 41). Like Ishiguro’s fiction *The Remains of the Day*, the narrators of *Nocturnes* have always questioned the identity of themselves, which means their deceiving the self-value of their talented arts perception, and finally turn out to be some “initial alienating split between the human being and his function is ultimately followed by the liberating split in the narrator, who suddenly becomes aware that his life has been a failure”(Terestchenko, 2007: 78). Through the paralleling structure of these stories, Ishiguro makes visible the similar fates both Lindy and Steve have encountered, which indicates their attempts to achieve the fortune and success through cosmetic surgery.

This kind of wish fulfillment or the reformulation of external and internal realities can only make the similarity of their predicaments more obvious, which is more so as “a moment of sudden and uncomfortable proximity, when boundaries become blurred and troubles shared”(Stanton, 2006: 17). The unreliable re-telling of Janeck’s and Steve’s episode about their own life, and especially about the ideal life of Tony and Lindy Gardner, has made even more visible the similarity and difference of human experience of facticity we have ever encountered before. Like Ishiguro's other novels, the first-person narrators of Nocturnes tend to conceal more connotations and implications than they have expected, which contributes to readers' reorganization of the gap between the narrators and the implied readers. In other words, what the narratee is supposed to know has somehow exceeded the knowledge of the implied readers, which has interrupted the delimitation of their own roles and set up some atmosphere of melancholy. Janeck, the narrator of "Crooner", encounters and accompanies Tony to serenades his wife Lindy before their scheduled divorce, which causes him to have recollected the role of Tony's music in comforting his beleaguered mother who "sat on the sofa, exhausted, or maybe heart-broken, while Tony Gardner's album spun in the corner of the room" (NOCT, 2009: 14). As for Janeck's performance outside in the piazza, he considers it "a relief, let me tell you, after all those stuffy hours performing from the back of the cafe" (NOCT, 2009: 3), which turns out to be the basic link between common people like readers and their talented musicians. In any case, this kind of doubling voice arouses the aesthetic perception that "the floating world also refers more broadly to an elaborate web of memories and epiphanies spun by narrators who are caught between two worlds"(Burton, 42). Just as the recounting of the "I" narrator, Eloise pretends to be one of the cello virtuosos herself who can tutor the Hungarian cellist and advance his career, and finally confesses her failure to play any music instrument, in case that the imperfect professionals would have damaged her talent. As Ingersoll has once commented, the discrepancy between the "I" narrators and the implied readers has somehow created "the comforting deceptions of the familiar, a familiarity that can turn itself inside out to reveal a radical otherness"(Ingersoll, 2007: 42). Despite the impression of drawing people into the experiences of the disappointments and even insanity they have suffered, the gap of such unconsciousness has been deepened through Ishiguro's presenting the failing or missed opportunity to fulfill their musical potentials, which has subverted readers' expectations of their consistency of themes and even recurring settings. Therefore, the similar condition readers have encountered in Nocturnes emphasizes the significance of reader-response, which can promote their understanding of human facticity with regards to their own life experience and convictions.

Even at the beginning lines of "*Cellists*", the first-person narrator comments that "you can't have it happen too often or they start suspecting you don't have a decent repertoire"(NOCT, 2009: 189), which echoes the awareness of another musician playing with him or belonging to the same category of musicians. For Eloise and Tibor, music presents and also promises the human idealism which has nothing to do with the cruel reality they have endured. Ultimately, Eloise marries the American golf merchant she doesn't love, and Tibor has to accept a second-rate job playing in "a small chamber group in the hotel dining room" (NOCT, 2009: 219). That is, the unfulfilled idealism they both have been pursuing contributes to the eventual conflicts between the promise of music and the facticity of human condition, which means that human beings "already find themselves transposed in their existence into other human beings, even if there are factically no other human beings in the vicinity"(Heidegger, 1995: 205).

Within the facticity of everyday life, boredom and anxiety are perhaps the most fundamental concepts which can demonstrate the essence of human condition. In the eyes of people like Lindy and Helen, choosing their husbands has always been some sort of transaction which can offer "what she'd dreamt of, what she'd planned to win for herself in that little diner. Whether she loved me or not didn't come into it"(NOCT, 2009: 29). Just as Ronell argues, the transience of human Dasein results in the mood of everyday boredom which "with its temporal slowdown and edge of anguish, is also an authentic mode of being-in-the-world. Boredom inflects a sonic quality, it attunes a murmur or an attitude of voice" (Ronell, 1992: 120). For example, the saxophonist narrator in "*Cellists*", like Janeck who plays in a piazza of Venice, observes how Eloise submits to the unjust fate or social reality and has to give up the self-belief of becoming a talented virtuoso. Therefore, Eloise, the self-deceived musician, like other musicians of this book, wanders in Central Europe with the hope of escaping the secular reality, which forces readers once again to mull over the lack of her understanding her own potential, or the cruel and uncanny human condition. Furthermore, most of the protagonists of this allegory Ishiguro has presented finally turn out to be such repressed and self-denied individuals that only plead for a place for themselves to escape the world.

The sense of participation in the plot of the novel has been strengthened through the "second addressee", that is, a kind of second vacuum is created, and the reader is drawn to fill in the fictional world as a participant. Just like his earlier novels, Ishiguro has projected the predicament of such floating strangers like Janeck and Steve onto an allegory of human condition, which indicates that "our poverty of experience is not merely poverty on the personal level, but poverty of human experience in general [...] We say this in order to introduce a new, positive concept of barbarism"(Benjamin, 1999: 732).

What fascinates us most is that all the stories turn out to end up with the protagonists' idealism of music talents submitting to the disappointments and compromises of human poverty. Like the novel *Never Let Me Go*, Ishiguro's recurrent exploration has also been applied to this allegory, in which the author arouses readers into questioning the values of creativity and artistry which involves the essence of human beings that "is a doubtless something peculiar, peculiarly circular or reflexive, to the 'essence' of man if, as it seems, he alone among the rest of living things can raise the question concerning his essence, can call his essence into question"(Winkler, 2007: 522). The structure of "Malvern Hills", through its realistic narration, presents the epistemology of allegory. Somehow, the scene of Malvern Hills offers him some belonging of cultural identity through which "I remembered from my childhood, I felt affection, even nostalgia, about this area"(NOCT, 2009: 94). That is to say, the self-narcissistic songwriting guitarist moves to Malvern Hills to querulously work for his sister in exchange of food and board, which involves similar resentment and complaint deriving from the Swiss couple and the professional singers who have admired and encouraged his music talent that he has possessed, through which one can experience the other's mortality in his finite existence.

Like such stories as "Crooner" or "Cellists", Ishiguro here describes the predicament when the narrator complains of his sister's positioning no appreciation of his music talent, even though she has "been, I happened to remember, a big music fan in her teens"(NOCT, 2009: 117), which somehow echoes the similarity of Tilo and Sonja's experience of his only son's misunderstanding. The atmosphere of hurtful sentiment Ishiguro has created reveals that the self-referential essence of allegory refers to the experience of boredom when "humankind is deprived of effective experience and becomes subjected to the imposition of a form of experience as controlled and manipulated as a laboratory maze for rats [...] the rejection of experience can provisionally embody a legitimate defence"(Agamben, 2007: 18). Just as what the Polish guitarist Janeck has always reminiscing about, the croon songs Tony Gardner's records have represented symbolize some kind of nostalgia of ideal past. As Janeck remembers, his performances of "going from band to band and playing 'The Godfather' nine times in one afternoon"(NOCT, 2009: 4) somehow seem to have echoed his mother's imagined escape from the cruel privation in Poland and resort to such consoling croon songs through which "we could leave things behind like that — I guess that's what my mother would have thought. If only sadness could be like that"(NOCT, 2009: 27). Despite their new necessity of choosing a new wife and husband to restart their career of fame and fortune, even Tony and Lindy can not avoid the romantic gesture which symbolizes their nostalgia of idealist past.

Like the butler Stevens in *The Remains of the Day*, who recounts a balanced structure of the world he has been involved in and the outside society he seems alienated from, the story *Nocturne* actually instantiates the paralleling relationship between the brilliant stardom Lindy Gardner's career represents and the boredom and anxiety Steve's life stands up for. Moreover, the frustrated experience of Lindy arouses readers' wonder about whether the success of her "Six years of manoeuvring, planning, putting yourself on the line like that.

Getting knocked back over and over again"(NOCT, 2009: 20) deserves what she has lost for her ambition. However, the power of facticity also rests in the possibility of refusing the public through the poverty of experience, because of "its existence in the form of a valuable resource which can be returned to them, either verbally or non-verbally, during subsequent interactions" (Mills, 1997: 673).

What this allegory presents through the facticity of everyday experience is to allegorize the human condition encountered with the confliction between such protagonists' musical talents and hopeless reality.Actually, readers have now realized that their feelings of familiarity derive from Ishiguro's unique technique that the characters still remain in their nostalgia of the ideal past, refusing to fit in with the changed reality in which "the people you started out with have long ago been replaced by a generation who gossip about different things, take different drugs and listen to different music" (NOCT, 2009: 40). The narrator Raymond, one itinerant English teacher who remains a jazz purist, moves to stay with his college friends, and finally turns out to be someone who has become the invited guest to rescue his friends' collapsing marriage through his presenting the qualities of a failed or collapsed life, resulting from his passing years which "have just left you high and dry. You're like a man on the precipice. One more tiny push and you'll crack"(NOCT, 2009:53). Notwithstanding the private and personal perspective of autobiographical memories, their functions have proved to be "simultaneously public because they usually involve other people. A primary function of reminiscing is social"(Reese and Farrant, 2003: 29).

The surprising elements that Ishiguro presents are the comic plot in which

Raymond has impersonalized a Labrador dog to cover up the mistake he has made, which causes the story to fall into pathologic and absurd condition of humankind. Like the surrealism of *The Unconsoled*, *Nocturnes* explores what makes humankind more human, which is determined by this projective character [...] what occurs is precisely a peculiar turning toward themselves on the part of whoever is projecting [...] this removal that pertains to projecting has the character of raising away into the possible"(Heidegger, 1995: 362-363).

Despite its absurdity and incongruity, readers can still recognize the sense of pain and hopelessness underneath the narrators' pretending not to question their inclination of croon music which has been beyond the facticity of their life. Just like the plot of *Nocturne*, Steve and Lindy, who have been divorced from their respective wife and husband, have to await up to recuperate in one Hollywood hotel and build up an awkward relationship beneath the mask of their heavily bandaged faces, which turns out to be an episode revealing their remaining in the fantasized idealism of past romantic love and nostalgia whose bond can be easily broken up by the cruelty of reality. In a word, love and talented creativity must share the similarity with its experience of humanistic facticity, in which "to be human is to have an interior self that is able to express what it feels, and that feels love in particular"(Seaman, 2007: 266). In a word, the book *Nocturnes*, which has categorized such short stories of similar theme together, contributes a lot to the formulation of an allegory about the facticity of common human life.

4.2 Non-human Identities of Cultural Ideology

As demonstrated in most of his earlier novels, Ishiguro tends to present his protagonists as artist or someone who has been infatuated with the functions of art. The narrators of his novels, such as An Artist of the *Floating World and The Unconsoled*, seem to raise the doubts about the effects the artistic or aesthetic values have performed in exploring the compensatory "imaginary homelands" for their exiled and deracinated identity. In *Nocturnes*, Ishiguro has chosen different settings such as Europe and America for the narratives. Just like what the narrator Janeck confesses, as a foreigner living in Venice he has always been regarded as one of the "gypsies".

Unfortunately, the distance between the aesthetic art and secular reality somehow leads to the narrators' bewildering about their responsibilities and memories of past losses or wounds. The narrator Janeck can be perceived as the same protagonist of both stories *Crooner* and *Cellists*, who embarrassedly discovers how "the bosom pals of today become lost strangers tomorrow, scattered across Europe, playing the Godfather theme or '*Autumn Leaves*' in squares and cafes you'll never visit"(NOCT, 2009: 190). In other words, Ishiguro carries into this book his consistent anxieties of artistic obligation and ability to evoke or to reshape the ordinary people's lives, which repeatedly confirms the mysterious power of their cultural and social identity of human beings.

Along the music journey of these narrators, we encounter musical dreamers, jobbing musicians and even bygone singers who foreground themselves from one Italian piazza to the Malvern Hills, from a London flat to an expensive Hollywood hotel. Like Ryder in *The Unconsoled*, the musicians like Tilo and even Tony Gardner still believe that "it's good that we perform to all kinds of people"(NOCT, 2009: 112), which nevertheless demonstrates their identities of being needed by people who encounter terrible problems. Nevertheless, these narrators have ultimately transformed into the strangers to their own consciousness and psychological identification, which arouses their "moments of self-awareness when each of the many poles of one's 'ambiguous' asserts [...] always involves denial of something which at times at least, we know to be true of ourselves"(Cooper, 1990: 119).

Through the similar theme of elegiac or croon music, readers have been reminded of the narrators' Kafkaesque wanderings across different cities and even countries, which points towards the humanistic dignity and even resignation to the mediocrity of human life. Despite the obvious desperation the narrators have encountered, they still tend to resolve the realistic cause which has destroyed their happiness of life. The predicament their floating life has caused has always been awaiting these lonely musicians and frustrated teachers, or coercing them to quit their usual identities and become others in order to achieve the fulfillment of their dreams. Janeck has been one of the "gypsies" moving around the piazza, and complaining the discrimination of tradition and the past. As Naipaul argues, the national prejudice of Englishness turns out to be "the product of fantasy, a work of national art; it will outlast England"(Naipaul, 2002: 215). That is to say, the dreamlike idealism these characters have pursued for their formulation of identities, such as Tony Gardner, Raymond and even Steve, has transformed them into the Hemingwayesque heroes who struggle against the compromise of secular life for their musical contribution to humankind.

As the creation of transcultural forms, the hybridity of human identity formulates one debatable notion of the individual status and position, which indicates a strong sense of dynamic contrariety, together with both regional and ethic implications. Because of their "not being Italian, never mind Venetian", such musicians like Janeck have to suffer the plights of not fitting the official bill as a regular band member, in spite of the fact that "We're well liked, we're needed by the other musicians"(NOCT, 2009: 4). Indeed, such Italian residents like the gondolier Vittorio prefer more to live in tradition or nostalgia, through which they "want something they recognise, maybe an old Julie Andrews number, or the theme from a famous movie"(NOCT, 2009: 4). In a word, music or song possesses a dynamic power that can present people the dreamlike life they have not deserved and even fulfill their self-affirmation in such an artistic and illusory world, despite its permeating a variety of different imperfections and pains.

In pursuit of their fame and fortune, the musicians and even music lovers have to suffer the suffocating and absurd reality of human life, which somehow reminds Janeck of Tony's influence upon his mother during the communist period. Realizing the fact that Tony Gardner's records have transformed his exhausted and even broken-hearted mother so much, the roving guitarist chooses to encounter and accompany this legendary American crooner to perform his extraordinary serenade before their divorce. That is, the affirmation of cultural identity has also reflected in the illusion of music world, which "contains more truth than does everyday reality [...] mystified in its institutions and relationships, which make necessity into chance, and alienation into self-realization"(Marcuse, 1978: 54).

Despite Janeck's belief in the fascination of music which certainly exceeds the limitations of different nations, such people still arouse the hostility from the extreme nationalists like Vittorio who would rather walk around saying "foreigners like me, we go around ripping off tourists, littering the canals, in general ruining the whole city. Some days, if he's in a bad mood, he'll claim we're muggers — rapists, even"(NOCT, 2009: 17). Furthermore, the juxtaposition of different national cultures somehow represents the confliction and even celebration of social hybridity, which results from the reconstruction of a post-modernist society. Suffering the narrators' floating status, they still choose to remain the belief that their artistic creation will certainly contribute to the humanistic idealism of society. Just like what Tony comments upon his encounter with Janeck, "what I intended to say to you, friend, what I meant was that coming from where you do, quite naturally, there are many things you don't understand yet. Just like there'd be many things I wouldn't understand in your country"(NOCT, 2009: 16).

Furthermore, the encounter of different cultures leads to no assimilation and compromise, but the prejudice and strangeness, which results in Janeck's anxiety of the following emergence that "when Mr. Gardner started singing, Mrs. Gardner would come to the window with a gun and fire down at us"(NOCT, 2009: 17). In fact, the characters like Tony and Janeck have tried to achieve their attempts to wipe off the barriers between sacred beauty of music and the filthy vulgarity of reality. In order to cover up the failure to communicate with his audience, Tony even needs to speak of the high standards of eating pork chops of a Milwaukee audience when appreciating his music, which somehow contributes to their understanding, through the way "the audience becomes someone you know, someone you can perform to. There, that's my secret"(NOCT, 2009: 18). Despite their suffering frustrating reality, these people still choose to restore the romantic illusion into their everyday life, which nevertheless confirms the consoling power of music. Faced with the pressure of social reality, people like Tony and Lindy prefer to transform their personal identities they have once been familiar with in order to follow the sound and fury of human life. For the pursuit of his musical career, Tony would rather choose to divorce from his wife than stay together for ever, and have "prepared to make a lot of changes, some of them are hard ones. You change the way you are. You even change some things you love"(NOCT, 2009: 30). Instead of keeping her love and matrimony, Lindy also prefers to "get out now, while she has time. Time to find love again, make another marriage"(NOCT, 2009: 31). Therefore, the suffering which belief in art has brought about does not disappear, and becomes even more obvious in the loss of human identities. Just as Anderson argues, the domination of secularism surprisingly becomes "a secular transformation of fatality into continuity, contingency into meaning [...] It is the magic of nationalism to turn chance into destiny"(Anderson, 1991: 11). All in all, the freedom of individual identity relies more on the rational reality, which has been ideologically circumscribed and even represented by the facticity of human life. Because of the fragmentary and superficial post-modernism, these people such as Lindy and Tony have been transformed into a unity of conflicts, which compete to control their cultural identities betokened by "our class origin, our jobs, the circuits of our friendships and desires, our ways of spending our leisure time, our literary predilections, our political affiliations — or lack of them" (Ahmad, 1992: 138). Accompanied by the dominating reality and its embodiments, what the art reveals is its groundlessness and fragility, which nevertheless arouses people's doubt about the polytropism of cultural identity reflecting their double-voicedness of human consciousness.

Indeed, all the stories in *Nocturnes*, except the second one *Come Rain or Come Shine*, foreground the itinerant working musicians, and even the narrator Raymond madly clings to such croon music of American Broadway singers in order to escape from "moaning" of his hopeless situation. Due to their cultural migrancy and rootlessness, these characters like Janeck have been estranged from any immigrated culture they have inherited in order to fulfill their spiritual requirements of "imaginary homeland". As Raymond claims, since his graduation from college, he has "spent years here in Spain, as well as in Italy and Portugal, while Charlie's [...] always flying off — to Texas, Tokyo, New York — to his high-powered meetings"(NOCT, 2009: 39). As the figures straddle different cultures, these people such as Raymond and Tibor represent a playful portrayal of cultural hybridity existing in postmodern society, which has been presented by the image of the one who "listens to reggae, watches a Western, eats McDonald's food for lunch and local cuisine for dinner, wears Paris perfume in Tokyo and 'retro' clothes in Hong Kong"(Lyotard, 1993: 42). The universalism of culture nevertheless points to the hybridity of identity, which is filled with ambiguity and contradiction undermining the dominant ideology.

As one itinerant language teacher, Raymond enjoys his life, in which he feels like "you're apart of a large network extending around the entire globe. You meet people fresh from their spells in Peru or Thailand [...] always you'd be part of this cosy, extended family of itinerant teachers"(NOCT, 2009: 40). However, the transition and transformation of his identity that can bridge the chasm of different cultures becomes "a process of displacement and disjunction that does not totalize experience. Increasingly, 'national' cultures are being produced from the perspective of disenfranchised minorities"(Bhabha, 1994: 5-6). Indeed, the cultural alienation of Raymond's floating life makes himself always feel slightly let down, and ultimately leads to his desperately imagining that "being godfather to one of their children would provide an official link, however tenuous, between their lives in England and mine out here"(NOCT, 2009: 41). Nevertheless, the influence Raymond has derived from his identity of cultural hybridity offers him some perspective to acknowledge his compromise with the current capitalist ideology. Instead of accepting the fate of being an ordinary bloke, Emily complains about the waste of Raymond's and even Charlie's potential, through which they have been destined for great achievements. Compared with the nostalgia of her past university life, Emily even thinks of her friend, and begins to dream about such wonderful figures like David bloody Corey and Roger Van Den Berg as her potential lovers because of their great accomplishments, which somehow results in their marital crisis, "what's so pathetically sad and ironic about all this, the point is, at the bottom of it all. She loves me. She still loves me"(NOCT, 2009: 61). With the emergence of increasing minorities, Europeanism and even Anglicism can't be imagined or reassessed without any reference to the otherness existing in Europe which acts as a hybrid creation of those who define themselves against or inside it. Perhaps through the portrayal of such identity-ridden wanderers between Britain, Continental Europe and America, Ishiguro attempts to present readers some pessimistic viewpoint of culture which leads to their wandering, which contributes to their post-Freudian tension inside human life.

In fact, the cultural identity Raymond represents has never transformed into the idealized 'third space' of hybridity, which can help "sustain me through my lousiest moments in strange and lonely countries"(NOCT, 2009: 62). Like Tilo and Sonja who are wandering musicians, Raymond and even Emily have to resort to the croon nostalgia music in order to shake off the sound and fury of secular culture, which nevertheless pushes the farcical comedy into a bittersweet drama. As pathetic beings, these characters have all suffered despondent things such as a total mess of work, estrangement of friendship and marriage, lingering around the edge of life, which somehow reflects their cultural status of marginality and placelessness beneath its simple imperial idealism of the so-called Englishness. Due to the confusing displacement of cultural identity, "the private and the public become part of each other, forcing upon us a vision that is as divided as it is disorienting"(Bhabha, 1994: 9). Because of the predicaments they have encountered, Emily anxiously regards the posture of his impersonating a dog to cover up the damage of her diary, and even his prepared cooking of one boot to make up the doggy smell as one symptom of despondence and wishful suicide, which betokens their never being contented with human facticity.

Most importantly, what has been left over for them to console their own injured souls is this croon music, and even brings them back to memories of past happiness which ultimately turns out to be a process of cultural "in-between spaces through which the meanings of cultural and political authority are negotiated"(Bhabha, 1994: 4). In a sense, Ishiguro has always remained influenced by his double identified life, which has, for one reason or another, been ready to penetrate into his portrayal of characters in his creation of universal writings. Due to his marginal or alienated status, the narrator of "Malvern Hills" has to suffer his usual old restlessness which exceeds the capability of grasping his idealistic dream of being a great musician. Despite the desperation at the musical reality, he still holds the belief in its redemptive power of musical idealism. Furthermore, the indifference of most bands in London to the original or talented music reflects the narrator's complaint about their stupidity, in which "there was something if not utterly rotten, then at least extremely shallow and inauthentic about what was going down here"(NOCT, 2009: 91). Like the characters Naipaul and Rushdie have created, Ishiguro equally presents various international figures of a floating world, which somehow foregrounds its transatlantic, transnational, cosmopolitan and postcolonial contexts that transcend beyond traditional notions of Englishness.

However, the facticity of life condition has ultimately transformed the narrator into someone who would rather complain or even hate his once teacher whose life is now falling apart, and even guest like Sonja who's lacking somewhat polite deportments. Due to their clothes and accents, our narrator even mistakes the Swiss couple Tilo and Sonja for "the Krauts", which nevertheless reveals the prejudice of other cultures deep down in his heart. Just as Foucault argues, the appearance or even apparatus has been "always inscribed in a play of power, but it is also always linked to certain coordinates of knowledge which issue from it but, to an equal degree, condition it"(Foucault, 1980: 196). The itinerant musicians like Tilo and Sonja, perform as a duo in so many strange and difficult conditions "though we like best to work in Switzerland and Austria" (NOCT, 2009: 108). More importantly, they have dedicated themselves to performing traditional Swiss folk music, despite their forced compromise to play such pop hits the audience is likely to appreciate.

What they have dedicated to the musical idealism ultimately turns out to have caused the personal tragedies resulting from their ignoring the human happiness their family demands. Under the influence of Swiss tradition and culture, Tilo and Sonja have demonstrated their somewhat unwilling reluctance to transform into some universal figures who can perform to all kinds of people living in not only Europe but also other countries. The acceptance of their changeable cultural identities can only descend into that void, wherein one may begin to come into confrontation with a spectre of invocation, whose freedom to participate in an alien territory and wildness has become a necessity for one's salvation. Just like the misunderstanding from the only son of Tilo and Sonja, the narrator nevertheless faces the similar scene, in which his sister and brother-in-law, Maggie and Geoff, equally despise his musical creation as something less than the simple chores of handyman.

Faced with his blighted dreams, the narrator of "Malvern Hills", like Steve, still prefers to insist on his idealistic dream of successful career in London music industry. Likewise, Steve equally regards himself as a serious jazz player in his innermost dreams. As Ishiguro states, his motif has always been concerned about such flawed individuals that "might highlight what is actually quite positive and valuable about being alive [...] they are capable of being very decent"(Shaffer and Wong, 2008: 220). In some sense, Steve possesses the somewhat talented gift and signature sound which contributes to his artistic pride to despise this stardom involving "image, marketability, being in magazines and on TV shows, about parties and who you ate lunch with"(NOCT, 2009: 131). Perhaps like Lindy, Helen is an ambitious and determined snob who regards her husband as her tools of obtaining fame and fortune, which leads to her divorcing with Steve and living with one successful lover. Meanwhile, facing the opportunity Helen's new lover offers, Steve begins to reestablish his dream of avoiding being a loser all his life and even possessing his own band one day, which represents his artistic integrity. Their facial surgeries have never perfectly promised the bright future they've expected, which somehow leads to their inevitable nostalgia of the past happiness and some sense of regret or disappointment. Therefore, the process of Steve's reconstructing his social identification somehow changes "the present's feeling of being 'at home' into an illusion [...] behind the back of the owner (the ego), or over its objections, it inscribes there the law of the other" (Certeau, 1986: 4), which nevertheless reflects Ishiguro's advocation of universal themes of cultural identity.

Steve nevertheless overcomes his nausea of facial surgery to "crawl after the Lindy Gardners of this world into Vacuous celebrity"(NOCT, 2009: 138), despite his much more radical ambitions of contributing to the musical welfare. Because of his longings and even regrets, Steve decides to belittle his once colleague Jack as something like nothing or bluffer who never knows music.

Actually, through the performance of his CD, Steve begins to be considered different from other musicians, which means his musical gift of being "really talented, someone who's just been blessed that way by God"(NOCT, 2009: 158) deserves Lindy's admiration and even the prize of *Jazz Musicians of the Year* she has stolen. Despite his talented potential of music, Steve has occasionally screwed up his performance of playing a solo which arouses the doubt of his seemingly reliable narration, from which the readers can somehow encounter his querulous complaints and even witness the traumatic experience, so that "If the demand for self-knowledge is willed by fate and is refused, this negative attitude may end in real death" (Jung, 1989: 474).

Lindy persuades Steve into believing the fairness of personal efforts, which presents the fact that "even if you were like me, one of the unblessed, there was still a chance for you, you could still find a place in the sun, you didn't have to settle for being just public"(NOCT, 2009: 175). Compared with the rational choice, Steve turns out to be one naive artist who desperately gains the returning of his wife through overcoming the nausea of his facial surgery. Furthermore, Lindy equally soaks herself in the nostalgia of her romantic love with Tony, which leads to her listening to his records continuously. Their attempts at mundane and pathetic self-assertion have nevertheless undermined and even baffled the integrity of humanity. All in all, the narration of these characters somehow undermines their own reliability of recounting the life facticity they have encountered, which reminds readers that life involves not just love and even art but also secular reality.

Surprisingly, the narrator of "Cellists" shares his similar longings and regrets with other characters like Steve and Janeck. Like Janeck, the Hungarian musician Tibor tends to appreciate a string of concerts around Europe, though he has to perform music he dislikes. However, his tutor, an American woman whose virtuosity has not been proved, nevertheless arouses his ambition of excavating the musical potential, through which "That woman's turned him into an arrogant little shit [...] He'll soon get a few corners knocked off him"(NOCT, 2009: 210). As a naive youth who remains ignorant of Western culture, Tibor enjoys Eloise's sense of mission to promote his musical talent, which leads to his regarding performing for people during their dinners as less than suitable for a music genius. Faced with her special gift, Eloise considers herself as one virtuoso. What remains most important is to protect the gift from being destroyed and then await somebody to unveil. Therefore, the artistic anxiety of our narrators nevertheless contributes to their attempts to justify the changeability of multicultural identity which "cuts into the plenitudinous notion of Culture splendidly reflected in the mirror of human nature; equally it halts the endless signification of difference"(Bhabha, 1994: 245). Through the narratives of such musicians or jazz fans, Ishiguro presents for readers the conflicts between secularity and artistry, through which each narrator has suffered some kind of identity crisis as an outsider of artistic market or the society. As Childs argues, in most of his work, Ishiguro has presented "themes of loss, trauma, dislocation, failure, and memory. A central theme is the narrator's self-deception"(Childs, 129) as a result of his own confused identities estranged between the musical idealism and realities on earth.

The struggling for the successes of these characters surprisingly echoes the author's efforts of music and songwriting before his turning to fiction, which compensates himself for his idealism of artistic perseverance. All in all, the search of these narrators for musical idealism is entangled with the psychological pursuit of their cultural identity, which reflects the hope of avoiding their feelings of "desertion, abandonment"(NOCT, 2009: 154). Just as McSweeney argues, the serious novelist should be concerned "not with nostrums but with diagnosis, with the painful and difficult work of understanding the social and historical reality he examines" (McSweeney, 1983: 191), which nevertheless confirms Ishiguro's purpose of universal writing to explore the predicament of these floating or marginal persons represented by himself.

What has always been haunting such characters as Steve and Tibor is the undertone of some metaphorical nocturnes filled with something of the impatience and even a kind of bitterness, which nevertheless reminds readers of whether or not the pursuit of music immortality deserves their sacrifice of human dignity. Unfortunately, such artists have to choose the compromise between the secular reality and artistic idealism, which echoes the connotation of Ray Charles' song in *Come Rain or Come Shine*, though the interpretation was heartbroken, resulting from the lack of redemptive guidance of positive ideology. Just as Ishiguro states, growing up in the late 1960s and the 1970s, his ambition of career has always been "to aspire towards being a rock star but part of me genuinely enjoys playing music and I think that is the part I am let with now" (Shaffer and Wong, 2008: 18). Despite their wandering between worlds, aimless and even rootless, the characters like Steve and Janeck are still struggling for some feeble artistic idealism which can nevertheless confirm their identities or cultural belongings, no matter how slim they turn out to be.

Chapter Five Conclusion

In the era of globalization, the communication and information technologies have innovated the forms of increasing cultural and economic interactions, and facilitated the transformation of migration, especially the postmodern configuration of migrants' existence. Global migration has grown in volume and importance since 1945 and especially since the mid-1980s. Nowadays, the notion of diaspora has broadened its semantic field so as to include such people as refugees, immigrants, guess workers and ethnic groups, etc. The interactions in industrial, marketing and cultural fields have compelled a symbiotic relation between the diasporas and their homelands. The dispersion of transmigrants, which is termed as the Greek word "diaspora" deriving from the Jewish dispersion during the Babylonian captivity, refers to communities moving away from their homelands, either forced or voluntary, to settle in a land of their host country struggling with the presentation of national culture. However, the notion of transnational diaspora no longer foregrounds the predicament of their existence, but "points to a structured whole where components interact despite their dispersion"(Ben-Rafael & Sternberg, 2009: 4). They not only participate in the daily life of their societies of hostland, but maintain the connections and even influence the homelands from which they have emigrated. Their dispersed experiences invite the postmodern thought to combine the feature of non-centre and hybridity with the recognition of heterogeneous identity.

Postmodernism allows readers to transcend beyond the orientalist view of oppositions between centre and periphery so as to appreciate their state of co-existence. For instance, Rushdie includes the character of Padma, Saleem's companion and also attentive audience for his story. She is not just the witness of his bodily deterioration seen as a metaphor for the post-independence India, but also essential for his storytelling project that brings about his concerns, "How to dispense with Padma [...] I have become, it seems to me, the apex of an isosceles triangle, supported equally by twin deities, the wild god of memory and the lotus-goddess of the present"(Rushdie, 1995: 170). The applying of Padma's role as an audience undertakes the function of necessary questioning and counterweights to the authorial miracle-laden omniscience. The diasporas create an imaginary space of "in-between", that is, "a travelling term, in changing global conditions", to combine the notion of "root" and "route" that presages the predicament between their compromise with and resistance to "host countries and their norms", wherein identities can be negotiated and the binary of self/ other breaks down (Clifford, 1994: 307).

The postcolonial identity can not avoid being contaminated by Eurocentric or cosmopolitan concepts and images, especially of immigrant writers. What is "contaminated" here is not only the postmodernist aspects of textuality or language, but also of cultural hybridization resulting from the multiple associations and interactions connecting people with their hosts and home societies. The cosmopolitanism, according to Thomas Schlereth, should be "be identified by an interest in, a familiarity with, or appreciation of many parts and peoples of the world [...] a readiness to borrow from other lands or civilizations in the formation of his intellectual, cultural, and artistic patterns" (Schlereth, 1977: xi). The writings of global travel in the eighteenth century, such as Montesqueu's *Persian Letters* (1712) and Oliver Goldsmith's T*he Citizen of the World* (1762) can signify the beginning of the European cosmopolitanism. The European colonizers regard novels of traveling, including knowledge of other cultures, as an educational tool that can contribute to the principles of enlightened thought. The ideal the cosmopolitan individuals advocate is that readers' knowledge and science should transcend beyond national boundaries. Since its articulation, cosmopolitanism has become a conscious choice of the upper and the middle classes, which enables them to appreciate varied cultures. Timothy Brennan acknowledges the concept of "cosmopolitanism" as "an act of avoidance if not hostility and disarticulation toward states in formation"(Brennan, 1997: 2), and even attributes its emergence to an outcome of the dominance of transnational corporations and the dissemination of American culture. However, Homi Bhabha focuses upon its post-colonial aspects, and advocates the term of "vernacular cosmopolitanism", which emphasizes "a dialogic relation with the native or the domestic", through the method of "introducing the global-cosmopolitan 'action at a distance' into the very grounds-now displaced-of the domestic"(Bhabha, 1994: 48). Bhabha's main concern is transferred from its oriental aspects to the everyday interactions of diasporic community united not by nations but by global capitalism. Its lack of national identity not only avoid the parochial stance of the local or the universality of European culture, but also emphasize the interaction of human societies and the openness to cultural difference. As for the settings of

Naipaul's earlier novels, Trinidad is a refuge and metaphor of heterogeneity and diversity for its ethnic tolerance and cosmopolitan perspective, wherein all the people, including Chinese, Indians, Portuguese and blacks, all are native to this soil as a result of its creolizing process of local forces. According to Stuart Hall, the creolisation of the Caribbean migrants, that is, "the cultural mix of different elements, which is a kind of 'cosmopolitanism at home'"(Hall, 1992: 351), can be regarded as a true diasporic society. Here, Hall also emphasizes the vision of transcending the local parochial stance to partake of a transnational community, which features itself in the emergence of multilingualism along with an explosion of various cultures that leads to not the result of scattering or mutual dilution but that of the accented and free sharing.

Despite the neighborliness of different cultural communities, the reality of Trinidad is actually a microcosm of colonial society devoid of any opportunity for a fuller life. What awaits for Trinidadian people is the choice of either resisting against or escaping from a milieu that can not satisfy their ambitions of meaningful life and human dignity. Naipaul suggests in *The Middle Passage* that "the Trinidadian is a cosmopolitan. He is adaptable; he is cynical; having no rigid social conventions of his own; he is amused by the conventions of others"(Naipaul, 2002: 74). In the eyes of Bhabha, Naipaul's recounting of Trinidadian society demonstrates the success of British colonial cultural discourse that has been effected on the residents, as well as its failure to relieve the cultural apathy between the blacks and the Indians which now exacerbates into political hostility. His preference stands aside with the oriental cosmopolitanism, with which the characters of his earlier novels always privilege their empirical education and take refuge in the printed worlds. Naipaul's trajectory stands for the process of alienating from his Indian community to embrace a satisfactory and dominant culture, which can prompt him to receive English education in Oxford and later change into a worldly-wise traveler and writer. As a colonial who received English education, Naipaul can not shed off the doomed identity of subaltern subjects who uphold the values and visions of the mother country. Furthermore, Rushdie also attributes this oriental perspective to the city of Bombay, in which people can tolerate each other based on the principle of openness to all forms of otherness. Madelena Gonzales claims that is "a postmodernist rather than a postcolonialist, but the postmodernism he practices is indubitably part of the grand narrative of capitalism still firmly hegemonic in the world"(Gonzales, 2005: 17). That is, his work contains many elements of patronizing Orientalism probably resulting from his status of being a Western intellectual. In reality, the immigrant writers, who are ashamed of their cultural backgrounds, strive for embracing the superior culture of host country, and judge the hybrid colonial world from their Eurocentric perspective.

Postmodernism presents a matter of aesthetics in which its political attitude is ambivalent as a result of its complicity with the cultural dominants. It turns out to be "aesthetizing of the political", which is compared with postcolonialism that "foregrounds the political as inevitably contaminating the aesthetic"(Brydon, 2003: 137). The immigrant writings mentioned above provide a sense of belonging and communality that transgresses the national borders, and deconstruct their national myths and traditions. However, the migration that took place in the nineteenth and early twentieth centuries was unidirectional and resulted in a cruel assimilation into the culture of host nation. Once settling in the destined land, the migrants had no other choices but to either disentangle or return to their homeland. The pre-globalized migration ultimately gave birth to a huge population that dispersed in such parts of the world as America, Europe, Africa and Caribbean islands, etc. More often than not, the migrants lived with a lamentable status that relegated themselves to second-class citizens. Rogers Brubaker points out that the identities of these migrants are determined by the congruence of state territory and citizenship. Thus the old diasporas are denied of their citizenship wherein "a distinctive national culture should be diffused throughout the territory of the state, but it should stop at the frontiers of the state; there should be cultural homogeneity within states but sharp boundaries between them"(Brubaker, 2015: 132). The alienation they suffered makes them either unable to transcend beyond their own cultural backgrounds or bear some insufferable pains while assimilating into the culture of the host nation. That is to say, the migrant communities tend to see the countries they left behind as their own homelands and nations, and adhere to their specific religions or ethnic habits. Their works also provide an important insight into nostalgia in the construction of autobiographical life-writings, because two writers respectively choose to draw on the significant events of childhood and the recuperation of the past trauma. The word "nostalgia" is derived from Greek works of "nostos" and "algos", which respectively means "return" and "suffering". It is originally applied for diagnosing the mental illnesses of soldiers in the nineteenth century, but now more associated with thc longing of regaining the childhood or reuniting with the lost homelands. As opposed to the historical facts that can be found in the archives, nostalgia is based more upon a rendition of the past that excludes others to create as a retroactive construct from the present point of view.

Even with its supposed veracity, history is still seen as a construct that is contaminated with selective amnesia, so that it has changed into a double voicelessness of both the oppressed and the official history that can not properly express themselves. Svetlana Boym claims that nostalgia is presented as “a symptom of our age, a historical emotion”, that can relate to people’s “unrealized dreams of the past and visions of the future that become obsolete”(Boym, 2001: xvi). Boym further divides nostalgia into two forms, that is, restorative and reflective. Whereas the former focuses on a return to origins, often in relation with religious and national myths, the latter emphasizes its negotiation between the official national history and collective memory, often regarded as “ironic, inconclusive and fragmentary”(Boym, 2001: 50). Within the corpus of these immigration novels, Rushdie’s ones come closest to a representation of a reflective nostalgia. Its interrogation of the officially national and religious history makes him an ironic and controversial writer. The novels of Naipaul and Ishiguro, on the other hand, contain a more restorative nostalgia, which is more premised on a sense of identity anxiety. While Ishiguro’s earlier novels focus upon the history of World War II and its consequent influence upon ordinary people, Naipaul portrays more about his family’s or his own migrant identity and its subsequent influence.

Unlike postmodern form of migration, the conventional existence of migrants is territorially confined by the lack of instant communicative tools that can defy the spatial restraints so as to connect the community they leave behind.

As depicted in Naipaul's novels, few Indians choose to return to their homeland during Apartheid in South Africa, so is the case with the immigrants of Carribean islands.

The self-portraits of immigrant writers reflect the trajectory they have undergone away from earlier narratives of nation to later cosmopolitan and multicultural works, that is, a literary expression of identity in a global but fragmental world. However, the postcolonial aspects are still obvious due to their imaginative retrievial of histories and homeland, and the controversial depiction of colonial stereotypes that move beyond the colonial presuppositions. It not only asserts local independence and global interactions, but also rely upon the contestation of cultural purity and homogenization versus hybridity and heterogeneity. As for Rushdie, his *Midnight's Children* criticizes the myths of purity and homogeneity by advocating Indian nation's heterogeneity. His other earlier novels such as *Shame* and *The Last Moor's Sigh* also mirror his conflicting attitude toward how to formulate a national allegory, that is, a demonstration of his Eastern homelands. Gradually, the author shifts from his national allegory toward the more cosmopolitan auto-fiction *The Satanic Verses*, although it does not entirely avoid the core-periphery paradigm of postcolonialism. Vinay Dharwadker states that "globalization of capital and material production and consumption after the fall of the Berlin Wall" and the changes of "economic and political relations among old and new nations"(Dharwadker, 2001: 1) are three major elements that stimulate the transformation of postmodern literary trend. Berthold Schoene also attributes this literary trend to the fall of the Berlin Wall that inspires the cosmopolitanism of the early 1990s, a departure from the "traditional internationalist perspectives while stressing the significance of local culture for the development of any meaningful and viable world-communal future"(Schoene, 2010: 1). The postmodern concept places the non-centre and hybridity, that is, the heterogeneous and diversified conception of identity in its changing global conditions. This is true of Ishiguro's and Naipaul's fictions in which the homelands have been transcended into the state of global themes and issues.

It is well-known that the revival of the national folklore or histories is essential for the formulation of cultural identities as an ongoing process of becoming that are shared by the homeland and its diasporic communities. Due to the alienation from both the hostlands and homelands, the immigrant communities share with each other high and popular cultures of consumption and religions, in particular the mainstream ideology of the host nation, and purposefully create the space of social and cultural coordination and communal solidarity, whatever their national origins and religious beliefs. Furthermore, the second generation or British-born immigrants are more willing to uphold the principles of tolerance, heterogeneity and cosmopolitanism. The religious or traditional images and ethnic existentialism are respectively mocked and satired in the writings of the immigrant writers mentioned above. Immigrant writers often mingle the indigenous legends or historical events with Western myths to either question the rationality of their living condition or help to redefine their new identities in their foster countries. Like Ishiguro also conceives of his hybrid mythology and chooses to embrace his multilayered heritage that he accepts as an international viewpoint for his later cosmopolitan novels. Moving away from the earlier portraits of his homeland Japan, the author gradually enters into the stage of depicting the fluidity and plurality of migrant identity. Perhaps resulting from his childhood of migration, his later cosmopolitan novels such as *When We Were Orphans* and *Never Let Me Go* can be regarded as a departure from his attachment to imagined homeland to a fabulous self-invented citizenry of homelessness and transculturality that is the price the immigrants have to pay for the emergence of global capitalism and culture.

As Suraj Kuma Saw points out, the previous diasporas have now "acquired new face, facet and feature under changing patterns of the global state membership. The children of migrants have developed a sense of multiple belongs without shedding their core diasporic identity"(Saw, 2018: 355). For instance, the immigrant writers such as Naipaul and Ishiguro all received their education in British schools, and later participated in the local cultures and public life while maintaining their social and cultural ties with their parents' homelands. The children of the 1980s and the 1990s, that is, the second generation youths "confront today a pluralistic, fragmented environment that simultaneously offers a wealth of opportunities and major dangers to successful adaptation"(Portes & Rumbaut, 2001: 55). This new tendency of cultural identification, which is quite different from what their parents uphold, offers a challenge to the assimilation and makes a passe. To take ishiguro's novel *A Pale View of Hills* as an example, the sisters Keiko and Niki, who respectively represents the first and second generation of immigrants, rccount their different youth life. Whereas the elder one encounters the discrimination and unequal opportunities she is subjected to, the younger one seems very optimistic about her future. Thus, Ishiguro shows readers the notion of new Britishness that permits the non-white immigrants like Niki to achieve his ideals of life in the hostland. The immigrant communities will continue their participation as a harbinger of plural identity, and try their best to integrate into the public lifc and activities of the multicultural host societies. Despite the rising of cosmopolitanism and its efforts of globalization, the fact that "in other cases nations and nationalism appear to be on the upswing"(Hannerz, 1996: 89) shouldn't be disregarded. The recent Brexit and the earlier Grexit affairs both continue to challenge the concept of globalization. The public in Britain and even Europe are all willing to make a reduction in the number of immigration. The writers such as Ishiguro, who both advocate the concept of cosmopolitanism and plural identity, can not refute the significance of nation-states and their national identities which exist in their "imagined homelands". Thus, the coexistence and of conflict between cosmopolitanism and nationalism still make a challenge of the way how the immigrants and their host societies treat the adjustment and formulate the harmonious principles of their future life. Perhaps, the approach of solving this predicament lies in what Naipaul claims as the notion of "travelling", which emphasizes not "roots" but "routes", that is, our focus should not rest upon their origins and parochialism as before but rather upon their movements and attachments.

Through the scribe character Salman the Persian, Rushdie casts doubts on the divinity of Mahound or the prophet Muhammad, and also highlights the absurdity of the rules that are laid out by the archangel to govern the faithful Muslims. Furthermore, Rushdie's later novel *Enchantress* explores the Mughal royal court of Akbar, which challenges the dominant Euro-centric history to assert the progressive politics and culture of Akbar's reign. Surprisingly, the emperor Akbar upholds certain controversial but progressive ideas, such as atheism and freedom of expression, which can offer an example of history famous for its more open and pluralistic attitudes to dissent and alternate faiths. According to Said's notion of Orientalism, Rushdie applies the past glory of Islamic history to overshadow the impotence and backwardness of the modern East so that "the European Orientalist found it his duty to rescue some portion of a lost, past classical Oriental grandeur in order to 'facilitate ameliorations' in the present Orient"(Said, 1977: 79). The revival of British heritage has been encouraged by the Margaret Thatcher's government to nostalgically focus on its lost prestige. The Thatcherite neo-liberalism prevalent in the 1980s and the 1990s witnessed the preservation of aspects and images of the past, especially the hierarchical Victorian and Edwardian values. While his earlier writings celebrate the "mongrelisation" of different cultures and religions, his later novels, especially since his fatwa affair, tend to uphold the discourse of West-versus-East Orientalism. Rushdie admits in his memoir Joseph Anton, "That thing needed to be fought and to fight it one had to name it and the only name that fit was Islam"(Rushdie, 2012: 356). Here he suggests that the religion itself should be responsible for the crimes committed by Islamic fundamentalists, that is, its incompatibility with the modern, Western and secular society is not only evidenced in his experience with the fatwa but also rooted in his postmodern persona as a voice of the Eastern diasporic for Western audiences. Rushdie is a modern embodiment, just like Naipaul and Ishiguro, an immigrant of Eastern descent now living in England and who has acquired a high level of multicultural competence.

This geographical distribution allows them to create a setting that is not just diasporal for the parent generation, but also a trend of cosmopolitan mobility of the children's generation. Taking Naipaul as an example, his earlier writings, including the first major work, *A House for Mr. Biswas*, are all concerned with the city of Port of Spain where he grew up and also knew best. In this novel, his father, in the disguise of Mr. Biswas, began to sense the evolving ethos of a hybrid community, but his state of in-between renders himself alienated from both sources of his heritage. The next generation Anand, a portrait of young Naipaul, further confirms his father's conviction that only colonial education can allow one a place as a writer to see the truth of the world, and that the colonial subject can not prosper by itself. The orientalist discourse the younger Naipaul received in his missionary school provides him with the internal consistency of Orientalism. With the surge of nostalgic images and representations of Britain's past, the narrative foregrounds its resurgent patriotism, of which "the countryside was [...] projected as a secure, nostalgic site infused with cultural and racial sanctity to buttress the influence of immigrants from the old empire"(Loh, 2010: 96). As a reaction of Thatcher's heritage policy, the immigrant writers mentioned above all re-examine the official traditions of imperial Britain and then address the experiences of colonization, migration and racial hybridity. They do not simply resist against the imperial heritage but remind readers of cultural relationship between different societies within the cosmopolitan context.

In his Nobel Prize speech, Naipaul admitted that his works reflected "my Hindu family, with its fading memories of India, there was India itself". The heritage of India renders himself a sense of traveler, stranded in a constant process of transition from ancestral Indian tradition to Western values. The postcolonial critics, such as Edward Said and Homi Bhabha, emphasize the aspects of migration, especially its process of traveling rather than cultural roots. Said explores the traveling theory as not a concept of traveling from one place to another, but a suggestion of "the possibility of actively different locales, sites, situations for theory, without facile universalism or over-general totalizing"(Said, 2000: 452). Naipaul is a tireless but reluctant traveler, portrayed in his writings as well as in real life, because his characters all share his own homelessness and separateness from Trinidad, India and even England.

Along with Rushdie and Ishiguro, Naipaul attempts to transform his experiences of migration, including his exotic homeland of Trinidad, into a cultural scrutiny of Britain's imperial heritage and tradition. Besides, Rushdie also recounts, through his auto-fiction *The Satanic Verses*, the experience of being an immigrant in Britain in the 1980s. That is, Thatcher's government encouraged migration of only those white or light-skinned people, which ultimately turns into an imperial ideology that defamilializes the space of home as location. The memory of displacement, according to Homi Bhabha, can be culturally translated into "a contingent 'in-between' space, that innovates and interrupts the performance of the present. The 'past-present' becomes part of the necessity, of the nostalgia, of living"(Bhabha, 1994: 7). The space of "in-between" can also be seen as a travelling term, which combines the notion of "root" and "route" that presages the predicament between their compromise with and resistance to host countries and their norms", wherein identities can be negotiated within the binary of self/other. The immigrant writers are poised between the two opposite presences of space, that is, whereas the metropolitan perspective of the Eastern homelands is proscribed as backwardness, the other one is to depict the metropolis as an automatic sovereignty through the penchant for European culture within the textually colonized East. The experience of migration, especially that of traveling from the marginal to the centre, transcends the previous notions of belong and dwelling beyond those who are excluded until the late twentieth century. Thus these cosmopolitan writers all encourage the public to transcend narrow loyalties and uphold the vision of shared colonial or post-colonial experiences with their appropriated forms of Western literature.

References of Chapter One

Anderson, Linda. Autobiography, London and New York: Routledge, 2001.

Barthes, Roland. The death of the Author, The Rustle of Language, trans. Richard Howard, Oxford: Basil Blackwell, 1986.

Beverley, John. The Margin at the Center: On Testimonio (Testimonial Narrative), De/Colonizing the Subject, ed. Smith and Watson, 91-114.

Billson, Marcus F. The Memoir: New Perspectives on A Forgotten Genre, Genre, 10.2, Summer 1977, 259-82.

De Man, Paul. Autobiography as de-facement, Modern Language Notes 94(5), 1979, 919-930.

Elliott, Anthony. Subject to Ourselves: Social Theory, Psychoanalysis and Postmodernity, Cambridge: Polity Press, 1996.

Groes, Sebastian. and Barry Lewis (eds). Kazuo Ishiguro: New Critical Visions of the Novels, New York: Palgrave Macmillan, 2011.

Hampel, Regine. I Write Therefore I Am?: Fictional Autobiography and the Idea of Selfhood in the Postmodern Age, Bern;Oxford: Lang, 2001.

Hampl, Patricia. Memory and Imagination, The Dolphin Reader, ed. Douglas Hunt, Boston: Houston, 1986.

Spence, Donald P. Narrative Truth and Historical Truth:Meaning and Interpretation in psychoanalysis, New York: Norton, 1982.

Hutcheon, Linda, A Poetics of Postmodernism: History, Theory, Fiction,

London: Routledge, 1988.

Jolly, Margaretta. Encyclopedia of Life Writing: Autobiographical and Biographical Forms, London: Fitzroy Deatborn Pubishers, 2001.

Naipaul, V. S. A Way in the World: a Sequence, London: Minerva, 1995. `

Polkinghorne, Donald. Ricoeur, Narrative and Personal Identity, Changing Conceptions of Psychological Life, eds. Cynthia Lightfood er al. Mahwah: Erlbaum, 2004, 24-48.

Ricoeur, Paul. Oneself as Another, trans. Kathleen Blamey, Chicago: The University of Chicago Press, 1992.

Ricoeur, Paul. Narrative Identity, Philosophy Today, Vol. 35 (1), 1991, 73-81.

Smith, Sidonie and Julia Watson. Reading Autobiography: A Guide for Interpreting Life Narratives, Minneapolis: University of Minnesota Press, 2010.

Wong, Cynthia F. Kazuo Ishiguro, Hordon: Northcote House, 2005.

References of Chapter Two

Adams, Tim. For me, England is a Mythical Place, Observer, 20 Febru ary 2005.

Anderson, Linda. Autobiography, London and New York: Routledge, 2001.

Atkinson, Rob. How the Butler Was Made to Do It: The Perverted Professionalism of The Remains of the Day, Yale Law Journal, 10, 1995, 177-220.

Auden, W. H. The Guilty Vicarage, Detective Fiction: A Collection of Critical Essays, ed. Robin W. Winks, Woodstock: Foul Play,1998, 15-24.

Beedham, Mathew. The Novels of Kazuo Ishiguro: A Reader's Guide to Essential Criticism, Basingstoke and New York: Palgrave Macmillan, 2010.

Bennett, Jane. The Enchantment of Modern Life, Princeton: Princeton UP, 2001.

Beverley, John. The Margin at the Center: On Testimonio (Testimonial Narrative), De/Colonizing the Subject, ed. Smith and Watson, Minneapolis: Minnesota University Press, 1992, 91-114.

Billson, Marcus. The Memoir: New Perspectives on a Forgotten Genre, Genre, 10.2, 1977, 259-82.

Bourdieu, Pierre. The Logic of Practice, trans. Richard Nice, Stanford: Stanford University Press, 1990.

Bradbury, Malcolm. The Floating World, in No, Not Bloomsbury, London: Andre Deutsch, 1987.

Buss, Helen M. Memoir with an Attitude: One Reader Reads the Woman

Warrior: Memoirs of a Girlhood Among Ghosts, a/b: Auto/biography Studies, 12.2, 1997, 203-224.

Chisholm, A. Lost World of Pleasure, Times Literary Supplement, 14 February, 1986, P. 162.

De Man, Paul. Allegories of Reading: Figural Language in Rousseau, Nietzche, Rilke, and Proust, New Haven: Yale UP, 1979.

Drag, Wojciech. Revisiting Loss: Memory, Trauma and Nostalgia in the Novels of Kazuo Ishiguro, Newcastle upon Tyne: Cambridge Scholars Publishing, 2014.

Eng, David L. and David Kazanjian. Introduction: Mourning Remains, Loss: The Politics of Mourning, eds. David L. Eng and David Kazanjian, Berkeley: University of California Press, 2003, 1-27.

Foucault, Michel. The History of Sextuality, Vol. 1, trans. Robert Hurley, New York: Vintage, 1980.

Freud, Sigmund. Mourning and Melancholia, trans. Shaun Whiteside, The Penguin Freud Reader, ed. Adam Philips, London: Penguin Books, 2006, 310-26.

Freud, Sigmund. New Introductory Lectures on Psychoanalysis, New York: Norton, 1965.

Furst, Lillian. Memory's Fragile Power in Ishiguro's Remains of the Day and W. C. Sebald's 'Max Ferber', Contemporary Literature, 48.4, 2007, 530-553.

Gilroy, Paul. The Black Atlantic: Modernity and Double Consciousness, London and New York: Verso, 1993.

Gorra, Michael. The Case of the Missing Childhood, New York Times Book Review, 24 September 2000.

Groes, Sebastian. and Barry Lewis (eds). Kazuo Ishiguro: New Critical

Visions of the Novels, New York: Palgrave Macmillan, 2011.

Guth, Deborah. Submerged Narratives in Kazuo Ishiguro's The Remains of the Day, Forum for Modern Language Studies, 35.2, 1999, 126-137.

Hall, Stuart.The Question of Cultural Identity, Modernity and Its Futures, eds., Stuart Hall and Tony McGrew, Cambridge, England: Policy Press, 1992.

Hart, Francis Russel. History Talking to Itself: Public Personality in Recent Memoir, New Literary History, 11.1, Autumn 1979, 193-210.

Horrocks, Roger. Freud Revisited: Psychoanalytic Themes in the Postmodern Age, New York: Palgrave, 2001.

Ishiguro, Kazuo. A Pale View of Hills, New York: Vintage, 1990.

Ishiguro, Kazuo. An Artist of the Floating World, London: Faber & Faber, 1986.

Ishiguro, Kazuo. Never Let Me Go, London: Faber and Faber, 2005.

Ishiguro, Kazuo. When We Were Orphans, London: Faber & Faber, 2000.

Ishiguro, Kazuo. The Remains of the Day, London: Faber & Faber, 1989.

Jolly, Margaretta. Encyclopedia of life writing: Autobiographical and Biographical Forms, London: Fitzroy Dearborn Pubishers, 2001.

Kamine, Mark. A Servant of Self-Deceit, New Leader, 13 November 1989, 21-22.

Kociatkiewicz, Justya. Towards the Antibildungsroman: Saul Bellow and the Problem of Genre, Frankfurt: Peter Lang, 2008.

Laing, Ronald D. The Politics of Experience, London: penguin, 1967.

Lang, James M. Public Memory, Private History: Kazuo Ishiguro's The Remains of the Day, CLIO: A Journal of Literature, History, and the Philosophy of History, 29.2, 2000, 143-165.

Lewis, Barry. Kazuo Ishiguro, Manchester: Manchester University Press,

2000.

Mason, Gregory. An Interview with Kazuo Ishiguro, Contemporary Literature, 30, 1989, 335-47.

Mason, Gregory. Inspiring Images: The Influence of the Japancse Cinema on the Writings of Kazuo Ishiguro, East West Film Journal, 3 (2), 1989, 39-52.

McCombe, John P. The End of (Anthony) Eden: Ishiguro's The Remains of the Day and Midcentury Anglo-American Tension, Twentieth Century Literature: A Scholarly and Critical Journal, 48.1, 2002, 77-99.

O'Brien, Susie. Serving a New World Order: Postcolonial Politics in Kazuo Ishiguro's The Remains of the Day, Modern Fiction Studies, 42.4, 1996, 787-806.

Poree, Marc. Kazuo Ishiguro:The Remains of the Day, Paris: Didier Erudition, 1999.

Punter, David. Postcolonial Imaginings: Fictions of a New World Order, New York: Rowman and Littlefield, 2000.

Quinby, Lee. The Margin at the Center: On Testimonio (Testimonial Narrative), De/Colonizing the Subject, ed. Smith and Watson, Minneapolis: Minnesota University Press, 1992, 297-320.

Robbins, Bruce. Cruelty is Bad: Banality and Proximity in Never Let Me Go, Novel, 40.3, 2007, 289-302.

Rose, Margaret. Parody: Ancient, Modern, and Post-modern, Cambridge: University Press, 1993.

Said, E. W. Culture and Imperialism, New York: Vintage Books, 1993.

Scanlan, Margaret. Mistaken Identities: First-Person Narration in Kazuo Ishiguro, Journal of Narrative and Life History, 3 (2&3), 1993, 139-154.

Shaffer, Barry. Understanding Kazuo Ishiguro, Columbia: University of

South Carolina Press, 1998.

Shaffer, Brian W. and Cynthia F. Wong (eds). Conversations with Kazuo Ishiguro, Jackson, MS: University Press of Mississippi, 2008.

Smith, Sidonie and Julia Watson. Reading Autobiography: A Guide for Interpreting Life Narratives, Minneapolis: University of Minnesota Press, 2010.

Suvin, Darko. Metamorphoses of Science Fiction, New Haven: Yale UP, 1979.

Tarnas, Richard. The Passion of the Western Mind: Understanding the Ideas That Have Shaped Our World View, New York: Ballantine Books, 1991.

Tookey, Christopher. Sydenham, mon amour, Books and Bookmen, March 1996, p.34.

Tyson, Lois. Critical Theory Today, New York: Routledge, 2015.

Vorda, Alan. and Kim Herzinger. An Interview with Kzauo Ishiguro, Mississippi Review, 20, 1991, 31-54.

Wall, Kathleen. The Remains of the Day and Its Challenges to Theories of Unreliable Narration, Journal of Narrative Technique, 24.1, 1994, 18-42.

Wong, Cynthia F. Kazuo Ishiguro, Hordon: Northcote House, 2005.

References of Chapter Three

Abbott, H. Porter. Autobiography, Autography, Fiction: Groundwork for a Taxonomy of Textual Categories, New Literary History, 19 (3), 1988, 597-616.

Alpers, Paul. What Is Pastoral?, Critical Inquiry, 8 (3),1982, 437-60.

Appadurai, Arjun. "Grassroots globalization and the research imagination, Public Culture, 12 (1), 2000, 1-19.

Benoit, Madhu. Cultural Representations: Strange or Stranger? Displaced Identities in V.S. Naipaul. Représentation, 3, decémbre 2007, 40-46.

Bhabha, Homi K. The Location of Culture, London: Routledge, 1994.

Bhattacharya, Baidik. V. S. Naipaul and Fictions of Subaltern Diaspora, South Asian Review, 32:3, 2011, 27-47.

Bové, Paul A. Discourse, Critical Terms for Literary Study, Ed. Frank Lentricchia and Thomas McLaughli, Chicago and London: U of Chicago P, 1995. 50-65.

Fanon, Frantz. Black Skin, White Masks, trans. Richard Philcox, New York: Grove Press, 2008.

French, Patrick. The World is What It Is: The Authorized Biography of V. S. Naipaul, London: Picador, 2008.

Gussow, Mel. The Enigma of V. S. Naipaul's Search for Himself in Writing, New York Times, 25 April 1987, 16.

Jorngarden, Anna. A Ruin Amidst Ruins: V. S. Naipaul Walking the English Countryside, Modern Fiction Studies, 64 (2), 2018, 209-238.

King, Bruce, V.S. Naipaul, Basingstoke and New York: Palgrave

Macmillan, 2003.

Mustafa, Fawzia. V. S. Naipaul, Cambridge: Cambridge University Press,1995.

Williams, Raymond. The country and the city, Oxford: Oxford University Press, 1975.

Naipaul, V. S. Prologue to an Autobiography, in Finding the Centre: Two Narratives, London: André Deutsch, 1984.

Naipaul, V. S. Words on Their Own, Times Literary Supplement, 4 June, 1964, 472-3.

Naipaul, V. S. A House for Mr Biswas, London: Picador, 2011.

Naipaul, V. S. Between Father and Son: Family Letters, Ed. Gillon Aitken, New York: Knopf, 2007.

Naipaul, V. S. The Magic Seeds, New York: Knopf, 2004.

Naipaul, V.S. Two World (The Nobel Lecture), Literary Occasions,ed. Pankaj Mishra, London: Picador, 2003, 181-95.

Naipaul, V.S. The Enigma of Arrival, New York: Random House, 1988.

Niven, Alastair. V.S. Naipaul Talks to Alastair Niven , Conversations with V.S. Naipaul, ed. Feroza Jussawalla, Jackson: University Press of Mississippi, 1997. 162-5.

Ramchand, Kenneth. An Introduction to the Study of West Indian Literature, London: Thomas Nelson, 1976.

Beecroft Simon. Sir Vidia's shadow: V. S. Naipaul, the Writer and The Enigma of Arrival, Journal of Commonwealth Literature, vol. 35 (1), 2000, 71 - 86.

Waugh, Patricia. Metafiction: The Theory and Practice of Self-Conscious Fiction, London: Routledge, 1984.

References of Chapter Four

Agamben, Giorgio. Infancy and History: An Essay on the Destruction of Experience, Infancy and History: the Destruction of Experience, trans. Liz Heron, London and New York: Verso, 2007.

Ahmad, Aijaz. In Theory: Classes, Nations, Literatures, London: Verso, 1992.

Anderson, Benedict. Imagined Communities, London: Verso, 1991.

Benjamin, Walter. Experience and Poverty, in Michael Jennings, Howard Eiland and Gary Smith (ed.), Selected Writings: Volume 2, 1927-1934, Cambridge and London: The Belknap Press of Harvard University Press, 1999.

Britzman, Deborah. On Being a Slow Reader: Psychoanalytic Reading Problems in Ishiguro's Never Let Me Go, Changing English, 13 (3), 2006, pp. 307-18.

Certeau, Michael. Heterologies: Discourse on the Other, trans. Brian Massumi, Manchester: Manchester University Press, 1986.

Cooper, David E. Existentialism, Oxford: Blackwell, 1990.

De Man, Paul. Allegories of Reading: Figural Language in Rousseau, Nietzsche, Rilke and Proust, New Haven and London: Yale University Press, 1979.

Drabble, Margaret. The Oxford Companion to English Literature, Beijing: Foreign Language Teaching and Research Press, 2005.

Bhabha, Homi. The Location of Culture. London: Routledge, 1994.

Foucault, Michel. Power/Knowledge, Brighton: Harvester Press, 1980.

Freud, Sigmund. The Uncanny, in J. Strachey (ed.) Standard Edition of the Complete Psychological Works of Sigmund Freud, 17, London: Hogarth Press, 1955.

Gilroy, Paul. The Black Atlantic: Modernity and Double Consciousness, London and New York: Verso, 1993.

Heidegger, Martin. Being and Time, trans. Joan Stambaugh, Albany: State University of New York Press, 1996.

Heidegger, Martin. The Fundamental Concepts of Metaphysics: World, Finitude, Solitude, trans. William McNeill and Nicholas Walker, Bloomington and Indianapolis: Indiana University Press, 1995.

Ingersoll, Earl G. Taking Off into the Realm of Metaphor: Kazuo Ishiguro's Never Let Me Go, Studies in the Humanities 34 (1), 2007, 40-59.

Ishiguro, Kazuo. Nocturnes: Five Stories of Music and Nightfall, New York: Vintage, 2009.

Jung, Carl. Mysterium Coniunctionis, trans. R. Hull, Princeton: Princeton University Press, 1989.

Krell, D. Farrell. Das Unheimliche: Architectural Sections of Heidegger and Freud, Research in Phenomenology 22, 1992, pp. 43-61.

Lyotard, Jean-Francois. Answering the Question: What is Postmodernism?, in Thomas Docherty (ed.) Postmodernism: A Reader, London: Harvester, 1993.

Marcuse, Herbert. The Aesthetic Dimension: Toward a Critique of Marxist Aesthetics, London: Macmillan, 1978.

McSweeney, Kerry. Four contemporary Novelists: Angus Wilson, Brian Moore, John Fowles, V. S. Naipaul, London: Scholar Press, 1983.

Mills, Marie. Narrative Identity and Dementia: A Study of Education and Narrative in Older people with Dementia, Ageing and Society 17, 1997, 673-98.

Moore, Michael. Scott and Michael Sontheimer. Spiegel Interview with Kazuo Ishiguro: I Remain Fascinated by Memory, Spiegel Online, 10 May, 2005, http://www.spiegel.de.

Naipaul, V. S. An Area of Darkness, New York: Vintage Books, 2002.

Nelson, Ed. Heidegger and the Ethics of Facticity, in F. Raffoul and E. Nelson (ed.) Rethinking Facticity, Albany: State University of New York Press, 2008.

Reese, Elaine. and Kate Farrant. Social Origins of Reminiscing, in Robyn Fivush and Catherine Haden (ed.) Autobiographical and Cultural Perspectives, Mahwah: Lawrence Erlbaum Associates, 2003.

Ronell, Avital. Crack Wars: Literature Addiction Mania, Lincoln and London: University of Nebraska Press, 1992.

Seaman, Myra. Becoming More (than) Human: Affective Posthumanisms, Past and Future, Journal of Narrative Theory 37 (2), 2007, 246-75.

Shaffer, Brian W. and Cynthia F. Wong (eds). Conversations with Kazuo Ishiguro, Jackson, MS: University Press of Mississippi, 2008.

Stanton, Katherine. Cosmopolitan Fictions: Ethics, Politics, and Global Change in the Words of Kazuo Ishiguro, Michael Ondaatje, Jamaica Kincaid, and J. M. Coetzee, New York and London: Routledge, 2006.

Terestchenko, M. Servility and Destructiveness in Kazuo Ishiguro's The

Remains of the Day, Partial Answers: Journal of Literature and the History of ideas 5 (1), 2007, pp. 77-89.

Vorda, Alan. and Kim Herzinger. An Interview with Kzauo Ishiguro, Mississippi Review, 20, 1991, 31-54.

Weber, Samuel. The Legend of Freud, Expanded Edition, Stanford: Clarendon Press, 2004.

Winkler, Rafael. Heidegger and the Question of Man's Poverty in World, International Journal of Philosophical Studies 15 (4), 2007: 521-39.

References of Chapter Five

Ahmad, Aijaz. Salman Rushdie's Shame: Postmodern Migrancy and the Representation of Women, Economic and Political Weekly, 26 (24), 1991, 1461-1471.

Ben-Rafael, Eliezer & Sternberg, Yitzhak. Transnationalism: Diasporas and the advent of a new (dis)order, Leiden: Brill, 2009.

Bhabha, Homi. The Location of Culture. London: Routledge, 1994.

Boym, Svetlana. The Future of Nostalgia. New York: Basic Books, 2001.

Brennan, Timothy. At Home in the World:Cosmopolitanism Now, Cambridge: Harvard University Press, 1997.

Brydon, Diana. The White Inuit Speaks: Contamination as Literary Strategy, The Post-Colonial Studies Reader (ed. Bill Ashcroft, Gareth Griffiths, and Helen Tiffin), London: Routledge, 2003.

Brubaker, Rogers. Grounds for Difference, Cambridge, MA: Harvard University Press, 2015.

Clifford, James. Diasporas, Cultural Anthropology, 9 (3), 1994, 302 – 338.

Dharwadker, Vinay. Introduction. Cosmopolitanism in Its Time and Place, Cosmopolitan Geographies: New Locations in Literature and Culture, New York: Routledge, 2001, 1 – 14.

Gonzalez, Madelena. Fiction After the Fatwa: Salman Rushdie and the Charm of Catastrophe, Amsterdam and New York: Rodopi, 2005.

Hannerz, Ulf. Transnational Connections: Culture, People, Places, London: Routledge, 1996.

Huggan, Graham. The Postcolonial Exotic: Marketing the Margins, London: Routledge, 2001.

Loh, Lawrence. Rural Heritage and Colonial Nostalgia in the Thatcher Years: V.S. Naipaul's The Enigma of Arrival. In: Hadley L and Ho E (eds) Thatcher and Her Afterlife in Contemporary Culture. Basingstoke: Palgrave, 2010, 96-114.

Naipaul, V. S. The Middle Passage: The Caribbean Revisited, New York: Vintage Books, 2002.

Hall, Stuart. The Question of Cultural Identity, Modernity and Its Futures, ed, Stuart Hall and Tony McGrew, Cambridge, England: Policy Press, 1992.

Portes, Alejandro. and Rubén G. Rumbaut, (eds.), Legacies: The story of the Immigrant Second Generation, CA: University of California Press, 2001.

Rushdie, Salman. Step across This Line, New York: Modern Library, 2003.

Rushdie, Salman. Shame, New York: Random House, 2005.

Rushdie, Salman. Joseph Anton: A Memoir, New York: Random House, 2012.

Said, Edward. Orientalism, London: Penguin, 1977.

Said, Edward. Reflections on Exile, Cambridge, MA: Harvard University Press, 2000, 436-452.

Saw, Suraj Kuma. Globalization and Migration in the Contemporary World Order: an Insight into the Postnational Condition and the Diasporas, Social Identities: Journal for the Study of Race, Nation and Culture, 24(3), 2018, 339-363.

Schoene, Berthold. The Cosmopolitan Novel, Edinburgh: Edinburgh UP, 2010.

Schlereth, Thomas J. The Cosmopolitan Ideal in Enlightenment Thought: Its Form and Function in thc Ideas of Franklin, Hume and Voltaire, 1694 – 1970, Notre Dame: U of Notre Dame P, 1977.

Rushdie, Salman. Midnight's Children, London: Vintage, 1995.

Bibliography

Abbott, H. Porter. Autobiography, Autography, Fiction: Groundwork for a Taxonomy of Textual Categories, New Literary History, 19 (3), 1988, 597-616.

Adams, Tim. For me, England is a Mythical Place, Observer, 20 February 2005.

Agamben, Giorgio. Infancy and History: An Essay on the Destruction of Experience, Infancy and History: the Destruction of Experience, trans. Liz Heron, London and New York: Verso, 2007.

Ahmad, Aijaz. Salman Rushdie's Shame: Postmodern Migrancy and the Representation of Women, Economic and Political Weekly, 26 (24), 1991, 1461-1471.

Ahmad, Aijaz. In Theory: Classes, Nations, Literatures, London: Verso, 1992.

Alpers, Paul. What Is Pastoral?, Critical Inquiry, 8 (3),1982, 437-60.

Anderson, Benedict. Imagined Communities, London: Verso, 1991.

Anderson, Linda. Autobiography, London and New York: Routledge, 2001.

Appadurai, Arjun. Grassroots globalization and the research imagination, Public Culture, 12 (1), 2000, 1-19.

Atkinson, Rob. How the Butler Was Made to Do It. The Perverted Professionalism of The Remains of the Day, Yale Law Journal, 10, 1995, 177-220.

Auden, W. H. The Guilty Vicarage, Detective Fiction: A Collection of Critical Essays, ed. Robin W. Winks, Woodstock: Foul Play,1998, 15-24.

Bakhtin, Mikhail. The Dialogic Imagination, (Ed. Holquist M; Trans. Emerson C and Holquist M), Austin: University of Austin Press,1981.

Barthes, Roland. The Death of the Author, The Rustle of Language, trans. Richard Howard, Oxford: Basil Blackwell, 1986.

Bartlett, Frederic C. Remembering: A Study in Experimental and Social Psychology, 1932, Cambridge: Cambridge UP, 1995.

Beedham, Mathew. The Novels of Kazuo Ishiguro: A Reader's Guide to Essential Criticism, Basingstoke and New York: Palgrave Macmillan, 2010.

Benjamin, Walter. Experience and Poverty, in Michael Jennings, Howard Eiland and Gary Smith (ed.), Selected Writings: Volume 2, 1927-1934, Cambridge and London: The Belknap Press of Harvard University Press, 1999.

Bennet, Jane. The Enchantment of Modern Life, Princeton: Princeton UP, 2001.

Benoit, Madhu. Cultural Representations: Strange or Stranger? Displaced Identities in V.S. Naipaul. Représentation, 3, decémbre 2007, 40-46.

Ben-Rafael, Eliezer & Sternberg, Yitzhak. Transnationalism: Diasporas and the Advent of a New (dis)order, Leiden: Brill, 2009.

Beverley, John. The Margin at the Center: On Testimonio (Testimonial Narrative), De/Colonizing the Subject, ed. Smith and Watson, 91-114.

Bhabha, Homi K. The Location of Culture, London: Routledge, 1994.

Bhattacharya, Baidik. V. S. Naipaul and Fictions of Subaltern Diaspora, South Asian Review, 32:3, 2011, 27-47.

Billson, Marcus F. The Memoir: New Perspectives on A Forgotten Genre, Genre, 10.2, Summer 1977, 259-82.

Bourdieu, Pierre. The Logic of Practice, trans. Richard Nice, Stanford: Stanford University Press, 1990.

Bové, Paul A. Discourse, Critical Terms for Literary Study, ed. Frank Lentricchia and Thomas McLaughli, Chicago and London: U of Chicago P, 1995. 50-65.

Boym, Svetlana. The Future of Nostalgia. New York: Basic Books, 2001.

Bradbury, Malcolm. The Floating World, in No, Not Bloomsbury, London: Andre Deutsch, 1987.

Brennan, Timothy. At Home in the World: Cosmopolitanism Now, Cambridge: Harvard University Press, 1997.

Brennan, Timothy. Wars of Position: The Cultural Politics of the Left and Right, New York: Columbia Press, 2006.

Britzman, Deborah. On Being a Slow Reader: Psychoanalytic Reading Problems in Ishiguro's Never Let Me Go, Changing English, 13 (3), 2006, pp. 307-18.

Brown, Merle. The Idea of Fiction as Fictive or Fictitious, The Bulletin of the Midwest MLA, 6, 1973, 62-73.

Brubaker, Rogers. Grounds for difference, Cambridge, MA: Harvard University Press, 2015.

Brydon, Diana. The White Inuit Speaks: Contamination as Literary Strategy, The Post-Colonial Studies Reader (ed. Bill Ashcroft, Gareth Griffiths, and Helen Tiffin), London: Routledge, 2003.

Burton, Rob. Artists of the Floating World: Contemporary Writings between Cultures, Lanham: University Press of America, 2007.

Buss, Helen M. Memoir with an Attitude: One Reader Reads The Woman Warrior: Memoirs of a Girlhood Among Ghosts, a/b: Auto/biography Studies, 12.2, 1997, 203-224.

Certeau, Michael. Heterologies: Discourse on the Other, trans. Brian Massumi, Manchester: Manchester University Press, 1986.

Childs, Peter. Contemporary Novelists: British Fiction since 1970, Hampshire: Palgrave Macmillan, 2005.

Chisholm, A. Lost World of Pleasure, Times Literary Supplement, 14 February, 1986, P. 162.

Clifford, James. Diasporas, Cultural Anthropology, 9 (3), 1994, 302 – 338.

Cooper, David E. Existentialism, Oxford: Blackwell, 1990.

Cundy, Catherine. Salman Rushdie, Manchester: Manchester UP,1996.

De Man, Paul. Autobiography as De-facement, Modern Language Notes, 94 (5), 1979, 919—930.

De Man, Paul. Allegories of Reading: Figural Language in Rousseau, Nietzsche, Rilke and Proust, New Haven and London: Yale University Press, 1979.

Dharwadker, Vinay. Introduction. Cosmopolitanism in Its Time and Place, Cosmopolitan Geographies: New Locations in Literature and Culture, New York: Routledge, 2001, 1 – 14.

Drabble, Margaret. The Oxford Companion to English Literature, Beijing: Foreign Language Teaching and Research Press, 2005.

Drag, Wojciech. Revisiting Loss: Memory, Trauma and Nostalgia in the Novels of Kazuo Ishiguro, Newcastle upon Tyne: Cambridge Scholars Publishing, 2014.

Elliott, Anthony. Subject to Ourselves: Social Theory, Psychoanalysis and Postmodernity, Cambridge: Polity Press, 1996.

Eng, David L. and David Kazanjian. Introduction: Mourning Remains, Loss: The Politics of Mourning, eds. David L. Eng and David Kazanjian, Berkeley: University of California Press, 2003, 1-27.

Fanon, Frantz. Black Skin, White Masks, trans. Richard Philcox, New York: Grove Press, 2008.

Foucault, Michel. Power/Knowledge, Brighton: Harvester Press, 1980.

Foucault, Michel. The History of Sextuality, Vol. 1, trans. Robert Hurley, New York: Vintage, 1980.

French, Patrick. The World is What It Is: The Authorized Biography of V. S. Naipaul, London: Picador, 2008.

Freud, Sigmund. Mourning and Melancholia, trans. Shaun Whiteside, The Penguin Freud Reader, ed. Adam Philips, London: Penguin Books, 2006, 310-26.

Freud, Sigmund. The Uncanny, in J. Strachey (ed.) Standard Edition of the Complete Psychological Works of Sigmund Freud, 17, London: Hogarth Press, 1955.

Freud, Sigmund. New Introductory Lectures on Psychoanalysis, New York: Norton, 1965.

Furst, Lillian. Memory's Fragile Power in Ishiguro's Remains of the Day and W. C. Sebald's Max Ferber, Contemporary Literature, 48.4, 2007, 530-553.

Gilroy, Paul. The Black Atlantic: Modernity and Double Consciousness, London and New York: Verso, 1993.

Gonzalez, Madelena. Fiction After the Fatwa: Salman Rushdie and the Charm of Catastrophe, Amsterdam and New York: Rodopi, 2005.

Gorra, Michael. The Case of the Missing Childhood, New York Times Book Review, 24 September 2000.

Groes, Sebastian. and Barry Lewis (eds). Kazuo Ishiguro: New Critical Visions of the Novels, New York: Palgrave Macmillan, 2011.

Gussow, Mel. The Enigma of V. S. Naipaul's Search for Himself in Writing, New York Times, 25 April 1987, 16.

Guth, Deborah. Submerged Narratives in Kazuo Ishiguro's The Remains of the Day, Forum for Modern Language Studies, 35.2, 1999, 126-137.

Hall, Stuart. The Question of Cultural Identity, Modernity and Its Futures, Eds., Stuart Hall and Tony McGrew, Cambridge, England: Policy Press, 1992.

Hampel, Regine. I Write therefore I Am?, Fictional Autobiography and the Idea of Selfhood in the Postmodern Age, Bern;Oxford: Lang, 2001.

Hampl, Patricia. Memory and Imagination, The Dolphin Reader, ed. Douglas Hunt, Boston: Houston, 1986.

Hannerz, Ulf. Transnational connections: Culture, people, places, London: Routledge, 1996.

Hart, Francis Russel. History Talking to Itself: Public Personality in Recent Memoir, New Literary History, 11.1, Autumn 1979, 193-210.

Heidegger, Martin. Being and Time, trans. Joan Stambaugh, Albany: State

University of New York Press, 1996.

Heidegger, Martin. The Fundamental Concepts of Metaphysics: World, Finitude, Solitude, trans. William McNeill and Nicholas Walker, Bloomington and Indianapolis: Indiana University Press, 1995.

Horrocks, Roger. Freud Revisited: Psychoanalytic Themes in the Postmodern Age, New York: Palgrave, 2001.

Huggan, Graham. The Postcolonial Exotic: Marketing the Margins, London: Routledge, 2001.

Hutcheon, Linda, A Poetics of Postmodernism: History, Theory, Fiction, London: Routledge, 1988.

Ingersoll, Earl G. Taking Off into the Realm of Metaphor: Kazuo Ishiguro's Never Let Me Go, Studies in the Humanities 34 (1), 2007, 40-59.

Ishiguro, Kazuo. A Pale View of Hills, New York: Vintage, 1990.

Ishiguro, Kazuo. An Artist of the Floating World, London: Faber & Faber, 1986.

Ishiguro, Kazuo. Never Let Me Go, London: Faber and Faber, 2005.

Ishiguro, Kazuo. Nocturnes: Five Stories of Music and Nightfall, New York: Vintage, 2009.

Ishiguro, Kazuo. The Remains of the Day, London: Faber & Faber, 1989.

Jolly, Margaretta. Encyclopedia of Life Writing: Autobiographical and Biographical Forms, London: Fitzroy Deatborn Pubishers, 2001.

Jorgarden, Anna. A Ruin Amidst Ruins: V. S. Naipaul Walking the English Countryside, Modern Fiction Studies, 64 (2), 2018, 209-238.

Jung, Carl. Mysterium Coniunctionis, trans. R. Hull, Princeton: Princeton

University Press, 1989.

Kamine, Mark. A Servant of Self-Deceit, New Leader, 13 November 1989, 21-22.

King, Bruce, V.S. Naipaul, Basingstoke and New York: Palgrave Macmillan, 2003.

Kociatkiewicz, Justya. Towards the Antibildungsroman: Saul Bellow and the Problem of Genre, Frankfurt: Peter Lang, 2008.

Krell, D. Farrell. Das Unheimliche: Architectural Sections of Heidegger and Freud, Research in Phenomenology 22, 1992, pp. 43-61.

Laing, Ronald. D. The Politics of Experience, London: penguin, 1967.

Lane, Richard J., Rod Mengham and Philip Tew, Contemporary British Fiction, Cambridge: Polity Press, 2003.

Lang, James M. Public Memory, Private History: Kazuo Ishiguro's The Remains of the Day, CLIO: A Journal of Literature, History, and the Philosophy of History, 29.2, 2000, 143-165.

Lee, Derek. The Politics of Fairyland: Neil Gaiman and the Enchantments of Anti-Bildungroman, Critique: Studies in Contemporary Fiction, 57.5, 2016, 552-564.

Lewis, Barry, Kazuo Ishiguro, Manchester: Manchester Univesity Press, 2000.

Loh, Lawrence. Rural Heritage and Colonial Nostalgia in the Thatcher Years: V.S. Naipaul's The Enigma of Arrival. In: Hadley L and Ho E (eds) Thatcher and Her Afterlife in Contemporary Culture. Basingstoke: Palgrave, 2010, 96-114.

Lyotard, Jean-François. Answering the Question: What is Postmodernism?, in Thomas Docherty (ed.) Postmodernism: A Reader, London: Harvester, 1993.

Marcuse, Herbert. The Aesthetic Dimension: Toward a Critique of Marxist Aesthetics, London: Macmillan, 1978.

Mason, Gregory. An Interview with Kazuo Ishiguro, Contemporary Literature, 30 1989, 335-47.

Mason, Gregory. Inspiring Images: The Influence of the Japanese Cinema on the Writings of Kazuo Ishiguro, East West Film Journal, 3 (2), 1989, 39-55.

McCombe, John P. The End of (Anthony) Eden: Ishiguro's The Remains of the Day and Midcentury Anglo-American Tension, Twentieth Century Literature: A Scholarly and Critical Journal, 48 (1), 2002, 77-99.

McSweeney, Kerry. Four Contemporary Novelists: Angus Wilson, Brian Moore, John Fowles, V. S. Naipaul, London: Scholar Press, 1983.

Merleau-Ponty, Maurice. Sense and Non-Sense, trans. Hubert L. Dreyfus and Patricia Allen Dreyfus, Evanston: Northwestern University Press, 1964.

Mills, Marie. Narrative Identity and Dementia: A Study of Education and Narrative in Older people with Dementia, Ageing and Society 17, 1997, 673-98.

Moore, Michael. Scott and Michael Sontheimer. Spiegel Interview with Kazuo Ishiguro: I Remain Fascinated by Memory, Spiegel Online, 10 May, 2005, http://www.spiegel.de.

Mustafa, Fawzia. V. S. Naipaul, Cambridge: Cambridge University Press,1995.

Naipaul, V. S. Prologue to an Autobiography, in Finding the Centre: Two Narratives, London: André Deutsch, 1984.

Naipaul, V. S. Words on Their Own, Times Literary Supplement, 4 June, 1964, 472-3.

Naipaul, V. S. A House for Mr Biswas, London: Picador, 2011.

Naipaul, V. S. A Way in the World: a Sequence, London: Minerva, 1995. `

Naipaul, V. S. An Area of Darkness, New York: Vintage Books, 2002.

Naipaul, V. S. Between Father and Son: Family Letters, Ed. Gillon Aitken, New York: Knopf, 2007.

Naipaul, V. S. The Magic Seeds, New York: Knopf, 2004.

Naipaul, V. S. The Middle Passage: The Caribbean Revisited, New York: Vintage Books, 2002.

Naipaul, V.S. Two World(The Nobel Lecture), Literary Occasions, Ed. Pankaj Mishra, London: Picador, 2003, 181-95.

Naipaul, V.S. The Enigma of Arrival, New York: Random House, 1988.

Nelson, Ed. Heidegger and the Ethics of Facticity, in F. Raffoul and E. Nelson (ed.) Rethinking Facticity, Albany: State University of New York Press, 2008.

Niven, Alastair. V.S. Naipaul Talks to Alastair Niven, Conversations with V.S. Naipaul, Ed. Feroza Jussawalla, Jackson: University Press of Mississippi, 1997. 162-5.

O'Brien, Susie. Serving a New World Order: Postcolonial Politics in Kazuo Ishiguro's The Remains of the Day, Modern Fiction Studies, 42.4, 1996, 787-806.

Polkinghorne, Donald. Ricoeur, Narrative and Personal Identity, Changing Conceptions of Psychological Life, Eds. Cynthia Lightfood er al. Mahwah:

Erlbaum, 2004, 24-48.

Poree, Marc. Kazuo Ishiguro: The Remains of the Day, Paris: Didier Erudition, 1999.

Portes, A., & Rumbaut, R. G. (eds.), Legacies: The story of the Immigrant Second Generation, CA: University of California Press, 2001.

Punter, David. Postcolonial Imaginings: Fictions of a New World Order, New York: Rowman and Littlefield, 2000.

Quinby, Lee. The Margin at the Center: On Testimonio (Testimonial Narrative), De/Colonizing the Subject, ed. Smith and Watson, Minneapolis: Minnesota University Press, 1992, 297-320.

Ramchand, Kenneth. An Introduction to the Study of West Indian Literature, London: Thomas Nelson, 1976.

Reese, Elaine. and Kate Farrant. Social Origins of Reminiscing, in Robyn Fivush and Catherine Haden (ed.) Autobiographical and Cultural Perspectives, Mahwah: Lawrence Erlbaum Associates, 2003.

Ricoeur, Paul. Narrative Identity, Philosophy Today, Vol. 35 (1), 1991, 73-81.

Ricoeur, Paul. Oneself as Another, trans. Kathleen Blamey, Chicago: The University of Chicago Press, 1992.

Robbins, Bruce. Cruelty is Bad: Banality and Proximity in Never Let Me Go, Novel, 40 (3), 2007, 289-302.

Ronell, Avital. Crack Wars: Literature Addiction Mania, Lincoln and London: University of Nebraska Press, 1992.

Rose, Margaret. Parody: Ancient, Modern, and Post-modern, Cambridge:

University Press, 1993.

Rosenblatt, Louise M. Literature As Exploration, New York: Modern Language Association of America, 1995.

Rousseau, Jean-Jacques. Confessions, New York: Penguin, 1953.

Rushdie, Salman. Imaginary Homelands: Essays and Criticism: 1981 – 1991, London: Vintage, 1992.

Rushdie, Salman. Joseph Anton, New York: Randon House, 2012.

Rushdie, Salman. Midnight's Children, London: Vintage, 1995.

Rushdie, Salman. Shame, New York: Random House, 2005.

Rushdie, Salman. Step across This Line, New York: Modern Library, 2003.

Rushdie, Salman. The Satanic Verses, London: Vintage, 1998.

Said, E. W. Culture and Imperialism, New York: Vintage Books, 1993.

Rushdie, Salman. Imaginary Homelands: Essays and Criticism 1981-1991, New York: Penguin, 1992, 129-139.

Said, Edward. Orientalism, London: Penguin, 1977.

Said, Edward. Reflections on Exile, Cambridge, MA: Harvard University Press, 2000, 436-452.

Said, Edward. Culture and Imperialism, New York: Vintage Books, 1993.

Saw, Suraj Kuma. Globalization and Migration in the Contemporary World Order: an Insight into the Postnational Condition and the Diasporas, Social Identities: Journal for the Study of Race, Nation and Culture, 24(3), 2018, 339-363.

Scanlan, Margaret. Mistaken Identities: First-Person Narration in Kazuo Ishiguro, Journal of Narrative and Life History, 3 (2&3), 1993, 139-154.

Schlereth, Thomas J. The Cosmopolitan Ideal in Enlightenment Thought: Its Form and Function in the Ideas of Franklin, Hume and Voltaire, 1694 – 1970, Notre Dame: U of Notre Dame P, 1977.

Schoene, Berthold. The Cosmopolitan Novel, Edinburgh: Edinburgh UP, 2010.

Seaman, Myra. Becoming More (than) Human: Affective Posthumanisms, Past and Future, Journal of Narrative Theory 37 (2), 2007, 246-75.

Shaffer, B. W. and C. F. Wong (eds). Conversations with Kazuo Ishiguro, Jackson, MS: University Press of Mississippi, 2008.

Shaffer, Barry. Understanding Kazuo Ishiguro, Columbia: University of South Carolina Press, 1998.

Simon, Beecroft. Sir Vidia's Shadow: V. S. Naipaul, the Writer and the Enigma of Arrival, Journal of Commonwealth Literature, vol. 35 (1), 2000, 71 – 86.

Sklodowska, Elzbieta. La forma testimonial y la novelistica de Miguel Barnet, Revista/Review Interamericana, 12, 3, 1983, 379, quoted from De/Colonizing the Subject, ed. Smith and Watson, 101-102.

Smith, Sidonie and Julia Watson. Reading Autobiography: A Guide for Interpreting Life Narratives, Minneapolis: University of Minnesota Press, 2010.

Spence, Donald P. Narrative Truth and Historical Truth: Meaning and Interpretation in psychoanalysis, New York: Norton, 1982.

Stanton, Katherine. Cosmopolitan Fictions: Ethics, Politics, and Global Change in the Words of Kazuo Ishiguro, Michael Ondaatje, Jamaica Kincaid, and J. M. Coetzee, New York and London: Routledge, 2006.

Suvin, Darko. Metamorphoses of Science Fiction, New Haven: Yale UP, 1979.

Tarnas, Richard. The Passion of the Western Mind: Understanding the Ideas That Have Shaped Our World View, New York: Ballantine Books, 1991.

Terestchenko, M. Servility and Destructiveness in Kazuo Ishiguro's The Remains of the Day, Partial Answers: Journal of Literature and the History of ideas 5 (1), 2007, pp. 77-89.

Tookey, Christopher. Sydenham, mon amour, Books and Bookmen, March 1996, p.34.

Tyson, Lois. Critical Theory Today, New York: Routledge, 2015.

Vorda, Alan. and Kim Herzinger. An Interview with Kzauo Ishiguro, Mississippi Review, 20, 1991, 31-54.

Wall, Kathleen. The Remains of the Day and Its Challenges to Theories of Unreliable Narration, Journal of Narrative Technique, 24.1, 1994, 18-42.

Waugh, Patricia. Metafiction: The Theory and Practice of Self-Conscious Fiction, London: Routledge, 1984.

Weber, Samuel. The Legend of Freud, Expanded Edition, Stanford: Clarendon Press, 2004.

Winkler, Rafael. Heidegger and the Question of Man's Poverty in World, International Journal of Philosophical Studies 15 (4), 2007: 521-39.

Wong, Cynthia F. Kazuo Ishiguro, Hordon: Northcote House, 2005.